ACPL ITEM
DISCARDED

D0461486

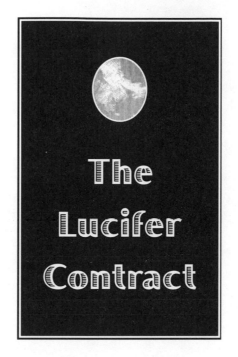

The Lucifer Contract

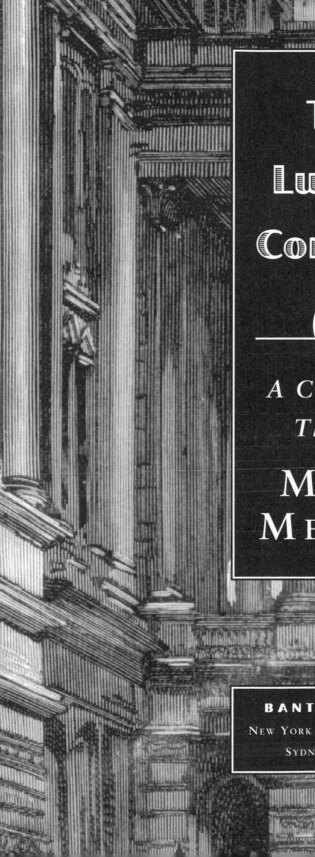

The Lucifer Contract

A Civil War Thriller

MAAN MEYERS

BANTAM BOOKS

NEW YORK TORONTO LONDON

SYDNEY AUCKLAND

THE LUCIFER CONTRACT

A Bantam Book / January 1998

Book design by Laurie Jewell
Genealogy chart by Laurie Jewell

Library of Congress Cataloging-in-Publication Data
Meyers, Maan.
The Lucifer contract : a Civil War thriller / Maan Meyers.
p.   cm.
ISBN 0-553-09707-5
I. Title.
PS3563.E889L8   1998
813'.54—dc21   97-35660
CIP

Published simultaneously in the United States and Canada

Bantam Books are published by Bantam Books, a division of Bantam Doubleday Dell
Publishing Group, Inc. Its trademark, consisting of the words "Bantam Books" and
the portrayal of a rooster, is Registered in U.S. Patent and Trademark Office and in
other countries. Marca Registrada. Bantam Books, 1540 Broadway, New York,
New York 10036.

PRINTED IN THE UNITED STATES OF AMERICA

BVG   10 9 8 7 6 5 4 3 2 1

*This book is dedicated
to the mystery booksellers,
who have given us their
support since* THE DUTCHMAN
series began.

Heartfelt thanks to Loring Lawrence, our source for New York Central and Hudson River Line information. To Sarah Smith, for sharing. To Katie Hamilton for her books *House and Home* and *Healthy Living*. ≼

To Canada's own Lynn Slotkin and Medora Sale. ≼

To Richard McDermott and *The New York Chronicle*. ≼

Thanks also to our agent, Chris Tomasino, and to the library and librarians of the New-York Historical Society. ≼

THE TONNEMAN FAMILY

⤙ 1 8 6 4 ⤚

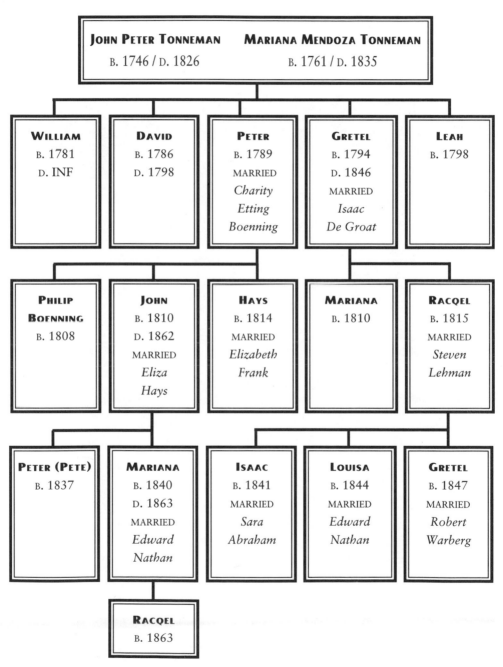

JOHN PETER TONNEMAN
B. 1746 / D. 1826

MARIANA MENDOZA TONNEMAN
B. 1761 / D. 1835

WILLIAM
B. 1781
D. INF

DAVID
B. 1786
D. 1798

PETER
B. 1789
MARRIED
*Charity
Etting
Boenning*

GRETEL
B. 1794
D. 1846
MARRIED
*Isaac
De Groat*

LEAH
B. 1798

**PHILIP
BOENNING**
B. 1808

JOHN
B. 1810
D. 1862
MARRIED
*Eliza
Hays*

HAYS
B. 1814
MARRIED
*Elizabeth
Frank*

MARIANA
B. 1810

RACQEL
B. 1815
MARRIED
*Steven
Lehman*

PETER (PETE)
B. 1837

MARIANA
B. 1840
D. 1863
MARRIED
*Edward
Nathan*

ISAAC
B. 1841
MARRIED
*Sara
Abraham*

LOUISA
B. 1844
MARRIED
*Edward
Nathan*

GRETEL
B. 1847
MARRIED
*Robert
Warberg*

RACQEL
B. 1863

The mechanics of the city, the masters,
well-form'd, beautiful-faced, looking you
    straight in the eyes,
Trottoirs throng'd, vehicles, Broadway,
    the women, the shops and shows,
A million people—manners free and
    superb—open voices—hospitality—
    the most courageous and friendly
    young men,
City of hurried and sparkling waters!
    city of spires and masts!
    City nested in bays! my city!

WALT WHITMAN
Mannahatta, 1860

CITY INTELLIGENCE

A man named Campbell, of 87 Crosby Street, carried to the headquarters of General Dix, this morning, two boxes curiously containing three bottles.

Officers who handled the bottles could find no reason for the curious situation and wondered if the boxes were a drummer's display.

Campbell, the carpenter, said they were taken in his shop in October by a stranger, who asked him to make boxes for them.

Not knowing what the bottles were, he made the boxes, and in them he packed the bottles which were never called for. The only reason Campbell brought the bottles to the Army was because of the strange chemical smell they gave off.

The carpenter did not see the man who brought three bottles. A person who worked in his shop took the order for the boxes. Campbell adds, from descriptions, that "the stranger was not a laboring man nor a New Yorker." In stature he was tall, his hair was brown, his mustache thin, and he wore summer clothing.

The particular uses for which the bottles were intended do not appear.

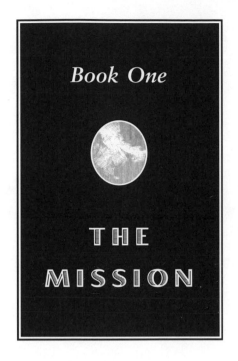

Book One

THE

MISSION

PROLOGUE

⌒September 17th, 1862. Near Sharpsburg, Maryland.

BULLETS CUT THE LEGS out from under the man to his left and shattered the head of the man to his right.

Duff kept moving forward, the 69th's banner flying.

Suddenly, out of the dust and smoke, a Reb officer appeared, brandishing a saber in his left hand. The blade glistened red in the autumn sun. The Reb was smiling, so happy was he at the scent of blood, and the chance to kill. It was clear to Duff that it was his particular blood this enemy was seeking.

The Reb was coming directly at him, his saber point aiming for Duff's throat.

You'll be a stuck pig, Duff told himself. *Run, you fool.* But his feet refused to swerve.

The two advanced, saber to flag.

With a terrifying Rebel yell, the officer thrust his blade. Using the flagstaff as a spear, Duff parried the thrust and jabbed hard at his opponent's head with the butt of the pole. His enemy, bloodied, foundered, falling away. Limbs twisted, he sprawled like death, his left hand still gripping his saber, his gray hat on the trampled, bloody ground.

Duff noted the man's gory face and twisted limbs without passion. But he was mesmerized by the Reb's full head of jet black hair which was divided neatly by a white streak straight down the center.

Duff crossed himself. *The Devil. I've fought the Devil and I've won.*

But the Devil now hurled his saber at him. Duff parried again, but not in time.

ONE

PRICE, JOHN. LIEUTENANT,
TENTH KENTUCKY CAVALRY.
ARMY OF THE CONFEDERACY.
WOUNDED IN HEAD AND LEFT
LEG. MORGAN'S RAIDER.
PAYMASTER, LUCIFER.

November 1st, 1864, Tuesday, midafternoon.

DAVID CORWIN WAS COMPACT, small in stature. He set his newspaper aside on the seat next to him and moved down the aisle to the door, balancing himself against the rocking with his hand on the seat backs. At the door he stretched, as if that were his only purpose for rising. When the train rolled into Catskill Station, he slipped casually out the door.

At the back of the car a second man, just as casually, got to his feet, adjusted his hat, and followed Corwin. The man jumped to the gravel. Except for the stationmaster with his red flag, he was the only one to be seen on the ground. *Where'd the little bastard go?* A quick gust snatched his broad-brimmed black hat, spinning it in the air, then slamming it to the gravel.

"Damn," the man said, retrieving the hat, but still seeking his prey. He dusted his hat on his long coat and squared it on his head.

·   ·   ·

⟳THE TRAIN WHISTLE wailed, shattering the quiet pastoral scene. The conductor, master of his domain, blew his own sharp whistle. " 'Board! All aboard for Manhattan, Thirtieth Street Station." In this manner, the train left Catskill Station. "Next stop, Germantown. Germantown, next stop."

The train picked up speed. The man who had followed Corwin swung himself aboard. After a quick inspection of his hat and coat and the knife sheathed in his boot, he strode down the aisle, plucking up the newspaper Corwin had left, and continued to his own seat at the back of the car.

He didn't notice the man in the herringbone mackinaw and spectacles.

And neither man saw the youth who was watching them both.

⟳IN A DITCH, not three yards from the tracks, among a patch of yellow weeds, Corwin lay, legs bent like broken twigs, throat cut from ear to ear. A lucifer friction match was jammed between his clamped teeth.

T W O

MARTIN, ROBERT. LIEUTENANT
COLONEL, TENTH KENTUCKY
CAVALRY. ARMY OF THE
CONFEDERACY. RODE WITH
MORGAN'S RAIDERS. WOUNDED
IN RIGHT LUNG, MAY '63. IN
COMMAND OF LUCIFER.

⁓November 1st, Tuesday, midafternoon.

SAM GREGORY, the stationmaster, spent too much time alone, which led him to serious thinking. He moved with a heavy step and a grave manner. Watching the train disappear from view on its way to New York City, leaving behind only a trail of black smoke, Sam was savoring the two things he'd share with his Bertha that night over the pork roast. Not the War news he was prone to talk about of late. Tonight, he would offer lighter fare.

First he would tell her about the passenger who'd been so anxious to send a message to General John A. Dix in New York. Never saw a man so frantic as when he found out the wires were down, but then, short people were that way sometimes, Sam had observed. Sheriff Jed Honeycutt was that way, getting angry enough to fight over nothing at all.

Bertha would like the second observation better. She didn't cotton to violent folks. But Bertha was interested in people. She'd truly relish to hear about the other man who got off the train for a spell. Sam had never seen a streak of white hair like that before, and he was pretty sure Bertha never had neither.

⁓ON THE TRAIN heading for New York at full chisel, a man sat straighter in his seat, set aside his worn copy of Mr. Hawthorne's *The Scarlet Letter,* and peered out the dusty window at a colt frisking about while its elders grazed. "The work begins, Toby," the man said softly to his young companion. "In just one week, Lucifer strikes." The speaker was tall and slender, swarthy-complected with a hawklike countenance. His name was Robert Martin.

"Dingdong," Tobias Garner exclaimed. "I'll be as happy as a pig in shit just to stretch my legs for longer than five minutes."

"If you don't keep your boyish enthusiasm in check, Toby, they'll be stretching more than your legs."

"Yes, Colonel."

"And don't call me Colonel."

A couple of grub butchers had come aboard two stops before and were now selling their wares in the aisles. "Sandwiches, hot coffee, apples. Fresh apple pie, made this morning."

Toby Garner lifted his hand. Neither man had eaten since before four when they had arrived in Albany, where they were required to take the ferry across the Hudson and change from the New York Central to the Hudson River Line, with still a hundred and forty-four miles to New York.

The Colonel kicked Toby's foot.

"Ow. What I do now?"

"Don't talk more than you have to. Just get your food and eat."

"Yes, sir. I do love my pie, sir."

The boy was barely eighteen, but acted more like fourteen, and had no business being in the Army, let alone being a lieutenant. But so many had died, and this one had come to him with a letter of recommendation from Robert E. Lee himself, who'd been a friend of the boy's dead father. The War was going poorly for the South: The Confederacy took what it could get.

Martin unfurled from his seat, shaking his head. He ambled down the aisle to another man, three rows along, who had covered his face with his hat and was dozing.

"Streak," the Colonel whispered, "put on your hat and keep it on. That skunk mark of yours makes you too damn easy to remember."

Smirking, John Price sat up and squared his hat on his head. "Calm down, Martin. Keep on like that and you'll have apoplexy before we strike the first Lucifer." Price screwed up his face and gave a mighty sneeze.

"You're the one who sounds sick."

"Just some New York weeds blowing in the wind." Price sneezed again. From another part of the car someone else sneezed. Price turned sharply but couldn't calculate.

TOBY GARNER WIPED his nose with a large red bandanna and leaned back in the wicker seat. He took a huge mouthful of the thick slab of apple pie he'd bought from the grub fellow and let his thoughts float back to the previous evening across the Canadian border, in Saint Catharines.

THE MAN CALLED Streak, John Price, settled into the pitch of the train and tried to sleep. He was an ordinary man who, but for the white streak in his hair, could blend into any crowd.

As sleep relaxed his body his mind wandered to a day in '62. The streak was a souvenir from that day, the result of a Yankee bullet that had creased the top of his skull.

Had he been an inch taller or wearing thicker boots, Price would have been dead. It was after Antietam, when he'd come out of the hospital, that he'd joined up with Morgan's Raiders and first met Colonel Martin.

Now his thoughts caught up to young Toby's. Only two weeks before, Senator Jacob Thompson had sent Price to Richmond to get the money from Judah Benjamin, the Secretary of State of the Confederacy. Though a Jew, Benjamin was a friend of Jeff Davis's and a loyal son of the South.

Much to Streak's surprise and pleasure, Jeff Davis had been there, too. It was Price's great pride that the President of the Confederacy had shaken his hand and wished him and Lucifer well.

John Price was paymaster for Lucifer, and he took his job seriously. The money—$300,000 in all—was in captured Yankee currency. Price would be in charge of the gold eagles; the greenbacks Colonel Martin would carry.

After spending the night in Benjamin's fine house in Richmond, Price awoke to find his clothes had been brushed and pressed. He was provided with papers and train tickets that would take him to Canada. The greenbacks were secured in the false bottom of his large carpetbag.

Less two thousand dollars, which in the form of one hundred gold double eagles had been sewn into the lining of Price's coat.

IN SAINT CATHARINES the weather was raw, a far cry from the warmth of Richmond. Immediately on arrival, Price hired a hackney to drive straight to the Front Street address that Colonel Martin had given him. An icy wind blew harsh off Lake Ontario.

TOBY WAS THINKING of blood. The night before, the fire had snapped and crackled, feeding voraciously on a new log, casting its flickering light across the faces of the men gathered in the sitting room of the house on Front Street. Outside, the wind howled and tore at the closed shutters.

John Price had been the last to arrive. He stood warming himself at the fire. There were eight of them. The Colonel passed the knife; one by one, they drew blood. Beside his bloody thumbprint each signed his name to the contract:

Robert Martin, Colonel.

John Headley, Lieutenant.

John Price, Lieutenant.

James Chenault, Lieutenant.

Robert Kennedy, Captain.

James Harrington, Lieutenant.

John Ashbrook, Lieutenant.

Tobias Garner, Lieutenant.

"As this fire burns," Colonel Martin had said, "so will New York."

The Lucifer Contract was in force.

THREE

⌒November 1st, Tuesday, midafternoon.

'T WOULDN'T DO, 'twouldn't do," Meg Clancy murmured to her-self as she went about her job, changing linens, dusting, scrubbing floors.

In her fourth year as a chambermaid at the LaFarge House on lower Broadway and in the twenty-second year of her life, Margaret Mary Clancy had fallen in love.

She scoured the tiles and tubs in the fancy bath chambers—one to each floor—till everything gleamed. No, it absolutely would not do.

What with Ma a widow practically crippled by the rheumatism and her two cop brothers and a younger sister married, Meg's pit-iful small earnings were counted on to keep the wolf from the door.

As she worked, she hummed to herself, thinking how shocked Ma would be if Meg didn't stay with the plan Ma had for her life.

The plan was Meg would see them through till the young ones married, then Ma would move in with one of them and Meg would become a nun.

"That'll be the day," Meg said aloud, gathering up the soiled linen. She looked about to see if anyone heard; more impishly than piously she made the cross. Locked up in a convent, saying novenas the livelong year, let out only to do good deeds, and no men but priests for company . . . "That'll be the day," Meg said again.

The object of Meg's affections was a recent widower with a young daughter. Though still grieving, he was the answer to a maiden's prayer, and a man of renown. The rub was he was also a Protestant.

She'd known who he was before she'd really met him. Everyone in New York did. She'd first encountered her Protestant some months back.

Meg's chambermaid work was from five to eleven in the morning, every day but Sunday. For this she received the grand sum of one dollar a week. Back in '60, when she'd started, the rate had been one-fifty. But what with the War and all, in spite of more customers every day and night, the rate had come down. In September, she'd been offered an extra fifty cents a week to clean up the George Washington Room, the public saloon of the LaFarge House, each day after she was done with her chambermaid duties.

The fifty cents wasn't the all of it. A stomach-filling midday meal in the kitchen came with it. Within a week a third job presented itself. When needed, Meg tended the bar. Ten cents every night and tips. Drinkers tipped better than hotel guests and for that Meg was grateful. It was the tips that Meg kept for herself, secreted away. "Oh, blessed Mary, Mother of God," she whispered each night, "thank you for the tips."

Margaret Mary Clancy was saving for the day she would escape from her life.

FOUR

November 1st, Tuesday night.

MANHATTAN," the conductor proclaimed. "Thirtieth Street Depot, Manhattan, next." But it was hardly necessary; passengers had already started collecting their baggage. "Thank you for riding with us on the Hudson River Line. I'm obliged by the Army's Department of the East to draw your attention to the posted notices on the platform pertaining to all arrivals from insurgent states. Thank you again for riding Hudson River."

"What's that all about, Colonel?" Toby whispered as they descended the steps to the platform.

"Toby!"

"Sorry, sir. *Mr.* Martin."

But Martin's attention was on Bob Kennedy who, just like Martin, was wearing a black frock coat over a checked vest and necktie, in the guise of a businessman. Kennedy was reading a notice pasted to a pillar. Very deliberately he spat on the tracks, then walked off without looking back. Martin shook his head, for he was a fastidious man and didn't care much for Kennedy's manners. Or lack of them.

Kennedy's stay at the Ohio Penitentiary with Colonel Morgan had left him a bitter man. Martin had pushed to get Kennedy on this mission. Now he hoped it wasn't a mistake. He shrugged. A man played the cards dealt him and that's the way life was. Martin took in a deep breath and immediately started coughing.

"Are you all right, sir?"

Martin pulled the handkerchief from his sleeve and held it to his mouth for several seconds until the attack was over. He inspected the handkerchief. No blood. This time. He picked up his bag and strode to the pillar.

Toby, hard on his heels, read the notice out loud. " 'FROM THE DEPARTMENT OF THE EAST: *All arrivals from insurgent states are required to register at Department of the East Headquarters——No. 37 Bleecker Street.*' "

Looking about, Toby quickly saw that the platform was empty except for a beggar man. Toby tore the notice off the post and shoved it in his pocket.

Martin frowned. "That was unnecessary. You have to remember that we don't want to call attention to ourselves, son. Let's go. We have work to do."

"Some pennies for Shakespeare, sir?" The beggar stood before them, his cap in his hand.

Martin stared at the man. "What?"

"William Shakespeare, sir. We're trying to raise money for a statue of the noble bard in the Central Park to celebrate his three-hundredth birthday."

Martin doubted the fellow's words but didn't begrudge him charity in his pretended homage to the bard. He tossed a penny into the man's cap and kept moving.

Toby added his own penny and ran to catch up to the Colonel.

The two men now walked through the area where men, women, and children waited for their trains to be announced. The place seemed to be swarming with Federal troops.

They emerged into night on Thirtieth Street on the East Side of the City, though the time seemed to make little difference to the citizens of New York. People hurried along with surprising energy, smiling, apparently happy. Colonel Martin inspected the gaslit street. "Good. The others have probably all gone on ahead." They had agreed in Saint Catharines to meet in a particular house on Gay Street.

The Colonel never had been to New York, but their man in the City, Captain Eugene Longmire, had been here since July and had sent him a map. Longmire had come ahead early to confer with Southern sympathizers. It was he who had arranged the safe haven on Gay Street.

Martin held his hand up to the first in a line of hackneys at the curb. A barouche pulled by a pair of dappled grays came forward.

"As soon as we're settled," Martin told Toby, "I want you to walk around the City, get to know it." Toby was picking at the front of his red shirt. "Toby."

"Got some pie on my shirt."

Martin patted the boy on the shoulder.

"Where to?" the driver asked.

"Gay St—"

Martin overrode Toby. "We're going to Jones Street in Greenwich Village."

"I know where it is," the driver said. "One block long, but I know where it is." The bantam Irish driver peered down at Martin. "From the South, are you?"

A look of concern crossed Toby's open face.

Damn. Martin prided himself on his lack of accent. And yet here he was, noticed straightaway. "Yes, Kentucky, a Union state."

"Take it easy, Johnny," the driver said. "Get in. I don't care if you're Jeff Davis's son-in-law from the heart of Virginia and have a hundred nigger slaves. There's War and there's people. Welcome to New York."

F I V E

November 1st, Tuesday night.

HAVE YOU SEEN today's paper?" the driver asked, after Martin paid him. There was a stack of newspapers beside him on his seat.

"No," Toby said, exchanging a penny for a newspaper. He tucked the paper under his arm.

"Good evening to you then," called the driver and drove away.

A milk wagon rolled past, raising dust. Colonel Martin waited till the hack was out of sight before he started walking. "Come along, lad. Gay Street is just a short walk. You understand why I had the cab drop us on Jones Street and not at our destination?"

"Yes, sir," Toby replied, wanting to roll his eyes. He wasn't stupid.

Gay Street turned out to be a crooked little street, much the same as Jones. Trees slanted along the flagstoned sidewalks. The two men walked through piles of muddy leaves until the Colonel stopped next to a street lamp in front of a row of town houses as alike as peas in a pod.

A smart-looking brougham waited in front of one, its colored driver in livery at the carriage door. Martin hesitated. The house wore a brass marker, No. 9. No. 11, next door to it, was where he and his men would stay. These two buildings and No. 13 were of the same brown stone, each having white shutters. All three had window boxes which, with winter approaching, were barren.

"Anything wrong, sir?"

"Nothing, Toby, merely being prudent. We'll simply continue our stroll." They weren't ten paces past the carriage when the sound of piano playing and laughter spilled out onto the street. The door at No. 9 had opened. Martin stopped, brought out a cigar, and patted his pockets for a lucifer.

Taking his lead from the Colonel, Toby unfolded the newspaper the driver had sold him and flipped through the pages. "Good God," he said, holding the newspaper up to catch the light of the street lamp.

Throughout his pretense, Martin was watching the open door and the activity it generated.

"Sir," Toby said excitedly.

"Not now, boy."

A man, presumably in his cups, was taking his leave of a very large woman, a black feather boa wrapped in many turns about her thick neck. Her gown was also black. And glittery. The woman kept tapping the man on the chest with a pink fan, and giggling.

"See you next week, Nancy," the man called, as he stumbled to his carriage.

"I'll be waiting," Nancy trilled, waving her fan.

As he continued his spurious search for a lucifer, Martin noticed the people along the block, across the street. A man on his left stood on the corner staring at the fat woman and her departing visitor. By his bearing, Martin reckoned him for a soldier. An officer, perhaps.

"Sir?" Toby tried once more to get Martin's attention.

But Martin was looking at two men not fifteen feet from the possible soldier. The bespectacled man in a black herringbone mackinaw had stopped to drop a coin into a one-armed beggar's cup. The beggar's white mongrel dog barked at the man for his charity.

An old Negro woman, moving at a fair pace, considering she carried a large bundle of laundry on her head, bustled past, repeating, "Pardon me, gentlemens." Her progress led the Colonel's eyes to yet a fourth man on the opposite corner.

This one kept peering up and down the road, checking his watch and shaking his head in what Martin supposed was meant to convey annoyance. His poor performance gave Martin no doubt that this man was a policeman.

"Sir?"

"What?"

"I think you should see this newspaper."

Annoyed, Martin snatched it from the boy's hand. "Watching the street is more important than the newspaper."

"I'm not so sure of that, sir."

Now a milk wagon ambled along Gay Street.

"Sir?"

"Yes, Toby?"

"Wasn't that milk wagon just passing when we arrived?"

"Good boy, Toby." Martin, somewhat irritated at the boy's ill-timed persistence with his newspaper, was now pleased. For all his naive ways, the lad had an observant eye and a clear head on his shoulders.

"I know we're in strange country and they might do things a little different, but back home in Maysville they usually deliver the milk in the morning."

"Correct," Martin said.

A man pushing a cart with a grindstone appeared from around the corner. "Knives and scissors," the grind man called. "Sharpen your knives, your swords. Knives and scissors."

The grinder could be legitimate, but it troubled Martin that he wasn't stopping and waiting for customers. At this point even the whore and her client looked suspicious.

In fact, Gay Street had become so crowded with watchers it was amazing they didn't step all over each other. This collection of eyes didn't just happen to be on Gay Street to sell milk or sharpen knives or watch a whore and her client. What had brought all these eyes to Gay Street?

Martin pondered his choices. Enter No. 11, their destination, which would be foolhardy. Keep walking, which would be reasonable. Or go into No. 9, which would at least be confusing.

Without even glancing at the newspaper, Martin shoved it back at Toby, found his match, and lit his cigar. At that moment he realized someone was peeking from behind the curtains on the ground floor of No. 13.

"Sir, may I talk now? About the newspaper."

"What is it?"

Toby showed his Colonel the article. Across the top was printed:
REB PLOT TO BURN CITY TO THE GROUND.

The urge to cough burned Martin's lungs. The familiar pain followed. He felt for his Colt. "Steady, lad. We may have to make a run for it."

Toby could barely contain his laughter. "I don't think so, sir. Read on."

Martin did. At the end of the piece it said: *Democrats call Secretary Seward's account a tall tale and dub it a hoax to win the election.*

His need to cough vanished. Martin took a deep drag of his cigar. "Come on, Toby—we're going to pay a visit to a whorehouse."

WHEN THEY WERE led into the parlor, the first thing they saw was the rest of the Lucifer team sprawled on the carpeted floor, surrounded by whores, drinking beer, and reading the New York papers, spread out around them like at a picnic.

S I X

HEADLEY, JOHN. MUHLENBERG
COUNTY, KENTUCKY.
LIEUTENANT. TENTH KENTUCKY
CAVALRY. ARMY OF THE
CONFEDERACY. RODE WITH
MORGAN'S RAIDERS. SECOND-IN-
COMMAND OF LUCIFER.

November 1st, Tuesday night.

NOS. 9, 11, AND 13 Gay Street were typical of the attached brown stone houses that were being constructed in the City, each an exact replica of the others.

The ground floor was entered from the street, under the wide stone staircase. There was no alley; the way to the yard in the rear of each house was through the house itself. The yards were separated from each other and the street by low picket fences.

The parlor floor accommodated a parlor in front and a library in back. One flight above on the third floor was the drawing room that faced the street; at the rear was a formal dining room. The fourth floor contained the bedrooms. On the low-ceilinged fifth were the servants' quarters.

Eugene Longmire, who held the rank of Captain in the Army of the Confederacy, had been with Stonewall Jackson at Chancellorsville in May of '63, when the General was wounded. Chancellorsville was an outstanding victory for Lee, but General Jackson died eight days later, leaving Longmire, who had hitched his wagon to Stonewall's success, a lost man.

Longmire had let No. 11, fully furnished with a cook and a maid, from an attorney with Southern sympathies. Both the cook, Anna, and the maid, Heidi, were of German origin but had spent their first years in America in Richmond, Virginia. Both believed fervently in the Southern cause. In Richmond, however, Heidi had been a housekeeper and supervised the maids, who were all black.

Carrying his carpetbag, Lieutenant John Headley slipped cautiously out the back door of No. 9. Swinging his long legs over the low picket fence, he crossed through the garden patch to the one behind No. 11. Like the rest of the Lucifer squad, Headley had never met Longmire. He knew little about their man in New York except that he was Lucifer's liaison with the Sons of Liberty, a group of Southern partisans in New York.

For all his prudence, Headley almost laughed aloud when the back door to No. 11 swung open at his touch. He entered a kitchen fragrant with roasting birds and quickly closed the door behind him. Anna, the cook, a small barrel of a woman on tiny feet, was bent over, basting the birds.

"For the love of God," Anna gasped, clasping her throat with both hands. Her wooden basting spoon fell to the stone floor with a clatter.

Headley touched his fingers to his hat. "My apologies for startling you. I am John Headley, looking for Mr. Longmire."

"He's in the library, sir." Anna's face was florid. "Leave your bag here. Heidi will take it to your room. Mr. Longmire is expecting you."

"I'll keep my bag, thank you."

"As you wish, sir." She led Headley up a narrow staircase to the parlor floor, and pointed to the library door. "You're the second to arrive. Will the others march through my kitchen, too?"

"I expect so."

"For the love of God," Headley heard Anna exclaim as she labored down the stairs to her kitchen, "my birds!"

Headley knocked and entered. Inside he found two men smoking cigars and drinking brandy. Newspapers were spread on a table and on the carpeted floor. "I'm Headley."

Both men looked up, then rose to their feet. The first was tall and stood as if he had a ramrod up his arse. He had brown hair and a precisely trimmed thin mustache. "Longmire," he said. "May I present James McMaster?"

McMaster was a squat man with muttonchops and several chins. A gold watch chain swelled across his substantial paunch.

"McMaster publishes the *Freeman's Journal*," Longmire explained. "One of the strong hearts among the Sons of Liberty."

Pumping Headley's arm, McMaster said, "I can guarantee an uprising, sir. The Governor is with us. While the fire rages on Election Day, three thousand at least will rise up."

Headley's response was slow and measured. "That is unlikely now, sir. Our mission has been compromised."

"Oh, no," McMaster protested. "We must carry on."

"Of course we will." Longmire poured a third brandy from a crystal decanter that sat upon his desk. He handed the drink to Headley. "But not when they expect us to do it." Next to the decanter was a humidor with an elaborate cover: a man hanging from a gallows. Longmire pulled on the rope and opened the humidor lid. "Would you care for a cigar?"

"Thank you," Headley said, selecting one. As Longmire let the lid close, the hanged man swung back and forth, giving Headley the shivers. He took a hearty taste of the brandy, then bit off the end of his cigar and tossed it into the fireplace. The room was lavishly furnished; its windows were draped in heavy wine damask. "The street you chose, Captain, appears to be a busy thoroughfare. Full of people playing spy games. The rest of our men are next door in No. 9, where we were made most welcome and where the arrival of a group of men will not be questioned."

Longmire laughed, derisively, Headley thought. "It's not us they're after, man. The street is cluttered with watchers because of all the niggers being moved through next door in No. 13. It's a stop on the Underground Railroad."

Headley smoked, then peeled a shred of tobacco from his tongue. His response was thoughtful. "That doesn't make much sense. This is New York, not Virginia."

Longmire shook his head. "You'd be surprised how many New Yorkers agree with us about the darkies."

"Nevertheless," Headley said, "we have to accept that the enemy knows we're in New York. The newspapers make that extremely clear. With all those watchful eyes they might also know we're on Gay Street."

McMaster nervously crossed to the nearest window and put his hand on the draperies as if to pull them back.

"Don't," Longmire commanded. There was an edge in his voice.

Flustered, McMaster's hand dropped to his side.

"What we can hope," Headley continued, "is that they don't know we're in this house. Colonel Martin believes any attempt at flight would pinpoint us as being the men they're after. He feels the best tactic would be for you to remain here, as a diversion, and we continue in the brothel at No. 9. The Colonel has made arrangements for us to stay in the unoccupied top floor. No. 9 will be our back door, so to speak."

McMaster cleared his throat. "Won't the whores be suspicious of all the traffic?"

"Never knew a whore who didn't have a taste for money," Headley replied.

That Longmire was unhappy with this decision was obvious. It certainly wasn't the way General Jackson would have handled things. He said, "Colonel Martin seems to be an overly cautious man."

"It's his decision," Headley replied. "Now, if you'll excuse me . . ." He left the room and went back to the kitchen door, where he signaled.

The others drifted in, in pairs or singly. After they were all present in the library, Headley had Chenault take up a position at one of the windows. He sent Ashbrook back downstairs to the front door to keep watch on the street. Soon those not on guard duty were as relaxed as they could be with cigars and good brandy.

After a quick and brief introduction, McMaster was dismissed.

"Time for discussion, gentlemen." Martin closed the door behind McMaster and stood with his back against it in order to listen for any activity in the hall.

Price was the first to speak. "We can't just give up the mission and go home."

"They'll be watching for us, Colonel," James Harrington said. The short, muscular man clenched his teeth, making the tendons on his broad neck bulge. "We have to bide our time till they're not so vigilant."

"Toby?" Martin asked.

"I agree with Jamie. We bide our time."

"Of course we could surprise them," Price said. "The day *before* Election Day would catch them all napping."

Longmire nodded his head vigorously.

"Good idea." Kennedy helped himself to another brandy. "I'm for it."

"Chenault?"

Half turning from the window, Chenault said, "Whatever you think best, Colonel." He resumed watching.

The Colonel looked at Headley, who was sitting in front of the fire, his feet up on an ottoman. "What about you, Headley?"

Headley blew a smoke ring and said, "I'd wait."

Price raised a bushy eyebrow. "He would wait. He's met a whore who loves him."

Over the laughter Martin said, "I know this doesn't make you happy, Streak, but we wait. Lucifer will go forward. I promise you that."

"Hurrah," Toby shouted.

"Contain yourself, Toby."

"Yes, sir."

"The first thing we do is get familiar with the City," Martin said.

Longmire stirred and rose from an armchair in the corner. "May I offer an opinion, Colonel?"

"My decision is made."

Longmire shrugged. "Are we done here, then?"

Martin nodded.

Longmire rang for the maid. "Even though you won't be staying here, you do have rooms. Supper will be served here in the library at eight-thirty."

When the maid, a formidable woman in a black dress with white cap, collar, and cuffs appeared, Longmire said, "This is Heidi. She'll show you to your quarters."

Heidi nodded once; her blond braids coiled tight to her head under her white cap did not stray from their assigned place. She did not seem to have much use for smiles. "Gentlemen," she said, making Toby think of his first sergeant, "follow me."

"A word, Colonel," Longmire said.

When the other men had left, Longmire asked Martin, "You have the money?"

"The bills are here." Martin patted the carpetbag. "Price is carrying the gold."

"We're going to need it to pay for the firebombs, food, and two sets of accommodations for some length of time." Longmire spoke curtly, feeling he was being made the fool. This did not sit well with him.

Martin did not bother to explain why staying at the whorehouse was good tactics. If the man didn't understand . . . "We'll have enough. And you'd best find other places for us to stay. I doubt that Gay Street will be safe for much longer."

Longmire had worked diligently to secure the space on Gay Street and felt Martin's reaction was extreme. "This is a costly City, sir," Longmire objected, puffing fiercely on his cigar.

Martin studied the Captain through the haze of cigar smoke. Longmire was West Point, from Virginia, a cavalryman, yet there was something about him that made Martin uneasy. "Have no fear, Captain. Lucifer will go forward. *They* think it's a joke. We'll give them a joke they'll never forget."

SEVEN

⁓November 1st, Tuesday night.

THE NIGHTS SHE tended bar, rather than go home to Sixteenth Street, Meg would sleep in one of the empty ladies' maids' rooms on the top floor of the hotel. And didn't Ma have a conniption fit on those nights.

Jimmy Dawes, the head barkeep, had pointed the renowned man out and let her serve him his Kentucky bourbon whiskey. Sometimes he was alone, sometimes one or both of his brothers joined him.

The three were all actors as their father had been. John and Junius were very dashing, but it was with Edwin Booth Meg had fallen in love. The man had been a widower now since February of '63. A suitable amount of time had passed. His young daughter, Edwina, needed a mother. It was time for him to remarry.

Eddy Booth had given her a ticket for *Hamlet,* which he was performing nightly next door at the Winter Garden Theatre. She'd lied to Ma, said she was working, then confessed the lie and her love to Father Ryan.

Her friend Claudia had lent her a lovely blue dress for the occasion. What joy it was to sit among the upper crust. Oh, the grand noses that would have turned up if it were known they was sitting next to an Irish maid! Some of the looks she got made her wonder if they did know. Still, Meg was thrilled as she felt herself drawn into Hamlet's frightening and sad world.

She was going to be an actress. Actors were a lively lot, free of convention, unbound by religion. The theatre was the life for her. If only she could have it. She and Mr. Booth would tour the world together. Edwina would have a mother again.

It was her dream. Edwin was a quiet, gentle man and not open with his affection. But he knew how she felt and she knew how he felt and that was enough for Meg. For the moment.

There were problems, though. John Wilkes was attracted to her, too. And in a more fiery and animal way than his brother. She felt John's heat when their hands chanced to touch as she set his whiskey down or offered him the candle for his cigar.

Yet she would have none of him. John Wilkes reminded her of the restless, slightly mad Irish boys who clustered in the pubs in the old country and the new, boasting of what they would do in this world.

John had the Booth charm but not the character. Eddy had the character.

Meg bent over behind the bar to lift a tray of fresh glasses for the second time in the past hour.

"Ain't you the busy bee tonight," a familiar voice said.

"I might say the same for you, my girl," Meg answered, straightening, staring into the painted face of her friend Claudia Albert, who'd worked with her as a chambermaid during her first two years at the LaFarge House, until, in Claudia's own words, she "got wise and joined the order."

Tonight Claudia wore her vivid yellow taffeta dress that showed off the narrowest of waists. Her stays were so tight her breasts were pushed up and out, a display of her wares. Over her arm was a small black satin cape, certainly not enough to keep the November chill from all that bare skin. Her Jewish red hair was up and rolled and glittery jewels hung from her lobes.

A kidskin-gloved hand was tucked into the arm of a man whose head barely reached her shoulder; Claudia was taller than most women and many men.

"This is my friend, Margaret Mary," Claudia told her gentleman.

Meg bobbed her head. "What will you have, sir?" Claudia had her nerve, always coming round, flaunting her money and her trade.

Damn Claudia, she was forever trying to get Meg to "join the order." Israelite blasphemy.

Whoring was whoring, no matter how much money you made. It would be a cold day in Hell that would find Meg doing that. She'd as soon be a nun.

"A jug of your best Kentucky sipping whiskey," Claudia's gentleman replied. He spoke with a soft drawl. That his accent was Southern meant little; New York was filled with Southerners, all doing business of a sort. "Three glasses."

"Three, sir?"

"I'm expecting a friend."

Leaning into her gentleman, Claudia said in a loud whisper, "Two is better than one." She roared with laughter when she saw Meg's fair color go red.

Claudia and her gentleman took a table in the darkest corner of the room. This was the way Jimmy Dawes liked it. He didn't hold with whores in the saloon, but he knew Claudia. Her gentlemen were gentlemen, and they always had money. And, most important, he and Claudia had an arrangement.

Soon the second man joined Claudia and her Southern friend. All three put the sour mash away like there was no tomorrow.

"All right, Johnny," Claudia cried. "Here's a tune just for you." She clambered onto the table, her skirt purposely drifting up her robust thighs. She wore red stockings with black garters. Meg looked away, horrified.

Claudia sang, " 'When Johnny comes marching home again, Hurrah! Hurrah! We'll give him a hearty—' "

"No, not that song." The man Claudia had come in with slammed the table hard, rattling the glasses. The bottle went sliding but Claudia stopped it with the curved heel of her shoe.

"What's the LaFarge House coming to?" a regular patron muttered, storming out. He was followed by two others.

Jimmy Dawes went among those remaining, calming them.

"Sing 'My Old Kentucky Home'!" Claudia's gentleman shouted. His friend grabbed his arm but he cuffed it away. "Sing, damn it!"

"All right." Claudia flounced her lifted skirts at him. "No need to get testy. 'Oh, the sun shines bright . . .' "

"That's enough, now," Jimmy called.

" '. . . on my old Kentucky . . .' "

"Claudia!"

" '. . . home.' " Claudia laughed uproariously. "You're a spoil-sport, Jimmy."

Another regular stormed out, saying, "The next thing you know they'll be singing 'Dixie.' "

Claudia took her gentleman's hand and jumped from the table; the bottle fell; bourbon streamed across the floor.

With good reason, Claudia shrieked loud enough to wake the dead. Her escort's friend had dropped a lighted match into the spilled whiskey.

The sawdust at Claudia's feet swelled into a small blue flame. The few remaining customers hurried out the door.

"Are you crazy?" Claudia cried with frightened glee, while her two men did a wild dance about her chair, stomping out the flames. "You could have set the whole place on fire. The whole damn City."

When they heard that, the two men began to laugh like lunatics.

Jimmy Dawes rushed over with a bucket of water. Fire was no joke to him. "It's all right, folks," he called to an empty saloon. "Nothing to worry about." Still, he splashed water about just to make sure.

When the fire was out and he realized he'd lost almost every customer, Jimmy turned to Claudia, livid. "Look what you've done!"

Claudia's Johnny dropped a gold double eagle on the table.

"Well . . ." Dawes said.

Johnny's expression went calm, then his mouth curled into an angry sneer. "Don't be greedy. Be a good fellow and bring us more mash."

"Yes, sir," Jimmy said, fearing the animal look on the man's face as much as he esteemed his gold. On his way back to the bar, Jimmy rolled his eyes at Meg. "Another bottle of bourbon."

Meg brought the new bottle and three clean glasses to the table. Now she recognized Claudia's second escort as a man she'd seen before. He was staying at the hotel. She set the glasses on the table and opened the bottle. As she turned to go, her empty tray glanced off the brim of Claudia's gentleman's hat, tilting it back on his head. Meg scrambled to snatch the tray before it hit the charred and wet floor. "Beg pardon, I'm sure."

Meg moved away quick as she could. She knelt behind the bar to cross herself. "Jesus save us." Claudia had done it now. Claudia was consorting with Lucifer on earth, all right.

But what was going to happen to Meg Clancy? She had exposed the Devil and the white mark of his fall from Heaven for all the world to see.

E I G H T

⌐November 2nd, Wednesday, midnight and beyond.

NEW PATRONS ROARING IN kept Meg so busy she hadn't noticed it was past midnight. Sad to say, her true love Edwin had not appeared.

When Claudia's friend called for a third bottle, Meg asked Jimmy to deliver it. "It's Lucifer the Devil sitting with Claudia."

Jimmy Dawes smiled broadly. "OK. Take care of my friend Pete Tonneman, then, over there. Give him ale no matter what he asks for."

The place was filled to bursting now with a raucous late-night crowd. If Jimmy was concerned about the irate customers who had left the LaFarge House because of Claudia and her friends, he gave no sign.

Meg looked where Jimmy had pointed and saw a man with golden hair, lighter than her own. He sat at the bar, shoulders hunched over his empty glass. His frame was long and cadaverous.

"Sir?"

"Whiskey," he replied, staring at the bottom of the glass mug.

"I think not, sir."

He lifted his head, startling her. His eyes were the blue of a summer sky; haunted scars of despair etched his face. "What did you say?"

"I'm Meg, sir. Jimmy told me to serve you nothing but ale."

"Ah, Jimmy. Would there were more Jimmys in this world. Ale, 'tis."

His words were blurred. Their tone was what made her feel his pain. "You fought in the War, sir?" She took his mug and filled it with ale.

"Nothing so heroic. I'm a journalist. Correspondent for the *Evening Post*. You're a pretty little thing. I haven't seen you here before."

"I don't know why not, sir. I'm usually here. When did you come back?"

"The end of May."

"War is a terrible thing, sir."

"It is, Meg, it is."

She had other customers that took her away from Pete Tonneman, but some instinct made her look back to him every so often.

This time when the room began to empty out, Claudia and her friends rose as well and Jimmy went to collect on their tab. As the three left together, Claudia gave Meg a wicked wink. Meg shook her head. That Claudia.

"Claudia's friends paid for another bottle," Jimmy said. "They want someone to bring it up to room 506 in an hour. You can do it, on your way upstairs." At the frown on her face, Jimmy continued quickly. "I've got the sums to do. You'll make a nice tip, you'll see. He paid me with this." Jimmy held up a gold double eagle for her to see.

Meg didn't want to, would rather have died, but in their cups as they were, the man might give her a gold coin all for herself. She could hide it away for her wedding dress.

"OK." She went to work, wiping down the empty tables, doing as much as she could now, to make the next day's full clean-up task somewhat easier.

Finally, only Pete Tonneman remained, as if frozen to his bar stool. When Jimmy sat down to add up his chits, Meg swept up, washed all the glasses and mugs, except Tonneman's, wiped down the bar, and emptied the spittoons and filled them with water to soak overnight so she could clean them easier tomorrow when she mopped the floor.

Meg dried her hands and set the fresh bottle and three clean glasses on a tray. She was weary. Her lids were drooping, her feet hurt, and all she wanted was her bed. Making certain she had her candle stub and box of lucifers in her apron pocket, she called, "I'm off, then, Jimmy."

"Good night, Meg." Jimmy did not look up from his figures.

She climbed the dimly lit back stairs to the fifth floor. The hotel had been full since the War began. Visitors came and went and many returned again and again.

To them she was Meg, and she liked it. It made her feel part of it all, the bustle and the excitement that the War brought to the City.

On the fifth floor, the gaslight was up bright, and there was Claudia leaning against the wall next to a jet. The gaslight reflected little gold rays from the coin Claudia was holding high.

Startled at the sound of the stairway door opening, Claudia dropped the coin. She quickly scooped it up and slipped it deep between her considerable breasts. "Oh, Meg, you scared me half to death."

Claudia's makeup was smeared; her red hair trickled out of its roll and hung in a tangle down her back. She pulled her little cape about her bare shoulders. "They are my good boys," she said with a hard smile, blowing Meg a kiss, as she went out through the door Meg had come in.

Meg sighed. She hurried down the hall to 506 and raised her hand to knock. The door was open a crack.

She heard one of the men say, "We should carry newspapers with us." The one with the white streak, she was sure. "They'll help the fire." The man added, "Come election day, with God's grace we'll burn Billy Yank's New York town to the ground."

"All right," said the other. "I know what to do."

Silence, now. Meg was confused. She repeated the words in her head and was terrified. Surely she should run, tell her policemen brothers what she'd heard?

"Wasn't that Claudia something?" the second voice asked.

Meg backed down the hall toward the staircase door. Calm, she instructed herself. It was her Christian duty to return to the room and perhaps learn more. She stopped. Humming that Kentucky song loudly, she went back to 506.

When she knocked, the man with the Lucifer streak opened the door. Only this time he was wearing his hat. "It's the barmaid," he said over his shoulder. "Come along, girl, we're dried out waiting for you."

"Yes, sir." Meg bobbed her head, good as pie.

"Ask her in, Price," the man inside said. "I'm for it."

"Keep still, you fool," Price said. He pulled a silver coin from his vest pocket and gave it to her. "That's for you, girl." He took the tray from her. "Now be on your way." He stepped back into the room and shut the door. She heard the key turn in the lock.

Disappointed, Meg held the silver dollar with a shaking hand. They were plotting to burn the City. "Holy Mary, Mother of God," she whispered. She ran all the way down the stairs to the George Washington Room and burst through the door. "Jimmy! Help me!"

But Jimmy wasn't there. The public room was empty. At least she thought it was—until she heard a soft snore coming from a corner banquette. Pete Tonneman was lying flat out, fast asleep. He was the one, for sure. If her brothers were here she'd tell them. But it was the middle of the night. Her brothers were at home. Pete Tonneman would know whom to tell. "Mr. Tonneman, sir. Wake up. Wake up!"

He groaned. "Go away."

"Please, sir. You have to help me." She shook the journalist— nothing but a bag of bones—he didn't move. She ran back to the kitchen where she located a coffee pot sitting on top of the cold stove.

Meg poured the dregs into a beer mug and rushed back to the bar. Ignoring Jimmy's earlier admonition, she fortified the coffee dregs with a large dollop of bourbon.

She pinched Tonneman's nostrils between her fingers. He snorted and jerked his head away. She pushed and pulled and finally got him sitting up against the banquette, though he rolled against her like a helpless baby. Pinching his nose again and getting him to open his mouth, she forced the coffee down him. By the bottom of the mug he was sitting up on his own, blinking at her.

"Mr. Tonneman," she said urgently, "they're in 506, plotting to burn the City down."

"What?" He rubbed at his eyes with the heels of his palm and opened his mouth as if his tongue was too thick to be contained.

"A devil named Price with a white streak in his hair is going to burn down New York."

"Balderdash." He rocked forward, attempting to stand. "But some of my best stories have started as balderdash. And I've never ducked a story in my life. Let's have a look."

"It's not balderdash." Meg kissed her fingertips and lifted them high. "I swear to God."

By the time they'd climbed the back stairs to the fifth floor Tonneman had fallen seven times. On the last fall his long body draped along several steps. "Tired. Leave me be."

Outraged, she kicked the soles of his feet. "You're a journalist, you sot. For God's sake."

Rejecting her assistance, he climbed to his feet. They walked along the hall. At 506 he pressed his ear to the door. Without warning it opened; Tonneman tumbled to the carpet. He raised his head and peered around.

The girl, Meg, hovered in the background. Gaslight flickered. Room 506 was empty. The plotters, if they ever existed, were gone.

N I N E

⌒November 2nd, Wednesday morning.

I N THE CITY OF NEW YORK on this November day a certain sharpness to the wind was only one of the telltale signs of autumn in the air.

Already the leaves of the trees along Chambers Street had turned red and golden. Soon enough they would lie helter-skelter on the ground for the sweepers to gather.

On the second floor of City Hall John A. Kennedy, Superintendent of the Metropolitan Police Force and special provost marshal appointed by the War Department, poked a hole in his cigar with a lucifer match but did not light it.

The Superintendent was impatient to get on with his day. He and his aide, Sergeant Jerry Murphy, had been first to arrive for the meeting. Kennedy was seated at the head of the long table. Murphy stood behind him. They did not speak.

The two weren't there long before a commotion at the door told Kennedy that the Mayor had arrived. Finally. Sergeant Murphy leaned over and whispered in his boss's ear. Kennedy grimaced and moved to his seat, left of the head.

Mayor C. Godfrey Gunther bustled in with a contingent of Tonnemans. The Mayor was oversized, with a high forehead under brown hair. His gray beard and absence of mustache made his soft but square jaw seem round. He sat at the head of the table, the signal for the others to sit, also. Chief Hays Tonneman and Old Peter sat opposite Superintendent Kennedy.

Old Peter, though retired from the Force as a Chief, was still called upon for advice at critical times. These were critical times.

Old Peter's son, Chief Hays Tonneman, named for the late High Constable, Jacob Hays, sat to Old Peter's left. Hays, a keen-eyed hulk of a man, dark-haired, ox-broad, was a clear contrast to his father.

The old man's hair was pale gold, going to white, and while hardy for his seventy-five years, his build and bearing were more elegant than his son's.

"I'll be brief, gentlemen," Mayor Gunther began. "I've just received a telegraph message from Secretary of State William Seward. He has information from the British provinces that the Rebs plan to burn New York."

"Bunkum," Kennedy exploded.

Gunther ignored the Superintendent's protest and showed the telegraph message all around. "I have it on credible authority that on Election Day members of the Confederacy intend to put major Northern cities to the torch."

"That's bunkum, Charlie," Kennedy growled again. Kennedy called him Charlie because he knew the Mayor detested this shortening of his first name.

"Isn't that what you said when I warned you about the riots?" said Old Peter, who always spoke his mind. "And for that you got a broken head."

"There you go," the Mayor said, his chin whiskers bobbing. A smile played on his thin lips. The clean-shaven area above his mouth seemed always to be covered with fine dots of perspiration. He was pleased he had thought to invite Old Peter to this meeting, as he knew his Superintendent of Police was not. Actually, Gunther agreed with Kennedy. The forty-three-year-old Mayor, a wealthy fur merchant, had been the candidate of the McKeon Democracy, an antiwar reform group.

Kennedy fingered the deep scar on his forehead and glared at Old Peter. The scar was a souvenir of the Draft Riots in July of '63. He'd been so severely beaten that Commissioner Thomas Acton had to step in. It was weeks before he'd really felt right. To this day he was still subject to staggering headaches.

Kennedy bore Old Peter no ill will; he just wished the old man would stay home and tend to his knitting. Having Old Peter around was like having the ghost of Old Hays to contend with, always looking over his shoulder.

On the other hand, he hated Gunther with a passion. Kennedy believed the stories that Gunther had supported the draft rioters and considered him muddleheaded and the same as a traitor.

"I'll issue a confidential bulletin," Kennedy told the Mayor, "but I still think it's bunkum."

Gunther's beard bobbed. "Very well. General Dix will alert his men at Department of the East headquarters. But he seems to agree with you."

Kennedy nodded. "Dix is a good man."

Old Peter stood. His gut instinct told him this was not bunkum. "I take Secretary Seward's words very seriously," he said. "You and Dix won't be satisfied there's a problem until this City is burnt to the ground."

TEN

⌒November 2nd, Wednesday, early afternoon.

H E WAS FALLING . . . a bottomless pit, smothered in darkness.

Gabriel's horn blasted him from his dreams. "Fresh fish," the monger was tooting and calling on the street. "Mackerel fit for the pan."

He opened his eyes; closed them immediately. He recognized the ceiling spinning over his head as his own by the odd boot-shaped crack in one of the corners.

What an awful thirst. He forced an eye open. The ceiling slowed its revolutions, at last coming to a halt. The boot shape was in the left-hand corner, where it belonged.

He had to get up but he could scarcely raise his head for the pounding. A drink. What he needed was a drink. He opened both eyes a slit, a crevice. Gripping the bedpost, he pulled himself to a sitting position. He was all right. It was the world that was askew. The bile in his throat threatened to make him sick. Where the hell was the blessed bottle?

Experience had taught him it would be under the bed. But that was a heroic task, worthy of a Hercules: to lean over and snag the bottle from the pits of Hell. And he was no Hercules, especially not this morning.

A pitcher of water stood by on the night table. Seizing the

pitcher, holding tight, he lifted it to his lips and washed the vile taste away.

He gulped in deep breaths and waited patiently. After several long minutes, he reflected that he might be able to stand.

HE WAS WRONG. It took him another quarter hour to stand. He was also wrong about the time of day. He'd assumed it was morning. It was just after noon. Slowly his ears began to pick up the sounds of the house.

His was the smallest bedroom, on the top, a floor above the old folks. He'd lived here on Grand Street with his grandparents fifteen years, since the death of his mother.

His father, John Tonneman, had moved into the family home so that Grandmother Charity could see to Pete's and his sister Mariana's upbringing. John Tonneman was dead two years, and while Pete was covering the War, Mariana had died in childbirth, leaving a bereft husband and an infant, Racqel.

Grandmother Charity had found a wet nurse and moved Mariana's husband Edward Nathan and his baby daughter into the Grand Street house.

In the spring, just before Pete returned to New York, Edward had married Pete's cousin Louisa, and Edward and baby Racqel had left the house on Grand Street for their new home on East Nineteenth Street.

Grandmother Charity, already in her seventies, began to fail rapidly and now lay near death. Her beloved husband, Old Peter, was in constant anxiety about her health.

In a great cruel wave, the memory of the previous night came back. He'd been drunk, though that was every night. But not so drunk he didn't remember what the barmaid had told him. What the devil was her name?

The room in the LaFarge House had offered no proof of her claims of a conspiracy. Three glasses, but no bottle. Too bad, he'd needed a drink then. As now. As always. All he had was the girl's word of what she'd overheard. Hell, he'd written great stories before on less than a chambermaid's tale.

He'd have to question her friend, the whore. Tonneman scanned the room for his clothes. On the chair. He got up, found his soiled shirt. On the right cuff he'd written a name: *Claudia Albert*. That was the barmaid's whore friend.

Suddenly he was dizzy again. He sat, dropping the shirt to the floor. "I'll never drink again," he whispered, knowing this was a lie. As quick as it had come the dizziness was gone.

He grinned. His trusty notepad, his cuffs, never failed him. Having Claudia's name gave him new determination to shave. Though retired, his grandfather was still an important man to the Metropolitan Police. If there was any truth to the barmaid's story about a Confederate plot, Old Peter would know.

After cutting himself only once while he shaved, Pete dressed. In spite of everything, he managed to look almost presentable. But he felt the hollow man inside, a ghost.

Quiet as his steps on the stair were, Nellie heard him. The housekeeper, thin as a post herself, clucked at him. "Don't eat, you'll die," she sang, showing him her big buck teeth.

"I need to talk to Old Peter." Pete groaned. The sound of his own voice pained him.

"Then you should have got up earlier. He's up, et, and out for three hours now. How about some fried mackerel, fresh bought?"

Pete could smell the grease and the frying fish. He groaned again, stomach heaving, shook his head. "Nothing."

"You can't go out with nothing."

"Coffee." She handed him a cup, clucking all the time. In spite of its scald he drank the coffee down in two gulps and rushed out.

On Grand Street, umbrellas danced like pickaninnies, making it more difficult to get a hack. Pete, of course, was without an umbrella. He took shelter under the big oak on Willit Street. No leaves, but the thick old branches did the job.

"Grand Street, still a grand street," he mumbled, turning his collar up, his eyes squinting at the rain. This was yet a neighborhood of fine homes. Ah, a hackney. He yelled, whistled, and ran, nearly breaking his neck on the slippery cobble. The icy pour soaked him through and through.

"Where to?" the coachman asked from under his umbrella, on his roost up top.

"Three hundred Mulberry Street," Pete shouted, his head throbbing with every syllable. Goddamn, he needed a drink.

The landau's fold-down roof leaked, dripping water down his neck. Worse, the driver was a madman, taking corners too fast, rocking, spinning. It was a gamble which would kill him first, bad whiskey or the slick Belgian blocks of the streets, which made the horses slip and slide in rainy weather. "So help me," Pete muttered. "The War was easier."

When the hackman pulled short at Lafayette where he had driven into a blind alley, Pete called it quits. He yanked on the man's leather leg strap, got out, gave him fifteen cents, and walked the rest of the way in the pelting rain. He arrived at Police Headquarters soaking, chilled to the bone, and much the worse for wear.

He was gratified when Jerry Murphy told him he would have to wait, using the twenty minutes he sat on the bench outside the Superintendent's office to recover somewhat from his lunatic hack ride.

"You can go in now, Pete, lad," Murphy said.

There was a big wet mark on the seat when Pete stood. He neatened his sodden coat with faltering hands and walked into Superintendent Kennedy's office.

"You've cut yourself, Petey," the Superintendent said in his thick brogue.

Pete touched his right cheek. His fingers came away with a little streak of blood. "Shaving."

"Grow a beard then, you won't have to bother. You look like a drowned cat."

"I feel like one." Pete sat down opposite the Superintendent.

"You told Murphy this was important. Let's hear it."

"Yesterday, I was in the LaFarge House public room and got to talking to the barmaid. She overheard two men talking about a Reb plot to burn the City to the ground on Election Day."

"Ha!" Kennedy said. The sound was like a rifle shot. "Old news, Petey, my boy. The Mayor told us all about it this morning, and he got it direct from Secretary Seward. So you see, my grand journalist, the Metropolitan Police Force knows all about the conspiracy."

"What?"

"The Army knows about the conspiracy. Even Lincoln knows about the conspiracy. I'm certain General McClellan knows about the conspiracy. And worse, from your point of view, everyone in the City knows about the conspiracy and don't think much about it. The *Daily News* has a story out calling Seward's warning an electioneering trick." Kennedy shook his head, laughing at the expression on Pete's face. "You're going to have to get up a lot earlier in the morning if you're going to bring home the bacon."

ELEVEN

⌐November 2nd, Wednesday afternoon.

PETE, CLUTCHING KENNEDY'S COPY of the *Daily News,* walked away from Mulberry Street thoroughly mortified. No one was taking the threat seriously; they didn't even think there was a threat. It was all a big joke.

Yet urgency had pierced his armor for the first time since he'd come home in May. Even now, after more than a year, the sounds of cannonfire and the tortured cries of the wounded and dying were still in his ears. After the fighting at Lookout Mountain and Missionary Ridge in November '63, he'd drifted, seeing the country through the bottoms of whiskey glasses.

New York burning to the ground. It was a terrible thought. He'd had enough of seeing people suffering, dying horrible deaths. A fire would be worse than last year's riot. War brought out the worst in human nature at home, and on the battlefield. He was sick of it. Damn the Confederacy, he was not ready to brush this story aside as one would a gnat. There was the ring of truth in Meg's tale; he had to act on it.

Pete's feet took him automatically toward Printing House Square, where the *Post* building stood at Nassau and Liberty. A bottle waited for him in his desk drawer.

The *Evening Post,* established in 1801, was only one of more than a dozen daily newspapers printed for New York's voracious readers. Along with those in English, there were the German, and the French and the Russian, and languages Pete had never even heard of.

It was War news everyone wanted now. The telegraph had changed journalism forever, giving readers almost instantaneous information about events thousands of miles away. Anything that came over the telegraph they wanted to know about.

Pete climbed the stairs eagerly, not even giving way to fellow reporter Bob Payne, running down, most likely off on an assignment.

On the second floor Pete drew a deep breath. He loved the rich mixed smells of printer's ink and tobacco smoke. Coming to work was always like going home.

Other reporters called greetings. "Hey, Pete, got a match?" one asked, laughing. Apparently this was the joke of the day.

Pete did not stop to chat as he normally would; he had other, more important things on his mind. He made a beeline for his desk and slammed open the drawer. The bottle was there. And more than half full.

Some of his fellow tipplers would, at this moment, drop a pencil on the floor, kneel, bottle in hand, have a quick swallow, then come up for air. This was not Pete Tonneman's style. In full view of his colleagues he took a hearty taste, capped the bottle, and returned it to its nest.

The presses were quiet, a blessing. Shortly, the huge machines would begin to roll out the first of the evening editions. Pete removed his wet hat, ran his hand through his hair, and quickly set the hat back on his head. Reporters always wore their hats, to protect them from the lead that fell through the cracks in the floor from the presses above. Why no one ever thought of putting the presses downstairs boggled Pete's mind. He rolled himself a cigarette and strolled the width of the large room.

His editor, Everett Miller, greeted Pete as he walked into his office. "Have a nice night off?"

"Passable," Pete said, shamelessly. *Night off* was Ev's term for when Pete hit the bottle too hard. They were friends. And Pete was a good reporter. Most of the time.

"I just got this from Harvey Hewlitt up in Catskill Station." Ev spat cigar leaf at his spittoon and missed. He balanced the cigar on the edge of his desk and flapped a sheet of paper at Pete. "Man had his throat slashed."

Pete lit his cigarette from Ev's cigar and returned it to its perch. He yawned. "Very interesting." Pete took, but did not even glance at, the paper. "What about these arsonists?"

Ev scowled. "The only thing *that* story's good for is wrapping fish. Like everyone else, we've written it, rewritten it, and thrown it away. If you wanted a part of that, you should have turned it in last night. Today it's old news."

"Not if I have new information."

"Do you have new information?"

"I've got a girl who claims she saw the conspirators and over-heard something."

"Ha!" Ev shouted. "Give me a nickel for every one of those and I'll be rich."

"I'm serious. Let me tell you."

Ev retrieved his cigar and puffed vigorously. He pointed to the sheet of paper in Pete's hand. "The fellow was found near the railroad tracks."

"And?" Pete asked.

"That's it."

"That's nothing."

"I know. That's why I'm asking you to write it. Half a column will do."

"You'll be lucky to get that." Now Pete looked at the piece of paper. "White. Smallish. Strong build. About thirty. No identification. Harvey says the body doesn't appear to be a local man."

"Which proves?" Ev asked.

"He might have been thrown from a train."

"Interesting. Put that in your story."

"What story? There's no story here. I'll give the best I can, which won't be much, considering what little you've given me." Pete took a last drag from his cigarette and dropped it to the floor, grinding it into the wood boards with his sole. Lord, he'd finally remembered her name. "This girl Meg, she's the barmaid in the LaFarge House's George Washington Room. She says this high-priced whore who's a friend of hers was in last night with two out-of-town big spenders. The whore went upstairs with the men. One was listed in the guest register as Joe Jones."

"Original name," Ev said.

"Meg was sent up later with a bottle. When she got to the floor, the whore was already on her way out. The door to the room was open a ways and the barmaid overheard the two men talking about burning down the City on Election Day."

"Did you investigate? See any of this for yourself?"

Pete shook his head. "When I got up there, the room was empty. Only sign they'd been there was a mussed bed and three glasses."

Ev nodded to the newspaper in Pete's coat pocket. "You've got the *News*. Have you read it?"

"No, I was saving that joy for when I got home."

"I'll save you the trouble. It says Seward's letter about a plot to burn down the City is a palpable electioneering trick. It says the people are sick of conspiracy stories. Claims the Government is crying wolf, when all the time the real wolves are Lincoln and the lying Republican politicians and that if there's trouble in the City on Election Day, the Republicans not the Rebs would be the cause."

"I think there's something to the girl's story. I can feel it in my gut."

Ev shrugged. "For all I know the feeling in your gut came from the bottle she was taking upstairs." At Pete's narrowing eyes, he added, "Talk to that whore. Maybe go back to the clerk who registered Joe Jones. Follow the story where it takes you. But don't waste too much time on it."

Glum now, Pete went back to his desk and took another swallow from his bottle. Then he neatly wrote out a short piece on the dead man up in Catskill Station, ending with a request for any information about a vigorous white man, of short stature, about thirty years of age, wearing good clothing, who was supposed to arrive on a train from the north on Tuesday, the first of November, but didn't show up.

Pete went home to Grand Street. If his grandfather was home he intended to talk to him about what Meg had overheard.

Nellie stopped singing and dusting when she heard him come in. "You've written on your cuffs again," she said, accosting him in the foyer, waggling her dust broom at him. "How can I do the laundry when . . . ?"

Pete had warned her long ago not to wash his cuffs if there was writing on them. "Thank you, dear Nellie, I've already gotten the information from my cuff today."

"All right then," she said. "Those cuffs look just awful. I don't know if I can get all that scribbling out this time."

"Cuffs?" He thought back to earlier in the day. He'd read Claudia Albert's name and then gotten dizzy. He'd never inspected the other cuff. "Get the cuffs, please," he said.

The old woman's eyes twinkled. She always thought of Pete as a little boy and was tickled by how excited he got over his work. "I'll be right back."

Pete waited, listening to her light footsteps on the stairs. Nellie might be getting old but one couldn't tell it by her footfall. She'd been with the family since Pete's mother had died.

In fewer than five minutes Nellie reappeared and handed him his soiled cuffs.

One cuff he'd already seen: *Claudia Albert.* On the other the pencil writing was smudged, so he could scarcely read it. *Price. White streak. Burn New York.*

TWELVE

⁀November 2nd, Wednesday, early afternoon.

MEG'S SLEEP HAD BEEN FITFUL. Since she'd spent the night at the LaFarge House, she could have slept a little later, but she'd been up at dawn. She'd done her work cleaning the rooms and the George Washington Room lickety-split, then instead of taking her meal she went off to find her brother Michael, to tell him what she'd heard. He'd know what to do, whom to tell.

Michael Clancy, Jr., was a beat copper, as his father had been before him. He wore the blue uniform with pride and liked to stand on the street corners in his territory, twirling his club and smacking it into his palm, watching out for the citizens.

Mike Sr. was gone six years now, the Lord preserve his soul. He'd been on horse patrol when the fool nag got spooked by a stupid dago's dancing monkey. Da landed on his head, lingered for a week, then went to his Maker, content to know that both his boys, Michael and Dennis, were on the Force.

The rain was coming down by the bucketful, flooding intersections, making crossing the streets treacherous. Unless they changed Mike's route, he'd be as close as possible to the Black Heart Tavern Meg knew. But it was inside that she found him, eating salted hard-boileds with his beer.

"Well, looka who's here," he said to Fat Francis, the barman. "My baby sister." A frown creased his boyish face. "Ma okay?"

"She's fine, Michael. Ma and everybody. Can you come out?"

"In that mess?" He gestured at the downpour outside. "Are you daft? What's going on here? Let me hear the worst. Don't tell me you went and lost your job."

"No, Michael." Meg tugged at his sleeve. "Please—I must talk with you in private."

"Don't mind me," Francis said, cramming an egg whole in his mouth and waddling to the end of the bar.

"Michael," Meg whispered hoarsely, "the Johnny Rebs are going to burn the City."

Michael choked on his beer, spraying pieces of egg on her and over his trim blue uniform. "Margaret Mary, you are a dithering lunatic. That's in the *Daily News,* for Christ's sake."

"Oh, Michael." Meg crossed herself at her brother's blasphemy.

"Oh, yeah, sure." Mike crossed himself and made a face at his sister for taking him to task with her good example. "Everybody knows it. They're saying it's a lie, that Seward made it up so Lincoln will get reelected." He laughed so hard he had to set down his beer.

"It's not made up. It's true as the nose on your face. I saw two of them, heard them plotting."

"Oh, yes. Two drunks pulling your leg, is all it was." His eyes narrowed. "Or are you pulling mine, Margaret Mary? Well, pull the other and let me get on with my lunch."

"I thought you would help. You're a terrible man, Michael Timothy Clancy."

"Go back to work, little sister, or you'll lose that precious job, for sure. Do you really think some Rebs could come here and light a fire and get away with it? Grow up. This is New York."

Meg wailed, "Why won't you believe me?" She stamped her foot, turning crimson.

"What's to believe? And what in God's name would they accomplish? The War is almost over. They've lost." Mike looked down at her and rubbed his nose. "You saw these men?"

"One has a white streak in his hair."

"And where are these Reb boys now?"

"I don't know. They left the hotel in the middle of the night. What shall we do?"

"Someone was having their little joke, but you'd best let them who know take care of it. Don't worry that pretty little head of yours."

"Dennis will believe me."

"Dennis will give you more of the same."

"Michael, you got to listen—"

He spun her around and pushed her out the tavern door. "Go on now."

So Meg left Michael and ran to the hotel in the drizzling aftermath of the torrent. On the corner of Broadway she gave the newsboy a penny for the *News*. Sure enough, the whole story was there for all the world to see. A ruse, they called it. That was that. Still, she hadn't seen Claudia. If there was more to this, Claudia would know.

THIRTEEN

⁀November 2nd, Wednesday, early afternoon.

"YOU SEEK THE LADY CLAUDIA?" the high voice asked.

Pete turned, surprised. Standing in front of the LaFarge House was John Wilkes Booth, unremittingly fashionable in his wine-colored coat with velvet lapels, and his buff waistcoat. Tight gray trousers were tucked into his gleaming black boots and the usual wide-brimmed straw hat he affected no matter the weather sat roguishly tilted back on his head.

Booth's success with women of all classes was legendary. The well-known libertine had but to gaze into their eyes soulfully, smile, and they would throw themselves at him.

Pete didn't like John Wilkes Booth. The man was an outspoken Southern sympathizer with a consuming hatred for the President, whom he referred to as "The Tyrant in Washington City." As proper as his brother Edwin was, John Wilkes was the opposite. He cared for no one but himself, except perhaps the Confederacy.

Ruefully, Pete fingered the damp lapels of his own drab ink-stained coat and glanced down at the battered rubber military boots he'd worn since Chattanooga; though he and John Wilkes Booth were about the same age, Pete suffered greatly by comparison.

Pete Tonneman and John Wilkes Booth were only slight acquaintances. Edwin was Pete's friend. The two men had met at Delmonico's on Beaver Street one night when Pete had won at cards and had more money than he knew what to do with.

How did John Wilkes know he was looking for Claudia? In that instant, Pete wondered if perhaps Booth wasn't mixed up with the conspirators. "Why did you say that?"

" 'Lady Claudia'?" A mocking smile played at Booth's lips. "You said 'Claudia Albert.' You were talking to yourself. You must watch that, old man."

As if pulled by a magnet, without discussion, both men entered the smoke-filled George Washington Room from the street. Jimmy Dawes stood behind the bar, drying glasses with a cotton cloth.

The two sat. Each was served the Kentucky sour mash Booth favored.

"You know Claudia, Booth?" Though he wanted to swallow it down at once, Pete took a small sip of the whiskey.

The actor nodded. "Hebrew Claudia of the red hair? Of course. She has a flat on Grand, near Elizabeth Street, I believe."

Grand Street? Where the Tonneman family had lived for over fifty years? Where Old Peter still attended services, as Jake Hays, the late High Constable, had, in the Presbyterian Church? What a hoot. What a tragedy.

Not sharing Pete's restraint, Booth tossed his drink straight down. He cleared his throat. "Helps to loosen the voice." The handsome actor did not speak in the strong resonant tones his brother used. John Wilkes had a notoriously thin voice and his throat often felt the strain. "Alice?" he called. When he got no response he pounded the table twice and shouted, "Two more whiskeys, here."

Alice, a pale girl with feverish eyes, approached tentatively. "Mr. Dawes says no shouting, Mr. Booth."

Booth's hand was on her waist and moving up.

"Mr. Booth, you shouldn't do that when I'm carrying a tray."

"Why not?" Booth didn't remove his hand.

The girl had a mug of beer on her tray. She held it high over Booth's head.

Booth laughed loudly and raised his hands in surrender. "You come back to me after you deliver that mug, you hear?"

Alice tore admiring eyes from the actor. "How are you today, Mr. Tonneman?"

"You know me?"

"Yes, sir. You were in one night last week."

"Two more whiskeys, please."

"Yes, sir."

As the girl withdrew Tonneman said to Booth, "I would have thought you'd be home in Baltimore."

"I'm a roving player. I go where the stage is." Booth offered Pete a cigar.

"This great disagreement of ours is winding toward an end."

"The War is not yet over, sir," Booth said as Alice returned with their drinks. She set down the whiskeys and leaned over the table to light their cigars with a match from her apron pocket. When she let out a small squeak, Pete noticed that Booth's hand was squeezing the girl's rump. Libertine he was, and a very successful one at that. Alice walked away smiling.

Pete asked Booth, "What do you make of this conspiracy to burn the City?"

"I'm arranging to be safely out of town on Election Day."

"You have a performance that night?"

"No. But if we did, Edwin could play both Hamlet and Horatio. He usually does."

"Do you know a man named Price? He has a white streak in his hair."

Booth stared at Tonneman. "How very interesting. I think I'll affect that for the next villain I play. It should be quite striking. Is Price his Christian name?"

"I don't know. Are you really going to be out of the City on Election Day?"

"Of course not. I wouldn't miss that blaze for the world."

FOURTEEN

GARNER, TOBIAS. AGE 18.
BANKER'S SON. MAYSVILLE,
KENTUCKY. LIEUTENANT. TENTH
KENTUCKY CAVALRY. ARMY OF
THE CONFEDERACY. LUCIFER.

November 2nd, Wednesday, late afternoon.

THOUGH OF MIDDLING HEIGHT, John Price had a powerful physique. Any other man wearing a coat with a hundred gold double eagles sewn in its lining would be dragging. For John Price it was a coat of feathers.

In his left boot was a hand-fitted scabbard; in the scabbard, a bowie knife. Thick and long, the single-edged blade was hand-inscribed with the battle flag of the Confederacy, surrounded by the words, "Our flag and our RIGHTS."

John Price was proud of his weapon. And he enjoyed using it.

With his hat masking his white streak, Price could disappear into any group. His comrades worked for the Confederacy. While Price was a fervent believer in the Cause, he worked directly for Senator Jacob Thompson, Martin's superior. The others had come to burn New York, and a worthy mission it was. Price was the paymaster for Lucifer, but his other job was more to his taste. He was to protect the mission and, if necessary, kill anyone who got in its way.

Which was why in the teeming rain he was following the man with the spectacles. Price hadn't taken much notice of Specs the first time, on the train. But when he caught a glimpse of him on Gay Street, the day after they'd arrived, the only possible explanation was that he had followed one of them from the train.

Streak didn't know who Specs was, he only knew the man was a danger to the mission, same as the other one. Which meant he had to kill this one, too.

Specs was easy to follow. Price would enjoy playing poker with the man. Just as many poker players gave themselves away with tics and gestures when they bluffed, Specs had already twice given himself away when he turned to inspect the terrain.

He was doing it now, straightening the collar to his distinctive black herringbone mackinaw. Another mistake. He shouldn't be wearing a coat like that doing work like this.

Price ducked between two delivery wagons. Sure as the rain that was falling, Specs turned casually to check the pedestrians behind him.

A lad, seven at most, feet dangling from the back of the wagon on Price's right, looked at him with curious eyes. Price placed a finger over his lips. To his left, a very old brown mare nibbled at Price's shoulder, slobbering his coat.

Price pushed the dripping muzzle away, annoyed at the distraction. He stepped back to the sidewalk.

Specs was gone.

◆TOBY DIDN'T WANT to follow Price too closely. The Colonel had lent Toby his map of New York's crooked streets, so he didn't expect to get lost. Still, he hadn't counted on the beer wagon practically knocking him over.

◆PRICE LOOKED ABOUT. What had been an almost empty street was crowded now. People with signs streamed past him. The Loyal Ladies of the Union, one sign said. The other signs proclaimed their loyalty for Lincoln. Damn that monkey's eyes. Where the hell had Specs gone? He was losing daylight, would have to get back to the house fairly soon.

He made his way to the intersection, just as a deer's tail of black herringbone disappeared into an alley. Price's mouth twisted into a crooked smile. Most of the Lincoln scum were gone. Price reached down and drew the bowie knife from the sheath in his left boot.

FIFTEEN

⟞November 2nd, Wednesday, early evening.

DUFF HATED BEING LATE. He had promised the Loyal Ladies of the Union he'd be at the Lincoln rally in Chatham Square by now. He turned up the collar of his Union blue overcoat and quickened his pace. In spite of the cold, the rain felt good in his face.

Jew's Alley was the right shortcut. The street lamps provided no light in the alley, but Duff knew the way like the back of his hand.

The figure carrying the rolled-up bundle appeared out of nowhere: pasted down soap-locks combed forward, sparse growth of whiskers on his chin, and most telling, the huge metal medallion which showed the number of his fire company. Duff knew at once that this was a Bowery Boy, one of the City's toughs who had two loves, fighting fires and just plain old fighting. Duff braced himself.

But the Boy barely gave him a glance. He ran past Duff and blended into the darkness.

Not five feet along Jew's Alley, Duff stumbled. He knelt, felt something give . . . a hand. "Jesus," Duff muttered under his breath, though he was trying not to blaspheme since he came home from the War.

A man's hand. Soaked, he was. Duff lit a match, hunching to keep the flame dry. The poor sod either hadn't owned a coat or someone, most likely the Bowery Boy, had stolen it. But he'd left the man's hat. "Mister, wake up." Duff made to move the poor bastard under the shelter of the shed in front of the building.

The lack of a left eye made it necessary for him to cock his head to one side or the other to see things clearly. As far as he could determine, except for the two of them in the rain-swept alley, there was not a soul in sight. He tossed aside the spent match.

As he pulled the poor cull into the shelter under the street lamp, he saw that the fellow had a lucifer match clenched between his teeth. And that he was dead, through and through. His throat had been cut.

"Jesus save us," Duff gasped, scrambling to his feet. This was not blasphemy, this was praying. He crossed himself.

Duff leaned down and removed the corpse's broad-brimmed hat. This time he swore.

The November wind buffeted his blue overcoat about him. Suddenly he was whisked back to that day of September 17, two years before, when service to his country took him near Sharpsburg in the State of Maryland.

The Reb's blade was point forward, aimed at Duff's throat. Duff was going to be a stuck pig. The Reb thrust his blade. Duff parried and jabbed with the butt of the flagpole. The Reb foundered, falling away, limbs twisted. His gray hat flew off, exposing a full head of jet black hair, divided neatly by a white streak straight down the center.

I've fought the Devil, he'd thought in that moment. *And I've won.*

But he hadn't. The Devil had hurled his saber at him.

Now the man who had taken his eye lay before him, killed not in battle, but with his throat slit ear to ear like a farm animal in a slaughterhouse.

SIXTEEN

November 2nd, Wednesday, early evening.

THE TWO COPS, Malone and Donahoe, peered down at the corpse by the light of their kerosene lamp. The Irish more or less owned the Metropolitan Police Force in New York City. And for that reason Duff had often thought of joining the cops after the War. But that was before he'd lost his eye.

He'd found Malone and Donahoe eating in a tavern not half a block away. Donahoe had gotten a boy to run to the station house to fetch the wagon and the two had come along with Duff, grousing all the while about missing their dinner.

Malone, the taller of the two, held the lamp high in order to see Duff clearly. "Your name?" he asked.

"Patrick Duff."

Donahoe looked over at Duff and grinned. "You know this fellow, Mr. Duff?" He motioned toward the body.

"I was on my way to the Lincoln rally in Chatham Square," Duff replied, ignoring Donahoe's question.

Donahoe's grin bled away. "As a loyal Democrat and McClellan man I'm going to forget you said that. Where are your people from?"

"I was born in Kilkenny."

"So was my Da." Donahoe nodded at his partner. "He's Dublin."

Malone saluted Duff with a finger to his hat.

"What's a Kilkenny fellow doing with the likes of Abe Lincoln?"

"Leave the man be," Malone said.

Donahoe shrugged. "So what happened?"

"Before I went into the alley I saw a Bowery Boy," Duff replied. "He could have come out of Jew's Alley. When I went in, I stepped on this poor bastard."

"How'd you hurt your eye?" Malone asked.

"A Reb took it out with his saber at Antietam."

Malone looked pained. "I'm sorry."

"It wasn't your fault."

"No, it was Mr. Lincoln's, for sure," Donahoe said. "Will you look at that white streak in his hair. You ever see anything like that?"

"Never," Malone said.

Duff thought it wise not to comment.

"No coat," Donahoe said, going through the dead man's pockets. "Most likely the Bowery Boy you saw stole it. What'd he look like? Did you see his medallion number?"

"He looked like a Bowery Boy. I did not see his number," Duff answered precisely.

"Nothing here except for some change. What do you make of the match between his teeth?"

Duff shrugged.

"A gang matter," Malone said. "Revenge."

Donahoe ran his hand along the corpse's legs, then reached into the left boot. "What've we got here?" He held up the knife sheath. "Ain't that a fine piece of sewing?"

Malone took it. "Must have held a wicked blade."

"And where is it, I wonder?" said Donahoe.

"I'll have a look around," Malone said.

"You're lucky that Bowery Boy didn't slit your throat with it, Mr. Duff." The dead man's broad-brimmed black hat lay on the ground where Duff had left it. Donahoe picked up the hat and looked inside.

"I hear Lincoln keeps his papers in that stovepipe hat of his,"

Malone said, casting his lamp back and forth over the alley, still looking for the missing knife.

Duff nodded. "So I've heard."

"Is that why you wear a stovepipe, because you're a Lincoln man?" Malone's eyes twinkled.

Duff appreciated the policeman's humor. "A hat is a hat."

"No papers in this hat," Donahoe said. "Give me that light over here."

Malone illuminated the dead man's hat. "What you looking at?"

"The leather inside; it says, 'Expressly made for J. Price by Deems and Deems, Lexington, Kentucky.' Is Kentucky Union or Reb?"

"Reb," said Malone, going back to searching for the knife.

"No," Duff said. "Kentucky is a Union state."

Donahoe took off his helmet, revealing a shock of orange hair. He set the dead man's hat on his head. "It fits perfect," he said. "What do you think?"

"Quite dashing," Duff said.

"Hear that, Tom? Fellow here says I'm quite dashing."

"I heard, and I'll tell the world," Malone said. "Dick Donahoe is dashing, all right. That damn knife ain't anywhere to be seen. Now, where the hell is the blessed wagon?"

Donahoe tilted the black hat this way and that. He said to Duff, "What sort of work do you do, Mr. Duff?"

"Stonecutter, when I can get it."

Donahoe nodded. "I know what you mean. My cousin Fred is in the same boat. He's a hod carrier. Can't get a job. It's the niggers, taking all the jobs. You know what James Gordon Bennett said in the *Herald* the last election, that if Lincoln was elected we would have to compete with the labor of four million emancipated niggers? He's right. When the War's over it'll be worse. We'll have a whole lot of them freed slaves moving here and stealing Irish jobs."

Duff knew that back in the forties all sorts of work, like hod carriers, coachmen, longshoremen, waiters, and barbers, had been Negro jobs. Over the past twenty years, what with running from the Famine and all, the Irish had swarmed into America, and had taken the jobs from the Negroes. Again he thought it wise not to comment.

"Stonecutter?" Malone said. "You think one of them chisels you use could cut a throat like that?"

Duff shook his head. "Too messy. I should think the knife that fit in that sheath did the job."

"I say he's right." Malone finally stopped his search. He was holding the light on the shed, looking it over.

"Where do you live, Mr. Duff?" Donahoe asked.

"I have a room at Broome and Clinton."

"The Israelites are starting to move into that part of Mackrelville."

Duff grinned wryly. "It was good enough for Jesus."

"Right," Donahoe said, laughing. "You might as well go. We have to wait for the wagon, worse luck."

Duff gave up all thoughts of the rally. Turning over in his mind the events of the last hour, he walked slowly back to his room, attempting to make some sense of them.

It was a many-sided conundrum. The man who'd taken his eye had inexplicably turned up in New York, newly dead.

And for reasons he couldn't explain, Duff had to find out why.

SEVENTEEN

⌐November 2nd, Wednesday, early evening.

T HE METROPOLITANS had no love for reporters. Newspapermen always seemed underfoot, butting their noses into things that weren't their business.

Because of Old Peter and Uncle Hays, Pete Tonneman had practically grown up at 300 Mulberry Street. He was treated with a tad more respect than the other journalists sniffing out stories around Police Headquarters.

Still, Pete followed custom; he brought his offering to loosen lips. Today he carried with him a box of Havana cigars for Sergeant Ned Corrigan, keeper of the desk. Oddly, no other journalists were to be seen, either inside or congregating out on the steps.

"Where is everybody, Sergeant?" Pete asked, setting the tin box of cigars on the high desk.

The lardy copper with his fat lips and watery blue eyes was not Pete's idea of a thief catcher. It was common knowledge that Corrigan was one of those who'd bought his way in, and it would be a rare sight to see the Sergeant anywhere else but on his fat arse at this desk.

"If you're meaning your family, they're at the Hall." Corrigan squinted at the cigars. "Garcia. Them's good smokes."

"They're yours, Sergeant."

Corrigan's hand shot out and the box was gone, under the desk. "I meant the other reporters."

They both looked over at the street door. A large-boned, muscular man with a patch over his left eye had just entered and was looking around.

"Hennessy! Why the hell aren't you watching the door?" Corrigan yelled. "Over here, mister," he said to the man with the eye patch. Corrigan's voice was high and whining, not the sort to inspire confidence. And it didn't in the one-eyed man.

The stranger was about Pete's age and wore a tall, black Lincoln hat atop longish brown hair. Stepping up to the desk, he said, "Patrick Duff is the name. I've come about the murder last night in Jew's Alley."

"That's a precinct matter."

"They told me that murders are investigated by detectives at Mulberry Street."

"Well, yes. *Important* murders."

Duff cocked his head. "I thought the death of any man was important."

"What are you, a bloody priest?" Corrigan's pale eyes glared.

"I ask you, sir, polite and sincere, are you going to help me with this matter?"

"Yes," Corrigan said. "I'm going to tell you to go back to the precinct and leave me be. Can't you see I'm busy?"

"There's nobody here but this gentleman." Duff looked at Tonneman.

"Don't mind me," Pete said, backing away from the desk slightly.

"Shows you what little you know about police business," Corrigan told Patrick Duff.

"What about the Bowery Boy I saw leaving the alley?"

"What about him?"

Duff's face went red. "You can go to Hell."

Corrigan lifted in his chair. "And you can go to jail if you don't mind your manners."

"Shit," Duff said and made for the door.

"Just a minute," Corrigan whined. "Who the hell are you calling a *shit*?"

But Duff was gone, slamming the door behind him.

Corrigan grinned. "How do you like them apples?"

"You're a master, you are," Pete said. He was thinking how good a glass of ale would taste.

Outside, the sun was bright, but distant. However, the earlier chill in the air was gone. Pete Tonneman liked soft days and soft women and good whiskey. Sally's, a favorite haunt of the cops, was only halfway up the block. That's where he headed.

When Pete entered Sally's, he saw that Patrick Duff was at the bar staring gloomily at the healthy dose of whiskey in front of him.

"A man after my own heart," Pete said, changing his mind about the ale. "Whiskey, Sally."

The woman called Sally was built like a man. She wore wide pants and affected short hair. She set Pete's drink before him. Pete dipped a finger in his glass; pensively he licked the finger.

Duff nodded at him. "You want to gulp it all down, don't you?"

"We seem to be members of the same club."

Duff nodded once more.

Pete wiped his finger on his trousers and offered his hand. "Pete Tonneman, Mr. Duff. I'm with the *Evening Post*. Maybe I can help you with your problem."

Duff's handshake was strong and sure, his hand heavily calloused. "Pleased to meet you."

"Where'd you lose that eye?"

"Antietam."

"Infantry?"

Duff nodded and lifted his drink to the light, appreciating its color. Pete did the same.

"Lovely stuff," said Pete.

"Like a maiden's kiss."

"I'll drink to that."

Down the drinks went; Sally brought two more.

"I didn't fight," Pete told Duff, "but I was in it in '63. Missed Gettysburg, so I complained to my editor. That's how I came to be with General Rosecrans when he took Chattanooga—September, last year—without a fight."

Duff, feeling the good glow of the whiskey, smiled sadly. "Antietam was the end for me. I came back here glad to be alive and able to work. Some weren't so lucky."

"I know," said Tonneman. "There were nine of us—five corre-

spondents, three artists, and a Matthew Brady man with his cam-
era—in Chattanooga. One of the artists was killed, just standing on
a hill, admiring a sunset."

"Tops of hills are not good places to stand during war," Duff
said.

"We ate together, drank together, played cards, talked about the
War, women, and the mystery of life, but not always in that order."

Duff raised his hand to Sally for another round.

"We lived and ate as the officers did," Pete continued, rapt in his
drinking and his storytelling. "Same mess, same muddy fields. We
paid for our food. The mud they threw in for free."

Duff laughed but made no comment.

"What got the high-muck-a-mucks' goat was they couldn't tell us
how to behave. Sometimes they were right about us, though."

"Officers are like that," Duff agreed. "Especially high-rankers."

"Many was the time we felt slighted. We were working journalists, in the correct and proper pursuit of our vocation. We were on a
mission to tell the people what was happening, and we had every
right to be there. They rated us with the food- and whiskeymongers
and the whores who followed the camp."

Duff burped. "You had every right to feel that way, you did."

"To be fair, Mr. Duff, we often talked too much, got drunk too
much, and acted like buffoons. But in spite of our behavior, we
wanted respect."

"Every man wants that. Deserves that."

"Sherman said we were as good as traitors, for God's sake. Putting Federal intelligence in the newspapers for all the Rebs to see.
Many's the time he had me kicked out of the campsite."

"General Sherman is known for his black moods."

Pete had put several Garcias in his coat that morning. He offered
one to Duff and they lit up. Sally brought two more drinks. Pete
went back to his War story.

"Things got hotter when the Feds were attacked by a Reb army
commanded by General Bragg at Chickamauga Creek. Lucky for
me I wasn't with Rosecrans when his right and center gave way
before the Confederate assault. I was on the left with General
Thomas." Pete was making whiskey marks on the bar with his finger, laying the battle out. "Thomas stood firm. He prevented a complete rout of Union troops."

"Sounds like a rouser," Duff said.

Pete grinned. "When it was over, we retreated to Chattanooga, while Bragg took up positions on Lookout Mountain and Missionary Ridge."

Duff drained half his fresh glass. "You've seen history, my friend."

Matching his new pal swallow for swallow, Pete said, "When I found out that Grant—the new boss of Union operations in the West—was coming to Chattanooga, I made sure to be there. He arrived toward the end of October; next Sherman showed up with the Army of the Tennessee. The following month, Grant attacked. The battle lasted two days; Bragg's troops were driven from both Lookout Mountain and Missionary Ridge. Bragg then withdrew to Georgia, and Grant got his promotion to lieutenant general and the command over all Northern forces."

"You were there in the thick, weren't you?" Duff said, having another taste.

"Yes, I was," Pete said, exhilarated as the day it happened. "I was first to know and first to get the story over the telegraph."

"Good for you!" Duff shouted. "That calls for another drink."

Drunk as he was, Pete was still functioning. "You say you saw a murder?"

"No. I found a dead man in Jew's Alley tonight."

"And the Bowery Boy?"

"Coming out of the alley, just before I went in."

"Can you describe him? Did you see his company number?"

Duff arched the eyebrow over his good eye.

"All right. Tell me about your dead fellow."

"He was a man I knew from Antietam."

Pete's fingers felt thick as his brain. They itched for his pencil but he restrained himself. "Were you together before he got killed?"

"No, that's the odd part. I hadn't seen him since the battle. But I stumbled over him in the dark. If it wasn't for the white streak in his hair, I never would have recognized him."

Pete set his glass down so hard whiskey sloshed over the rim. "What?"

"He had a white streak in his hair."

"What was his name?"

"Price. J. Price. It was marked in his hat."

Pete's insides grew heated, more than the whiskey ever did for him. He didn't sober up, but he did get sharp. "You knew Price from the Army? Were you in the same outfit?"

Duff shook his head. "Oh, no, no, no. You don't understand. Price wasn't a Union soldier. He was a Reb."

Pete pushed his drink away, heedless of the whiskey he slopped. "I think you better tell me this again. From the beginning."

"This was at Antietam, remember. I can still hear Father Corby as if he was in this tavern with us right now." Duff's good eye closed. "He was brigade chaplain. 'Buck up, boys,' he told us. 'You're fighting for God and country.' Then he wheeled about nicely, for he was a fine horseman. Sitting tall in the saddle, he called out absolutions to those about to die. I put the rosary Kathleen Tierney had given me around my neck. I'd given up that stuff— religion—but I hadn't wanted to hurt poor Kathleen's feelings, sweet girl that she was, though she was a whore."

Pete was afraid to say a word for fear Duff would stop.

"The color guard, Matt Flynn, he carried the banner of the 69th. He stumbled and fell and didn't get up. I'm no hero, but poor Matt was lying there like a sack of potatoes. Someone had to carry our banner. I slung my rifle and caught up the flag. Now, by luck or God's will, I was the color guard." For no apparent reason Duff stopped talking. He stared at the wall.

Finally Pete could bear it no longer. "Go on, man. Please."

Duff wiped his mouth. "When we came to a sunken road, which later they'd call Bloody Lane, a column of Rebs moved onto the top of the plateau. I was in the front rank and just reached the crest when the Rebs rose up. It seemed as if all the Confederate guns at Antietam were firing straight at me." Out of nowhere Duff gave a shrill, keening cry that Tonneman imagined might be better suited to the bogs of Ireland.

He touched Duff's arm. "Are you all right?"

"Now, yes; then, no. Fifty-eight-caliber slugs chewed up the legs of the fellow to my left. The head of the boy to my right exploded like it was a shell. Jesus, Jesus." Duff began to sweat profusely. "I didn't fire, I didn't fight, I just kept going, carrying the 69th's flag."

Pete leaned on the bar for support. Duff seemed to pay him no mind.

"Out of the smoke came a man, left-handed he was, waving this big bloody sword at me. And the bastard was smiling, for Christ's sake. He had one thing on his mind and one thing only. My demise."

"What did you have on *your* mind?"

"To this day, I can't answer that question. I would like to answer 'God and country,' but I just can't remember. I don't know."

"Then what happened?"

"What do you think happened? The bastard had his sword pointed at me and he kept coming, aiming for my throat. He was going to stick me like a pig. Run, I says to myself, but I couldn't. I fended off the thrust."

"With the flagpole?"

"What else? I hit him hard with the end of the pole. The man fell, his gray hat flew off. That's when I first saw his hair. Ink black it was, with a stripe of pure white down the middle. I told you I'd given up on religion."

"Yes," said Pete, surprised to hear his voice so hoarse.

"I crossed myself. Over and over. In the heat of the battle all I could think was that this was the Devil. By defeating him I'd change my life. I'd saved it, of course, but now I'd change it. It was while these confusing thoughts were swimming in my battle-addled brain that the son of a bitch threw his sword and took out my eye."

"Amazing story. And you met him again?"

"Agh," Duff barked. "You've not been listening. I didn't *meet* him. I *stepped* on him. Earlier this evening, in Jew's Alley. Lying there like a beggar. His coat gone, his shirt filthy."

Knees wobbling, Pete lifted his glass to his lips and was disappointed to find it empty. "Sally!"

Duff lifted his hat and ran his fingers through his thick hair. "You know, though I never knew that fellow I feel I owe him something. Because of all that happened between us. I have to find out who did this. Maybe it's crazy. But I owe him."

"Even though he took out your eye?"

Duff chuckled. "What's an eye between enemies?"

"What now?"

"Mr. Price's life and mine are connected."

"But he has no life; he's dead. The connection is broken."

"No, it's not, don't you see? Not while he's wandering in Limbo."

"What the hell do you owe a dead man?"

"Peace. He'll not rest until his killer is found. And, therefore, Mr. Tonneman, neither will I."

EIGHTEEN

⌒November 2nd, Wednesday evening.

GASLIGHT BARELY CUT through the soft fog created by the sudden change in weather. The City was cloaked in warm, moist air.

Elated by his chance meeting with Patrick Duff, Pete wended his way home. He was stinking drunk, but his mind clung to what the veteran had told him about the dead man.

Meg had given him only bits and pieces; Duff's strange tale brought it substance. A Confederate soldier named J. Price had been heard by a barmaid on the night of Tuesday, November 1st, plotting the burning of New York in room 506 of the LaFarge House on Broadway. Price had been in the company of another man and previously both had been in the company of a prostitute by the name of Claudia Albert. On Wednesday, November 2nd, Price was found dead in Jew's Alley, near Chatham Square, his throat cut, his coat and perhaps his knife missing.

According to Meg, Claudia Albert had received a gold double eagle for her work Tuesday night. Tonneman wondered what sort of loyalty that sum bought. Probably none at all from a woman of her sort. But he certainly couldn't match it.

The Tonneman house stood on Grand Street, at Willet. Claudia Albert lived at the other end, on the other side of the Bowery.

Bees buzzed in Pete's brain. What cross street had Booth mentioned? Only when Elizabeth Street loomed ahead did he remember. He stopped and asked a blind beggar.

The fellow granted him a lascivious grin. "Going to get your stick wet, eh? She's just a block from here, corner Mott. This side." The beggar held out his tin cup and shook it, listening for the expected clink.

"No change," Pete said, chagrined. "I'm giving you a five-cent stamp."

"Thanks for nothing," the blind man called after, his fingers groping in the cup. He shouted louder. "She don't come cheap!"

The corner building on Grand at Mott was No. 205. Two fat old ladies sat like guard dogs on boxes in front of the building, chewing tobacco. Pete stepped back quick to keep from getting marked, nearly losing his balance on the edge of the curb.

"What do you want here?" one old woman demanded.

"I'm looking for Claudia Albert."

"*Who?*" the other old lady screamed. She lifted an ear trumpet from the ground and held it to her ear. "*Who?*"

"Claudia Albert," yelled the first. "He's looking for Claudia."

"Claudia Albert, my arse," the deaf woman shrilled. "I know her from when. Them Jew kids. They're all whores. Hanna Rappaport is who she is." The deaf woman stood, inhaled noisily, and shrieked, "Hanna! Man here wants to get his stick wet."

A window sash opened on the first floor. "Shut up, you old witch." A red-haired woman thrust her head out. "What can I do for you, handsome?" she asked Pete.

He craned his neck. He could see the woman's bare shoulders and that she was wearing a white corset with lots of lace. "I'm Pete Tonneman. A friend of Meg Clancy's."

Claudia laughed. "Come on, Meg didn't send you to me to get laid."

Pete felt like an idiot, talking from the street. "No, nothing like that. May I come up? I need to talk to you."

"Not tonight. I'm off to see a gentleman friend."

"Let me walk with you." Looking up like this made Pete dizzy; he leaned against the stoop railing.

"Do you think you can manage that?"

"What do you mean?"

Claudia laughed. "I mean, sit on the stoop; I'll be down directly."

'Down directly' meant one thing to Pete and something completely different to Claudia. Pete was dozing with his head against the stoop when he heard the whisper and inhaled the intoxicating perfume.

"Wake up, soldier boy."

He jumped up with a start, setting the old ladies cackling and spitting.

Claudia was grandly dressed in a gold brocade dress, a red velvet cape over her shoulders. Her red hair was piled high like the headdress of some pagan princess. She was as tall as Tonneman himself.

Pete offered her his arm. "Where to, my lady?"

"The St. Nicholas Hotel, Mr. Tonneman. Shall we hire a hackney? My poor shoes are not made for walking." She lifted her dress to reveal slim ankles in white hose and fragile red velvet slippers.

They found a hack on Broadway. Tonneman helped Claudia in and climbed in after, taking the seat opposite. Claudia's hoopskirt filled the small cab, spilling over on Tonneman. Claudia settled herself, maintaining an expression of amusement.

"What did Meg tell you I could do for you?"

Tonneman was amazed at her nice even teeth. No one had teeth like that. Even his own, which had had good care because Auntie Lee was a doctor, were crooked and yellowed. Claudia also had a dimple in her left cheek which became more pronounced whenever she spoke or smiled. It was hard to believe she was a prostitute. 'Twasn't hard to believe some men thought her worth twenty dollars.

"You were with two men last night," he began.

She laughed. "I'm with two men, or more, every night but the Sabbath."

"I'm talking about Tuesday night, November first, and the man with a white streak in his hair."

"Ah. The double eagle. Johnny Price and his friend . . ." She tilted her head. ". . . Kennedy. Southern boys, they were. For the Union."

"I think not," Tonneman said. The influence of the whiskey was wearing off and the headache and bilious stomach were just beginning. "John Price, did you say?"

She nodded.

"What was Kennedy's first name?"

"Didn't ask, he didn't say."

"Had you ever seen them before?"

"No."

"Since?"

"No."

"Did they tell you why they were in New York?"

"Business, is what they said. I never ask questions of my gentle-men."

"Do you know where they're staying?"

"Why, the LaFarge, of course."

"They left not long after you did."

"Then Meg didn't get her gold eagle?"

"I don't believe so."

"That's too bad," Claudia said. "Those boys were practically rolling in them."

"They showed them to you?"

She shook her head. "I don't miss much, I can tell you. When I helped Price off with his coat, I nearly fell down with the weight. They were sewn into the lining. There's no missing the feel of coins."

Tonneman pursed his lips. He'd found out why the dead man's coat was missing.

The hack driver pulled up in front of the St. Nicholas. Even though the hour was late a great many people, in particular men in evening clothes, were coming and going in carriages and cabs.

Tonneman squeezed gingerly past the hoopskirt and stepped out of the cab. As he helped the prostitute down, he knew she was pleased with the way he was treating her. Though he was sincere, he also knew it was the smart thing to do with a woman like Claudia.

He paid the driver and handed Claudia his business card. She slipped it into a slit of a pocket in her gold dress, and immediately brought out a card of her own. *Claudia,* it read, simply. *No. 205 Grand.*

Tonneman accepted the card and tipped his hat. "Thank you for your help, Claudia." He escorted her into the hotel, said good night, and went immediately into the St. Nicholas's saloon. This time Tonneman stayed with ale for the sake of his bilious stomach.

The conspirators had obviously come to New York with a great deal of money. Were they now turning on each other? Had this man Kennedy murdered Price and gone off with the coatful of gold eagles?

Or did the murder and theft have nothing whatever to do with the conspiracy? Was it merely Price's bad luck to be in that alley at that time?

Pete swirled the amber liquid in his glass and thought about leaving it. He drank it down. One of these days he had to stop.

No, the Confederate plot was real. And Price's death had everything to do with it.

NINETEEN

November 3rd, Thursday, early morning.

Colonel."

Robert Martin opened his eyes instantly, his Colt in his hand. On guard, but unruffled, he said, "Yes, Headley."

"They haven't come back, sir. Kennedy and Price."

The top floor of No. 9 Gay Street was one large attic room beneath slanting rafters. Except for the missing Kennedy and Price and James Harrington, who'd patrolled as outside sentry, all the men of Lucifer had slept there on the floor the previous night, under the dim glow of gaslight.

Harrington was keeping his vigil, watching the watchers. He would give warning should their behavior change.

As the two most knowledgeable about explosives, Price and Kennedy had gone to talk to the chemist, Henry Stout.

Longmire had arranged for the purchase of the self-igniting bombs made of the deadly combination of phosphorus in a bisulfide of carbon that the chemist Stout called Greek fire. Price and Kennedy had not yet returned.

Martin wiped the back of his neck. November it may be, but the ladies of the house liked to keep all their fires going and the attic was hot as an oven. "Gather the men in ten minutes, Headley."

. . .

⌒DETECTIVE TIM O'CONNOR rapped smartly on the door of No. 9 Gay Street. The door opened. The corpulent woman ran her black feather boa up and down her thick neck as if she were drying herself after a bath.

"Could I come in and talk to you? I'm a pillow drummer and I'd like—"

"Fiddlesticks. You're a copper and we both know it. Nancy's my name, whoring's my game. What's *your* name, dearie?"

"Uh, Tim."

"Well, uh-Tim, step in and we'll see what tickles your fancy."

"That's not what—"

"Of course it ain't. But we can make you very happy here." Nancy closed the door and pushed her fleshy body at him.

"I don't think—"

"Not many men do. What did you expect? To have your way with me?" Nancy lifted the skirt of her glittery black dress and flapped it at him. "Not too likely. You couldn't afford me. But now, seeing's you're a member of the Force . . ." She grabbed her fan from a table and tapped him on the nose with it. Facing the stairs she yelled up, "Linda!"

"No, that's not what I came in here for—"

"I believe you," Nancy replied.

Detective O'Connor was about to protest again when he saw the full-bosomed young blond girl trudging down the stairs. "Oh, well" barely escaped from his lips. It was all he could do not to drool. First he would fuck the tart, then he'd get down to business.

⌒MARTIN TOOK A drink from his canteen; his mouth soured at the taste of rubber. The gas fumes had given him a headache. He tugged on his boots.

"Toby," Headley called.

"Sir?"

"Empty those chamber pots. It stinks like an Army camp up here."

"Yes, sir."

In short order Headley, Toby, Chenault, and Ashbrook were dressed and gathered around Colonel Martin.

Martin looked each in the eye, then said, "As you can see, Kennedy and Price have not returned. There may be good and sufficient reason for this, but we have to consider the possibility that they've been captured."

"And the authorities could be on us any minute." A lean, intense man with keen features, Chenault's grim mood could be read in his dark eyes and the set of his jaw.

"I don't believe Price and Kennedy would betray us," Toby said.

"And God's in His Heaven," Chenault retorted.

"Amen," Toby said, seriously.

"At ease, gentlemen," Headley ordered.

"Sir," Toby said. "Price has the gold."

"Yes," Martin answered, "but it only represents two thousand dollars. If it's gone, we can still carry on."

"What I mean, sir, is if Price were tempted to spend one of those double eagles, it would be very tempting to find out if he had more."

"And hit him on the head to get them," John Ashbrook said.

Headley saluted the boy. "Good thinking, Toby."

"That is a possibility," the Colonel said. "At any rate we can't scurry out of our holes like frightened rabbits any time something goes amiss. We shall keep our heads, continue using this house as our base of operations. But we must remain vigilant."

A board creaked. "Colonel," Headley whispered.

All watched the landing as a Negress showed her round face at the top of the stairs leading to the attic. She was carrying two large pitchers of hot water. "Miss Nancy said there was a policeman nosing about but she took care of him. And if you want to see how, that knothole over there comes out." The Negress pointed with her chin to a plank on the floor not far from her feet. "Miss Nancy also said if you don't come down to breakfast in a quarter hour, she's going to feed it to the pigs."

"Thank you, Ruby," Headley said. "We'll be there directly, we are all respectable."

Ruby laughed, set the pitchers on a board laid across two sawhorses, and waddled back to the stairs. "In this house? Me-oh-my-oh-me-oh. That is a joke. Me-oh-my-oh-me-oh."

"Look at that, look at that, look at that," Ashbrook jabbered. He was flat on the floor, his eye to the hole.

"Let me see." Chenault pushed Ashbrook away. "Goodness gracious, the Lord preserve us, I'm going to tell your wife on you, Jamie. Oh, I've never seen the like."

"I have," Ashbrook said, pulling on Chenault's collar. "When my Aunt Betsy decided to breed her prize milk cow to Farmer Huston's bull."

"All right, men, enough of this tomfoolery," Headley said, pushing both men away and having a look for himself. "Oh, God. There's a man down there riding hell for leather."

"Headley!" A giant grin broke out on Colonel Martin's face. "Headley!"

"Sorry, sir," Headley said, scrambling to his feet. "Just getting a good look so I could report."

"Of course," Martin said. "Thanks to Miss Nancy, there's one officer of the law we don't have to concern ourselves about."

"Not for the next hour at least, sir."

"Breakfast is waiting. Unless you prefer lewd exhibitions."

"No, sir," came the responding mutters of his men.

"Very well, then. Time is too precious to waste. Everyone get to shaving as I speak. And leave that damn hole alone."

"Tell that to that cop down there," Chenault said.

"Enough," Headley said.

Martin waited a moment for the order to sink in, then said, "You've had your fun, now to business. After breakfast I want all of us to leave this house. That policeman being here proves the wisdom of that. And the less time we spend in one place, and together, the better. I want you to walk around the City—"

Another creak; Headley raised his hand in warning. This time it was James Harrington returning from guard duty. "Your turn, Toby."

Toby started for the stairs.

"Wait," Headley said, "the Colonel isn't done."

"First I want to hear Jamie's report," Martin said.

Harrington had deep circles under his eyes. "Yes, sir. After midnight they all left. Whoever is watching us, and I think it's more than one, they're doing a lousy job of it."

"That's good to know."

Toby had his hand up.

"Yes," the Colonel said, acknowledging him.

"Do we meet back here?"

Martin nodded. "Unless you get a message to the contrary. I'll be happier when we're rid of Gay Street. Too many eyes. Longmire is seeking different quarters. You'll each be on your own, two objectives in mind. First, study the terrain as you would a battlefield. We may have to pull back quickly when our job is done. I want a fighting chance. Second, Price and Kennedy must be found before that damn coat and its gold points a finger at us."

TWENTY

KENNEDY, ROBERT. CAPTAIN.
TENTH KENTUCKY CAVALRY.
ARMY OF THE CONFEDERACY.
RODE WITH MORGAN'S RAIDERS.
CAPTURED WITH MORGAN AND
SIXTY-SIX OTHERS AND SENT TO
OHIO PENITENTIARY RATHER
THAN MILITARY PRISON, AND
TREATED LIKE CONVICTS.
LUCIFER.

⌒November 3rd, Thursday, early morning.

PETE WAS UP EARLY, ravenous for once and not nursing his usual drinker's indisposition. Nellie had made a mountain of griddle cakes and eggs and coffee, enough for an army. "No sausage?" he asked through a mouthful of cakes and eggs.

"Not today."

"Grandpapa up?" Pete noted a thought on the back of an envelope. Nellie made good strong coffee. He was on his second cup.

"He's with your grandmamma and your aunt."

"Auntie Lee?" Pete had hardly gotten the words out when a door above closed and footsteps came softly down the stairs. No wonder no sausage. Auntie Lee, Grandpapa's sister, kept to the Hebrew customs. She ate no pork.

Pete left the table and hurried out to the foyer. Stepping off the last riser was a tiny woman who, on quick glance, might be mistaken for a young girl were it not for her startlingly white hair, parted severely in the center in the latest fashion. She carried a black leather medical bag. She not only practiced medicine, she taught it to other women at Elizabeth Blackwell's infirmary.

Blackwell had been the first woman in the United States to receive a medical degree, thus opening the door for Auntie Lee and others to follow. As one of the first women doctors in the State of New York, Leah Tonneman was carrying on a family medical tradition.

"Well, let's have a look at you," she said, squinting up at Pete, after accepting his hug.

"Will you have coffee, Miss Lee?"

"Thank you, Nellie." Lee set her bag on the sideboard and sat down.

"How is Gram?"

"She's failing, Peter. I've told your grandfather it's time to send for Philip." Lee's olive skin flushed for a brief moment.

Pete's Uncle Philip Boenning Tonneman was Charity Tonneman's firstborn, a child of her first marriage, to Philip Boenning. Boenning, an artist of some fame, had died before Philip was born. Old Peter was the only father Philip had known. Uncle Philip was a painter like his blood father and had lived in France for the past twenty-five years, making rare, brief visits home.

"She didn't know me last time I went in," Pete said. "Kept calling me John."

Auntie Lee peered at him critically. "You favor your father a good deal, my dear, and if you keep up this way of life, you'll drink yourself into an early grave."

"Auntie Lee—"

"I mean it, Peter. Find yourself a woman who'll make you rush home to her charms and arms instead of rushing to a tavern."

"Auntie Lee, I'm shocked. What is this world coming to when a woman of your class—"

"Applesauce." She shook her finger at him. "Don't attempt to worm your way around this, Peter Tonneman. You have the family curse; it's written all over your face."

"What is written all over Pete's face?" Old Peter shuffled into the room and sat down. Nellie placed a plate of griddle cakes and a cup in front of him, and poured coffee.

"I have to get back to the infirmary," Auntie Lee said. She drained her cup. "Mark what I said," she told Pete as she stood.

"Will someone tell me what you're talking about?" Old Peter's sharp eyes darted from one to the other.

"I'm talking about a wild young man, who happened to be my nephew, who many many years ago was enamored of taverns." Lee kissed her brother's cheek and, picking up her medical bag, strode to the foyer where her cloak and bonnet hung from a peg. "I'll be by tomorrow."

"Grandpa—"

"Wait till I taste my coffee."

This was a ritual; when Pete was a boy, Old Peter insisted that Pete learn to marshal his thoughts before he spoke. Old Peter thought it a necessary skill for a good policeman, which he hoped Pete would be. It was also an important skill for a good journalist.

"Grandpapa, yesterday a barmaid in the LaFarge House public room told me that she'd overheard two men talking about burning down the City on Election Day. One of the men was called Price, the other Kennedy. I know the story is common knowledge and considered a fraud and a hoax and that the Democrat newspapers deem it a Republican trick to win votes. But I believe this is serious business."

Old Peter seemed lost in the process of nibbling on a sweet roll. After a short time, he said, "Go on."

"The barmaid told me about a prostitute, Claudia Albert, who was with the two men."

The old man gave his grandson a piercing look. "Did you talk to the prostitute?"

"Yes, sir. She confirmed the barmaid's story. Price's Christian name is John. He wore a coat that had gold double eagles sewn in it. He paid her with one."

"Then he shouldn't be hard to find: a man who gives away double eagles."

"Somebody found him all right. Last night, a veteran, Patrick Duff, stumbled on a dead body in Jew's Alley. The dead man, whose hat identified him as J. Price, was the Confederate soldier who took Duff's eye out at Antietam. Both the barmaid and Duff noted that Price had a white streak in his hair. His coat with the gold in it was missing. That's all I have so far."

Old Peter leaned forward in his chair, his lined face solemn. "Keep me informed. I agree, this is no hoax. This is very serious business."

⌐THE NEWSBOYS HAD already collected their papers by the time Pete got to the *Post,* making passage into the building easier than usual.

His early morning appearance stunned the regulars so that all work ceased as he entered. Only the telegraph could be heard.

"Good morning, gentlemen," Pete sang, strolling through the newsroom, tipping his hat to one and all. When he came to Everett Miller's desk, he pulled up a chair, spun it around, and sat, leaning his chin on the backrest. "How are you this fine day, boss?"

"You look like the cat that swallowed the canary. Out with it, Tonneman." The editor searched for his cigar. When he found it on the edge of his desk, Ev jammed it in his mouth, reflamed it with a lucifer, and leaned back.

Pete wanted to say he had the first real arsonist story. But he knew Ev would throw up his hands and boot him out. Instead, he chose a flanking maneuver. "A one-eyed veteran, Patrick Duff, on his way to the Lincoln rally in Chatham Square last night, took a shortcut through Jew's Alley and stumbled over a dead body."

"That's hardly news in New York City."

"This veteran recognized the dead man as someone he knew from Antietam."

Ev leaned forward. "I like it."

"The dead man had no coat, but on the band inside his fine hat was written J. Price, Lexington, Kentucky." Pete paused for effect.

It worked. Ev sat up. "All right, carry on."

"You haven't heard the best. The dead man wasn't a Union soldier. He was the one man Duff never expected to see in New York.

He was the one that stabbed Duff's left eye during the battle. The dead man was a Reb."

"Good."

Pete took a breath. Now came the ticklish part. The Rebel arsonists. "And . . . he had a white streak in his hair just like the fellow Meg Clancy, the barmaid, told me about."

"Damn," Ev said, flinging his cigar at the floor. It set off a small burst of flying sparks that both men ignored. "You're doing it again. That arsonist bunkum."

Pete was not deterred. "You have a Southerner named Price, who has a white streak in his hair, tossing around gold double eagles and talking about burning the City. Then a man with a white streak in his hair and hat from Kentucky, with the name J. Price in it, is found dead. And that dead man turns out to have been a Reb soldier."

"Go on." He had Ev's interest again.

"I know this Price carried the eagles sewn inside his coat."

"How do you know that?"

"From a whore who spent time with him at the LaFarge."

"Impeccable sources, a barmaid and a whore. Continue."

"The whore confirmed that the dead man's first name was John. The dead man's coat was gone. Stolen for the gold is my guess."

"Now we're playing guessing games."

"There was another man with Price at the LaFarge House. The whore told me his name was Kennedy."

Ev clapped his hands together. "You've got it. Stop the presses. Put out a special edition. Superintendent of Police Kennedy suspected of planning the burning of New York."

"Amusing, Ev. Very amusing."

TWENTY-ONE

⁀November 3rd, Thursday, midafternoon.

TOBY TURNED ROUND and round looking at the people, the buildings, taking in Broadway. He'd been acting like the biggest of yokels, first getting on the wrong accommodation—what they called their omnibuses—and going halfway to Yorkville, wherever that was.

He saw Kennedy before Kennedy saw him. As Kennedy shambled out of a low dive called Joe's Luck, a handbill was thrust at him by a red-suited lad wearing a peaked cap. Printed on the cap in as large letters as it could hold was the word BARNUM. The handbill went into more detail. Toby knew this because he had one just like it in his own hand.

P. T. Barnum's American Museum was one of the first places a visitor to New York wanted to see. The City's primary place of amusement stood five magnificent stories on the corner of Ann Street and Broadway.

Along the roof ensigns of many nations fluttered in the breeze. Above all the other flags was the largest: A brand-new United States banner with thirty-six stars, including one for Nevada, which just had been admitted to the Union at the end of October. Jutting out over the entrance was Barnum's own twin-pointed white pennant, trimmed in red.

The rest of Ann Street near Broadway was occupied by saloons, cheap dining halls, gambling dens, thieves, pickpockets, malefactors of every stripe, and, feeling very much at home, brokerage houses.

As Toby thought to approach his comrade he recalled what the Colonel had told them at the outset: Assume nothing and get the lay of the land before plunging in where angels fear to tread.

So Toby did not make contact; he followed Kennedy to the Barnum entrance, and when Kennedy bought a ticket, he did the same.

According to the paper, Barnum's American Museum had jugglers, ventriloquists, industrious fleas, dogs with human intelligence, living statuary, tableaux, rope dancers, live "Yankee" pantomime, gypsies, singers and dancers, instrumental music, dioramas, panoramas, models of Niagara, Dublin, Paris, and Jerusalem, mechanical figures, fancy glassblowing, and knitting machines, as well as freaks of all kinds: albinos; fat boys; giants; dwarfs. Its Lecture Hall was a huge theatre.

The main attraction was still the life mask and clothing of Albert E. Hicks, a notorious thief and murderer. In 1860, Hicks had been drugged and shanghaied off the streets of Manhattan, only to wake up on a Virginia-bound sloop.

The sloop was later discovered off the New Jersey coast, adrift, unmanned, and spattered with blood. Pockets stuffed with the ship's officers' money, Hicks made his way home. Eventually apprehended in Providence, Rhode Island, Hicks confessed that he'd axed all hands to death. He was hanged on Bedloe's Island a few months later.

Only when he saw Kennedy take a seat near the back of the Lecture Hall did Toby sit behind him and whisper, "Howdy, Captain."

Kennedy turned, snapping his right hand forward.

At the sight of the bowie knife, Toby jerked back. "Friend, sir. It's me, Toby." Until now, the boy hadn't known that Kennedy, like Price, favored the bowie. It could have been the twin of Price's blade, but then, all bowies were related, and had a family resemblance. More to the point, Toby'd never seen Kennedy draw the heavy single-edged blade before. It was impressive. And frightening. "It's me, Captain."

When Kennedy grinned, a gold incisor flashed. He smelled strongly of whiskey. "Not following me, are you, boy?"

"No, sir. I just came in and saw you sitting here."

"Where are the others?"

"Around town. The Colonel says there are too many eyes on Gay Street. Longmire is looking for other places." Toby bobbed his head. "Colonel Martin is a cautious man."

"Too cautious," Kennedy growled. "Wrongheaded, too. Why the hell are we waiting? We should go forward, come hell or high water. They'll be their most vulnerable on Election Day. If you ask me, Martin is afraid."

"No, sir, Robert Martin is not afraid. I'd stake my life on that."

"You may have already done that, boy."

A man slipped in past Toby. Toby put his mouth to Kennedy's ear. "The Colonel thinks the authorities would be waiting for us. Then where would we be?" Toby drew an imaginary knife across his own throat.

Kennedy beckoned; Toby moved to the seat in front of the Captain. Kennedy had taken a pint bottle from his coat and was drinking. "Wrong, wrong, wrong," he said, with no regard for the people coming into the hall and sitting all about them. "Mark my word. If we did the deed we were ordered to do on Election Day, we'd escape in the confusion." He snapped his fingers. It sounded like the crack of a whip. "As sure as that."

Toby looked around nervously.

"Now, who can figure what will happen?" Kennedy mumbled. "Damn!" he shouted suddenly.

"Sir?"

Kennedy nodded. "I know, I know. Mum's the word." He leaned forward and gripped Toby's shoulder. "I didn't survive battle and the Ohio Penitentiary to end up dangling from a rope in Yankee Town just because some coward couldn't act."

TWENTY-TWO

⁓November 4th, Friday morning.

T HE MORGUE, at Tenth Avenue and Thirty-sixth Street, was one of many in the City; ten blocks downtown and on the shore of the East River was Bellevue Hospital and its more modern morgue.

The Thirty-sixth Street location had once been a warehouse. Whenever Pete came here he had to smile. It wasn't that he found dead people funny. Not at all. What amused him was the slaughter-house across the street and the vagrant thought of one place's carcasses going to the other. All and all, this area of Tenth Avenue had a particularly savage stink.

The Tonneman family history was tied into the coroner's office. Old Peter's father, John Tonneman, and his father before him both had been coroners of the City of New York. But at this moment Pete's only interest in history was the War. And he was in a great hurry.

Unclaimed dead like Price didn't stay long at the City morgues. As soon as possible they were planted in Potter's Field at 115th Street, north of the Central Park, along with New York's poor and other unwanted.

Pete pushed open the street-level door. "Anybody home?"

"Just me and the dead." That would be the coroner. He said that every time.

"It's me, Finney," Pete called. "I want to have a look at one J. Price, found with his throat cut two days ago."

"Ain't that a coincidence?" Finney, a fleshy, cheerful fellow, was saying as Pete walked into the storage room. Here, in this room, the bodies were put into pine boxes before being sent up to Potter's Field.

"Why's that?" Pete asked, as he spotted another man, a red-faced old fellow with hair sprouting like weeds from his large head.

"Because," Finney said, "Sheriff Jed Honeycutt here just come from Catskill Station for the same express purpose. Sheriff, this is Pete Tonneman. He's a newspaperman for the *Post*."

The old man stood less than five feet in height but plainly was truculent as hell. He had a wad of tobacco stuffed in his cheek. "You know anything about *him*?" The Sheriff hooked his thumb at the body on the table. By the cadaver's white-streaked hair it had to be John Price.

"Yes," Tonneman replied. He moved closer to the body. A matchstick was jutting out of the corpse's mouth. "What the hell is that, Finney?"

"That's how he was brought in. With the lucifer clenched between his teeth. After I looked inside his mouth, I put it back the way I found it for the photographer."

Damn, thought Pete, Duff hadn't told him about the matchstick. People didn't realize how important little things like that were. "I wrote the story," Pete explained to Sheriff Honeycutt.

"I come down because of it. About him and the one-eyed soldier. A conductor on the Hudson River Line gave me the *Post* last night as I was making my rounds near the tracks." The Sheriff crossed to the window, opened it, and spat. "We had a man," he said, walking back, "a stranger, David Corwin, killed pretty much the same way this fellow was. Throat cut ear to ear."

"I wrote a few lines about that." Pete brought out his pencil stub and an old envelope. "But I didn't know his name." He wrote the name down.

"Well, I never would have put it together with this fellow, but

our stationmaster, Sam Gregory, saw Corwin get off the south-
bound train. He saw another man, too, about the same time from
the same train. A man with a white streak in his hair."

Pete nodded. "That is interesting."

"I'll tell you something else, City boy. This dead man, Corwin,
had papers hidden in his boot saying he was a member of the Federal Secret Service. And Sam told me he was trying to send a telegraph message to General Dix in New York, but couldn't because
the line was down."

"Have you informed the Government of this?" Tonneman
asked.

Honeycutt shifted his wad of tobacco from left cheek to right and
seemed ready to spit again. "Don't try to teach an old man how to
suck eggs." The Sheriff pulled out a large handkerchief. He blew his
nose.

Pete nodded toward the corpse. "You reckon this fellow killed
Corwin?"

Taking deliberate time to fold his handkerchief and tuck it away
in his coat, Honeycutt finally said, "Yes. And I thank you for finding my murderer."

"How do you know Price is your murderer? Both were killed the
same way. Why not by a third man?"

The Sheriff shook his head. "Corwin could have been killed by
anybody on God's green earth who happened to be in Catskill Station that day. Or passing through on a train. But this one and mine
certainly weren't sliced by the same killer. Maybe your one-eyed
soldier killed yours."

"I don't think so." Pete was hot on his arsonist conspiracy.
Nothing would please him more than having the two victims done
in by one murderer. "What makes you say the two weren't killed by
the same man?"

"My man, Corwin, was cut from the back, right to left, by a left-
handed man. This one was cut from the back, too, but by a right-
handed man."

"How can you be so sure?"

This time Honeycutt didn't bother with the window. Tobacco
juice splattered the stone floor under the dead man's table.
"You're starting to vex me, City boy. I been butchering hogs since

I was knee-high to a frog. . . ." Honeycutt quit talking and stomped away in disgust. "New Yorkers," he muttered. "Well, that's it for me." Then he stopped. "There's one thing that bothers me, though. Our dead man had a matchstick in his mouth, too."

TWENTY-THREE

November 4th, Friday afternoon.

MEG FOUND THURSDAY'S *Evening Post* tucked behind one of the chairs in the George Washington Room when she was cleaning up. She stood reading it, at first unaware of the soft rapping on the window. Looking up belatedly, she peered through the etched glass. Claudia.

Claudia pointed to Meg's newspaper and mouthed words Meg couldn't understand. She motioned that she was coming in. Meg glanced at the paper and saw what Claudia was so excited about. There it was, right in CITY INTELLIGENCE. A man named John Price, who had a white streak in his hair, had been found with his throat cut in Jew's Alley.

Meg read the brief story twice. It probably didn't mean anything to most anybody, except maybe her and Claudia. And the man who'd written it had to be Pete Tonneman.

Well, that's what came of carrying all those gold double eagles. Murder. Meg shuddered. A third time, she read the article. It didn't mention the other one. Price's friend, Mr. Kennedy. Now there was a man with a nasty look to him. Most likely he sliced Price's throat and ran off with the gold.

So Michael had been right all along. Meg hated to admit it because her brother never gave her credit for having a brain in her head.

"Did you see?" Claudia demanded, rushing into the barroom. She was carrying a small valise. "You're the only one I told. You told Pete Tonneman, didn't you? And he put it in the *Post*. What are you two trying to do? Ruin me? Get me killed? I have a business to run, a life to live."

"I don't understand," Meg said, surprised at her friend's distress.

"I'm a prostitute, Margaret Mary. A whore. A highly paid whore, but still a whore."

"Shh," Meg said, looking about the empty room.

"*Shh* yourself. Men kill whores as easy as people swat flies. There are gold coins involved. That alone can lead to trouble. Somebody killed John Price. It had to be for his gold. He was a stranger here. He told me he knew no one except his friend Kennedy."

"But the story doesn't mention your name—"

"Thank you for little favors. Kennedy knows my name. He'll know that's how the story got in the paper."

"Oh."

"Oh, positively. Who the hell do you think they're going to come for next? Me, you simpleton."

"Holy Mary, Mother of God—"

"I've got no time for that. I just want to tell you that you and that Tonneman, you've ruined my life. I've got to hide. I think I can be safe at my uncle's. No, you never heard that, I never said that." Claudia clutched Meg's forearms and squeezed with all the power of the fear that possessed her. "Swear. I'm begging for my life. Swear. In the name of your precious Jesus Christ. Swear you won't give me away, again."

"I swear."

"Thank you. You're a dear soul, and not a bad person for an Irisher." Claudia ran outside. Meg watched her through the window as she hailed a hackney on Broadway. Then she was gone.

Meg rubbed her arms. Claudia was sure to have left nail marks. "I never . . ." How could Claudia say such things? Meg let out a deep sigh. Claudia's agitation and Pete Tonneman's story had nearly put a damper on the wonderful event that was to come. This very night—November 4th, 1864—Margaret Clancy was to make her stage debut with Mr. Edwin Booth.

TWENTY-FOUR

HARRINGTON, JAMES.
LIEUTENANT. TENTH KENTUCKY
CAVALRY. ARMY OF THE
CONFEDERACY. MARRIED, WITH
A SON. LUCIFER.

November 4th, Friday, late afternoon.

THE DECISION was made: They were to stay in several different places. In that way, should any one of them be captured, those remaining could complete the mission.

The Colonel and Headley were to be quartered in Jane McDonald's rooming house above the Hamburg Drinking Club on Stanton Street at the Bowery.

Harrington was the first to go. Longmire had assigned him to a butcher shop on Sullivan Street. The butcher, though born in New York, was friendly to the Cause. He was a widower with a ten-year-old boy who could carry messages.

"It's lily-livered," Bob Kennedy muttered. Nonetheless, he stood up and shook Harrington's hand.

"I didn't decide this lightly," Martin said. "We all agreed."

"I didn't, Price didn't." Defiant, Kennedy cast his eyes about the attic, seeking support.

"If you'd have been here, you would have had your say, Kennedy. However, it wouldn't have changed my mind—"

Kennedy interrupted. "Where's Price?"

Seeing Harrington pause on the stairs, Martin said, "Go ahead, Harrington." It was as Martin had thought initially. Kennedy and Price were the wild cards, unpredictable and unreliable. Two more than he needed on a mission like this. Price had been forced on him by Senator Thompson.

Kennedy, on the other hand, was Martin's own responsibility; he had chosen the man because the two of them had ridden with Morgan. Still, Martin was beginning to wonder if Kennedy and Price weren't from the same barrel.

"Anybody here seen Price?" Kennedy persisted.

"I thought," Martin said, "you would know where he is." He dismissed the subject. "Toby's gone out to look for him."

"That green—"

Kennedy's words were cut short by Toby's voice on the stairs, then Harrington's. The two came back up. Toby carried a folded newspaper.

"Harrington!" Headley barked. "For God's sake, man."

"He can leave after Toby gives his report," Martin said.

Toby set the newspaper on the board across the sawhorses and crossed to the Colonel. "Not much to report, sir. I wasn't followed going out. I made wide circles, looked in at the LaFarge House . . . ."

Kennedy nodded. "Price might have sniffed his way there again."

Ashbrook had his carpetbag open; he was searching frantically through his belongings. "He'll come back and we'll be gone."

"Longmire will watch for him."

"Claudia," Kennedy said. "The whore Price had was called Claudia. The bartender will know where she is. Price's probably off with her. I'll get him." He started for the stairs.

"No," Martin said. "They're sure to know your face."

"I'll go," Toby offered.

"I found it." Ashbrook displayed a daguerreotype. "John's picture."

The stairs emitted their tell-tale squeak. Headley stepped forward, peered down, then announced, "Longmire."

The room was filled with nervous energy; the men, unable to contain themselves, had begun to move around.

Chenault picked up Toby's newspaper, unfolded it, and held it close to an oil lamp; with all the men complaining of the stink, Colonel Martin had turned off the gaslight.

Longmire's head appeared, then his torso. He, too, carried a newspaper. "Have you heard?"

"Damn it all to Hell," Chenault cried out.

Martin saw the look on Chenault's face. "What is it, James?"

"Price won't be coming back. It's here in the *Post*."

Headley took the newspaper and read aloud. " 'Dead Man Found In Jew's Alley.' Dear God."

"The Secret Service must have caught up with him," Kennedy said.

"We're all dead men," Harrington blurted, collapsing on the top step.

"Be quiet," Martin ordered. "Carry on, Headley."

"Yes, sir." Headley read on. " 'The dead body of a white man approximately thirty years of age, identified as John Price, a Confederate officer, possibly from Lexington, Kentucky, was discovered by Patrick Duff, a veteran of Antietam, early Wednesday evening in Jew's Alley, near Chatham Square. An unidentified Bowery Boy was seen leaving the scene of the crime. Price's throat had been cut from ear to ear. The dead body will be sent to the City Morgue on Tenth Avenue and Thirty-sixth Street, and should no one claim it, thence to Potter's Field for a pauper's burial.' "

"Hellfire!" Ashbrook exclaimed.

"In a straw shanty," Kennedy agreed.

"The story makes no mention of the gold," Longmire said. When Martin gave him his attention, Longmire added, "It makes no mention of Price's coat."

"None at all," Headley agreed. "The coat may still be on him."

Kennedy laughed. "Not very likely. Billy Yank would steal the pennies from a dead man's eyes, let alone a coat loaded with gold double eagles."

"What are we to do?" Longmire asked Colonel Martin. "There have been too many dark signs."

"We go forward," Martin said. "Nothing else for us to do. We have our orders. We will deal with each exigency as it occurs."

Headley said, "Sir, let me go and look at Price's body. If he still has his coat, I'll get it. Claim it or steal it."

Martin shook his head. "I'll not jeopardize this mission for two thousand in gold."

"May I speak, sir?"

"Of course, Headley. We've never acted like a line outfit, why start now?"

"Permission to go, sir. I'd like to look at Price's body. See how he died. Someone out there killed one of us. If it was the Secret Service or the police, they wouldn't have left him in the alley."

"It's foolhardy," Martin said. He thought for a moment. "Permission granted. Take Toby with you as lookout. That way if you're caught, he can report back. And Headley—don't take any unnecessary chances."

"Yes, sir."

"It may be a trap," Longmire said. The man was edgy, nervous, pacing back and forth. "I'm worried."

"If I think it's a trap I won't go in," Headley told him.

Longmire removed his hat. "McMaster has gone old woman on us. He believes we should call off the mission."

"McMaster!" Kennedy exploded. "He's nothing but a Yankee turncoat. What the hell . . ."

"I'd like to cut his cowardly throat," Chenault said.

Martin raised his hand. "We carry on."

"Hurrah," Toby said softly.

"Very well," said Longmire. "I have a young couple named Anderson on Irving Place and Fourteenth Street. Who goes there?"

"Chenault," Martin said. "Harrington, you should be halfway to Sullivan Street by now."

"Yes, sir," Harrington said, chagrined.

"Chenault, wait ten minutes," Headley said.

Headley made arrangements with Longmire about where to find him should returning to Gay Street be impossible. When Chenault slipped out the back door, Headley and Toby left by the front. They walked several blocks before they hailed a hackney to take them to the morgue.

Martin felt strangely reassured. He was worried about Toby. He felt an odd bond with the boy, as if he were his own son. So why had he let him go into what he feared might be a trap? The boy was

a soldier. And a soldier had to do his duty, no matter the conse-
quences.

"The whore killed him for the gold," Kennedy growled. "You'll
never find the coat."

"What are you talking about?" Martin asked sharply. "Did she
know about the coat?"

"She knew about the gold. A gold eagle can buy a great deal of
happiness between a red-haired woman's legs."

"You bastards," Martin said, "squandering the mission's gold on
a whore."

"Why, Colonel," Kennedy said insolently, "I'm beginning to
think you don't like me."

TWENTY-FIVE

⌒November 4th, Friday, late afternoon.

THE BAY PULLING the hackney trotted slowly out of the heart of the City onto country roads, poking along beside the railroad tracks, the docks and piers bordering the Hudson River. The driver, who had the mournful face of a hound dog, seemed in no mood to urge the bay to greater speed. Making no complaint, Headley used the time to ponder the mission and the kernel of doubt that had bedded itself in his thoughts. Truth was, he found New York stimulating.

Toby, thinking of his father, watched as they passed clusters of shanty whites and farther still, shanty Negroes. Children and adults stared at them as if they'd come from the moon.

"So much for freedom," Headley muttered, breaking his silence.

"Sir?"

"The darkies." Scrawny children sat beside the roadway, listless in the coach's dust.

"I thought you were against slavery," Toby said.

Headley didn't respond.

They passed a small, well-cared-for farm with a red barn on which an advertisement for Haley's Tobacco had been painted. Outside a chicken coop, a dozen or so hens pecked the ground. A cow and five goats grazed on barren earth searching for the occasional spike of winter grass.

Toby tried again. "You rode with Morgan, didn't you?"

"You know that. Same as the Colonel, Kennedy, and Price."

"Morgan was a slave man."

"He was," Headley replied, still looking out the window. "Sold and rented them."

"My Pa hated slavery. Always said so."

Headley nodded. A man had principles or he had nothing. The colored man had rights, but so did he. "I joined the Cause because I don't think the Federalists should tell me or Kentucky what to do. We are a league of sovereign states."

A grisly smell abruptly surrounded them.

"Here you be, gentlemens." They were in the middle of the road. A wagon laden with coffins rolled out as the hackney driver pulled up in front of a warehouse. The warehouse door had a small sign over it, proclaiming it City Morgue, No. 5. They climbed out of the cab.

"Damn," Headley said, watching the coffin wagon disappear in the dust. He hoped Price wasn't in one of those coffins.

"You think we're too late?" Toby asked. "Where's that wagon going?" the boy asked of a ruddy-faced oldster, who was smoking a corn pipe and watching them.

The old man didn't answer. He stirred himself and went around the side of the warehouse.

"Driver, wait here," Headley shouted to the hackman. "I won't be long."

Toby watched Headley go in. To his relief the dreadful stink came from a slaughterhouse just across the road, where wagons were arriving and departing.

When Headley entered the morgue, there was no one about. He proceeded down a hall and entered a dismal room, divided in two by a partition of iron with glass windows. The room, about twenty feet square, would have made a good jail. The floor was tile, the walls unfinished timber. Headley stepped into one section which held two desks and two chairs. He looked through a window at four stone tables, resting on iron frames in the second section. Laid out on the tables, their naked toes toward him, were four bodies, each covered to the chin with a sheet. A stream of cold water, from a movable jet, spilled over the faces of the four corpses. Headley felt his muscles lock. He'd seen dead men on the battlefield, but this display was obscene.

The sound of hammering returned him to his senses. He called out, "Anyone here?"

"In the back."

Headley reentered the hall and walked toward the hammering.

"I'm Finney." The words came from a corpulent man, his head half-hidden behind a newspaper. A boy about fourteen continued hammering nails into a pine coffin. "Headmaster, hereabouts." Finney had a rolling laugh that dissolved into a phlegmy cough. "What can I do for you?"

Headley said, "Why the flowing water?"

"Oh, you've been in the dead room? It stops them from rotting too fast." Finney sniffed. "Doesn't help. Still stinks. You get used to it. Well?"

"We're in New York on business," Headley answered. "My brother went out for a walk two nights ago. He didn't return."

Finney clucked his tongue and shook his head, but he never set his paper aside. "Probably walked in the wrong direction. He'll turn up. Maybe." Another laugh. "You better hope not here."

"I'm concerned. I saw the story in the *Post*. My brother's name is John Price. He has a white streak. . . ."

Finney ran his fingertips over the center of his own close-cropped white thatch.

"Yes, that's John."

The coroner screwed up his face. "That makes four of you already."

"Four?"

"Yes. The reporter what wrote the story. What's his name? Tonneman. The one-eyed soldier, Duff, who was with Price in the War."

"John Price is my brother. I'm Henry Price."

"Well, my condolences, Mr. Price. I guess you've found him."

"This will kill my folks." Headley drew a white linen handkerchief from his pocket and dabbed at his eyes. He looked around the storeroom. It wasn't much more than four walls and a window.

Various pine coffins were stacked halfway to the ceiling. "Which one? And can you give me the loan of a wagon to get him to the train station?"

"Sorry to say . . ." Finney let one end of his paper go to pull a watch from the top pocket of his coat. ". . . your brother's already halfway to Potter's Field." The watch dropped back into the pocket. Finney retrieved the paper, then added, "That's on One Hundred Fifteenth Street."

"This is appalling." Headley made a show of sorrow behind his white linen handkerchief. "I have to get John back, give him a Christian burial in our family plot."

"Hire a cart and go on up to Potter's Field. If you catch them before they plant him they'll be glad to see you. One less hole to dig."

"His clothing," Headley said, as if the thought had just occurred. "Was it all there?"

Finney frowned. "As far as I saw."

"Doc!" someone yelled. "Delivery!"

"Come ahead!" Finney called.

Headley decided he'd overstayed his welcome. He started out, then stopped. "You said four people were interested in my brother. Who was the fourth?"

"Excuse me, mister." Two husky Negroes with bandannas over the lower portion of their faces, like bandits, stood at the door with a large wicker hamper. An oilcloth-wrapped arm hung over the side of the hamper.

"An old guy. Sheriff he was, from Catskill Station. Jed something or other. Looking into a killing up there."

"A killing?" Headley said. "What would John have to do with that?"

"How the devil would I know? Why don't you ask that reporter, Tonneman? Now if you don't mind, my colored boys need to get on with their work."

Troubled, Headley left the morgue.

Toby saw Headley's grim expression. "Appears like things aren't too hunky."

"Not hunky at all. Driver, do you know where the *Evening Post* is located?"

"Off Printing House Square, gentlemens," the driver answered, "Nassau Street."

As they drove off, neither Headley nor Toby noticed that they were being followed by a cart driven by a red-faced old fellow with iron-gray hair sprouting like weeds from his large head.

TWENTY-SIX

November 4th, Friday, late afternoon.

H EADLEY CONTEMPLATED the hustle and bustle that was Printing House Square this evening. Only in New York would there be no difference between the commercial activity of the night and the day. Especially here.

It pleased him to contemplate how much all the people inside these newspaper buildings would give to know who he was and what he was doing in their City. He'd provide them with something to write about very soon, he and the rest of Lucifer. Maybe not on Election Day, but soon.

Toby came out of the *Post* building shaking his head.

Headley grinned. "Not too hunky?"

"Not hunky at all. The Tonneman fellow's not there. Nobody knows where he is. Or when he's coming back. What now?"

"Now we have something to eat."

"And then?"

"Potter's Field."

"SHERIFF. I'D THOUGHT you'd be back to Catskill Station by now."

"Go away." Jed Honeycutt, sitting in a cart behind a gray geld-ing, spoke out of the corner of his mouth without moving his lips.

Pete Tonneman, whose intuition had told him to follow the Sher-iff, peered at the diminutive lawman. "That's no way to act."

"Leave me be, City boy."

"You look exactly like a cat ready to pounce on a bird." Tonne-man turned and stared through bleary eyes at the object of Honeycutt's rapt attention. A man and a boy stood talking next to a carriage outside the *Post* building. The pair got into the carriage; the carriage pulled away.

Honeycutt's gnarled hands were ready at the reins.

"What's going on here?" Tonneman demanded.

"Read it in the papers tomorrow, scribbler." The Sheriff agitated the reins; the cart followed the carriage.

Tonneman raced after the cart, calling, "Wait a minute, Honeycutt. You can't do this."

"Shut up, damn you." Honeycutt's reply came in a guttural whisper. If that fool didn't stop making noise, those two he'd heard through the morgue window asking after Price's body would get away.

"Sheriff, wait for me." Tonneman ran alongside the cart, hanging onto the gelding's leathers, breathing heavily.

Honeycutt slowed the gray. "Shut up, you damned fool, and jump on." He kept his eyes on the carriage as it lengthened the distance between them.

Satisfied, Pete Tonneman climbed on board the rolling cart. "What are you waiting for? You don't want them to get away, do you?"

Jed snorted as the cart began to pick up speed. "Confound it, Tonneman. You are one pain in the arse."

Smiling, Pete asked, "By the way, who are they?"

TWENTY-SEVEN

⁀November 4th, Friday, late afternoon.

Y OU'D BEST STAY out of it," Jimmy Dawes said when Meg told him about Price and his friend and the gold eagles and showed him the story in the *Evening Post.*

"But that dead man, he's the one with the gold eagles."

"Stay out of it. What's fit for Claudia ain't fit for you."

"What does that mean?"

"You know good and well."

"No, I don't. And I don't want you telling everything to my brother," Meg said resentfully. It was because of her brother Mike that Dawes had put in a good word for her, which was how she got the bar job. Meg didn't trust that Dawes wasn't telling Mike about what she did, whom she talked to.

Wiping down the tables vigorously, she muttered under her breath. "I've half a mind to go off with a touring company of actors." She rubbed a particularly grimy table harder. "Or circus performers," she shouted, then looked around, embarrassed at her outburst, glad to see Dawes had left the room.

"You OK?" he called from the kitchen.

"Just fine." She concentrated fully on her polishing till the wood surfaces gleamed.

Mike thought Jimmy Dawes was the best. Outside the cops,

Jimmy was Mike's closest friend. Well, the man was no choirboy. What would Mike say if he knew his pal had come to her room one night? The spalpeen had a LaFarge House master key.

When he groped for her, she smashed him with a police club Michael had given her. Broke his nose, blacked his eye.

He'd never tried anything again. Smart thing, too, because Mike would have killed him and she would have had to look for another job.

This very morning Meg finally had told Dawes that if he didn't stop running to Mike every two minutes telling on her, she would tell Mike about Dawes's key and his visit.

"What was that yelling about?" Dawes said now, coming in toting a case of bottles.

"Never you mind." She went behind the bar where she had stashed last night's *Post*. Meg picked up the paper and stared at the story.

"Stay out of it, I say." Dawes poured himself a whiskey. "Where's your friend been lately?"

"Claudia? She's scared. Gone off, maybe for good." Meg's eyes teared. "I might never see her again."

"Good riddance," Dawes muttered.

After wiping her hands on the bar rag, Meg removed her apron, folded it, and placed it under the counter. "I'm working for Mr. Booth tonight."

"Another one of your elf-and-fairy stories. If it's not dead men with gold coins, it's Booth. The stage life is no life for a sweet Irish colleen. Edwin Booth is a dark-mooded man with a motherless child. He drinks, too," Jimmy added, sucking at the last of his whiskey.

"Except for the child, you just described every Irishman I know. Mr. Booth has a good soul. And he's a great man. A great, gentle man."

In response, Dawes spat into her freshly cleaned spittoon.

Meg glared at him. "And I'll thank you not to make remarks about him in my presence." She pronounced her words with dignity, speaking the way Edwin had taught her. She concluded, "A sensible woman would be daft to marry an Irishman."

"Well, ain't you the fine lady?" Dawes said loudly, mimicking her elongated words. "You mix with them actors, you'll get your comeuppance. Wait and see. They'll use you and spit you back so the only choice you'll have will be your friend Claudia's life. But don't you worry, Miss Prima Donna Clancy," he brayed. "Your friend Jimmy Dawes will be your first customer."

☞LATER, WHEN SHE went next door to the Winter Garden, Meg could still hear Dawes's laughter ringing in her ears.

She stood out front of the theatre, awestruck with her good fortune. Before Edwin, she had been to the theatre only once in her life, with her Aunt Lucy. They had stood outside on a cold rainy night and had come into the place through a door around the corner, trudged along dirty stairs to broken-down benches up in the second balcony.

Aunt Lucy had brought chicken and beer and lemonade, so they had a good time watching the show. But now Meg knew there was better than that. And better could be for her.

Not only the poor people, actors too were supposed to go in by the side door. But because this was the first time, Meg went in through the front. The sight took her breath away. It was like, God help her, entering church.

The lobby looked as if someone had melted a bunch of those gold eagles and poured it all over. Except where it was marble and polished wood like the tables in the George Washington Room.

Crystal chandeliers hung overhead looking so much like branches of heavenly trees where angels would perch.

Everywhere she looked were shapes and images she'd only imagined and dreamed of.

☞FLORETTE CHANDLER WAS old now, and hunched. Her white hair thinned daily. Her hands were crippled with arthritis, her knees were stiff, but her eyes were still a blinding green. Fine cheekbones, jaw, and brow gave hint of the luminosity men still talked of, albeit old men.

Florette had been a member of one or another acting company for over thirty years, with her father and mother and brothers, first in England, then in America. The only one left, she still found work now and then.

More often than not she was at liberty, but she lived simply in a boardinghouse for actors doing bits of sewing when she could.

Edwin Booth had grown up knowing Florette. There was always room in his company for Florette Chandler. If not onstage, then behind the scenes, as a dresser. It was Edwin who had kept the old actress from the poorhouse, and she was grateful to him.

"Now, girl, have a look at yourself." Florette held the hand glass up for Meg to see.

"Oh, my." Nowhere in the reflection could the girl find Meg Clancy, the bog-trotting chambermaid from Cork. Whom she saw was Margaret Clancy, great lady of the theatre.

Soon she would stand on the grand stage and accept the applause and adulation she was meant for. It was in God's plan for her.

The old actress took the mirror from Meg's reluctant hand and set it glass side down on the table. Then she removed the smock that covered Meg's costume and draped it over her arm. Meg stood and examined herself in the cheval glass.

"Sit, please," Florette ordered.

Meg obeyed. She was in awe of Florette and the occasion and her new self. Florette fitted the frilled cap over Meg's blond hair and pinned it in place. "Will I do, Miss Florette?" she asked breathlessly.

"You'll do. Now we must work."

In the next half hour, Florette shepherded Meg through her performance, taking her onstage, showing her where to stand, and stressing important cues.

Stagehands went about inspecting ropes and sandbags while others sat against the brick wall behind the set and talked.

"Remember," Florette said, "never stand in front of Mr. Booth. You could be his daughter and he'd still knock you down and step over you. And if you find yourself behind him, don't move a muscle, not even your face."

"What if he says something funny or sad? Shouldn't I react?"

"Oh, for Heaven's sake, child. Never react."

⌒AN HOUR BEFORE performance, Edwin Booth came onstage and found them still rehearsing. "How is she?" he asked Florette.

"Ready."

"I'm very grateful, Mr. Booth," Meg said with true humility. "I pray I won't fail you."

"You'll not, child." In the same motion Booth patted her on the shoulder and shunted her toward the wings. "When Florette brings you down, wait here for your first cue." With a tilt of his head, he indicated to Florette that he wanted to speak to her.

Meg walked slowly toward the staircase. Her heart began a mad flutter. Suddenly overwhelmed at what was about to be, she leaned against the banister post and closed her eyes, entreating Jesus not to let her forget anything.

"Well, well, what do we have here?" The high voice of the other Booth broke into her prayer.

Meg opened her eyes. John Wilkes, in his usual elegant attire, was standing before her. "Perhaps," he said, caressing the velvet of his opera cape, "we'll come round for you after the performance. You'll be famished. A bird and a bottle will be just the thing."

A shadowy figure moved behind the actor.

". . . that is, if my brother allows it," Booth said.

"I'm my own woman, John," she said, savoring the sentiment and the use of his Christian name. "And I'll have none of you. I've seen the way you take and cast off women—"

"Not so fast, my pretty," Booth declaimed, on stage even when he was off. "We—all three Booths—are going to do a benefit performance of *Julius Caesar* in about three weeks." He raised his head like a rooster about to crow. "I play Marc Antony. There's a small part of a servant that hasn't been cast yet. I could see that you get it."

"I believe," Meg said stiffly, "that decision is your brother's to make."

John Wilkes fairly snarled. "My *brother*!"

Activity around them ceased. Silence.

The man behind Booth emerged from the shadows and placed a restraining hand on Booth's arm; he smiled at Meg.

Meg started to smile back, for he was a good-looking chap, somehow familiar. Then she remembered; the smile froze on her face. This was the other man. Price's friend.

TWENTY-EIGHT

⟆November 4th, Friday evening.

MAJOR GENERAL Benjamin F. Butler read the report with utter contempt. "Is that it?" he asked, dropping the papers on his desk. Newly arrived that day to New York from Virginia with his troops, Butler had set up his headquarters at the Fifth Avenue Hotel. He was dissatisfied with the accommodations and already had his aide scouting a better location.

"Yes, sir!" Lieutenant Smith boomed in his best parade ground voice. Theodore Smith was on slippery ground and he knew it. Butler's jurisdiction and that of his superior, General Dix, was vague. But Butler wasn't known as the "Beast of New Orleans" for nothing. This was a tough and tyrannical man.

"Precious little."

"Yes, sir!"

"It won't do. Lax, careless, negligent. As of noon today, I am the military commander of New York City. Secretary Stanton has given me a job to do, and by the Eternal, I'm going to do it. Dix has been coddling you men, letting you get away with murder. I won't stand for such sloppy behavior. Seven thousand additional troops are arriving today to ensure an uneventful Election Day. I have no more officers to spare for this 'arsonist' chore, only one noncommissioned officer and nine enlisted men." He glared at Smith's partner.

Lieutenant Carl Ridley felt the glare right down to his polished boots. "Sir . . ."

"Damn it, I'm not done. If I had an officer to spare, your souls would belong to Jesus and your bodies to Unconditional Surrender Grant. You'd be under Grayback fire, with Grant's boot up your arse, and that rumpot yelling at you to attack, attack, attack. Understood?"

"Yes, sir!" the two junior officers snapped out, Ridley's words overlapping Smith's by a beat.

"You're supposed to be soldiers and military policemen. From your report you've been acting like neither. Worse, embarrassing news of Army personnel, Secret Service, and local coppers running into each other and stepping all over each other's feet is common knowledge. Dix may tolerate such behavior, but I'll be damned if I will."

"Yes, sir!"

"Thus far you've had a cushiony job, but gentlemen, I have news for you. That day is over. From now on you two and anyone under you will *soldier*. Do you hear me?"

"Yes, sir!"

"Then we understand each other." Butler moved an errant inkstand to a position at the left-hand corner of his desk. "Now. This entire situation seems bogus. You say that the majority of men observed went into the brothel at No. 9?"

"Yes, sir," Ridley said.

The General fixed Ridley with another of his lethal stares, then continued. "No. 13, it's mostly coloreds, the address being a known stop on the Underground Railroad. And you say . . ." Butler fingered the papers on his desk until he found the one he wanted; he read it aloud. " 'It stands to reason that any whites seen entering No. 13 would not be Southern sympathizers.' Did you write that, Lieutenant Smith?"

"Yes, sir, I did."

"I don't want reason, I want facts and results. Ridley?"

"Sir?"

"You noted traffic through the backyards between No. 9 and No. 11."

"Yes, sir."

"Well, what you have are niggers and lecherous bastard whoremongers running rampant. Worse, you probably have mingling of the races. How anyone could equate this activity, shameful as it may be, to espionage and arson I'll never understand. The local cops are chasing their arses and Secretary Seward says he can't spare any Secret Service. Still, I want you to raid all three houses tonight. Clean out this mess so I can get on with my job. Election Day will come and go without a catastrophe." General Butler delivered his next words with relish. "Superintendent and Special Provost Marshal Kennedy lost control of the City last year with the Draft Riots. I will not allow anything like it to happen again. Understood?"

"Understood," Smith and Ridley said. Smith knew that twelve men were not enough for the operation the General had described. But he was a soldier and he knew enough to say yes, sir, and follow orders.

"Don't kill anybody you don't have to. The point is to stop any trouble before it begins."

"Understood, sir," Smith and Ridley said.

"Any new word from Minstrel, sir?" Smith asked.

"None whatsoever," Butler replied, seemingly made more sour by the question. "Get the hell out of here. Dismissed."

THEY FEASTED ON a rich oyster stew in Gilbert's Public House, one of many such in and around Printing House Square. Afterward, while Toby ate both of their portions of custard pudding, Headley savored Kentucky sour mash and a cigarette rolled with Kentucky tobacco. It amazed Headley how much of home was available in New York City.

Toby scraped his dish noisily as Headley rolled another smoke of the thin-leafed tan tobacco from the pouch and lit up again. It had been a long time. Headley hated to admit how good it felt.

Through the haze of smoke he examined his companion, who was still more boy than man. Toby seemed tense, distracted. His eyes darted about the room. "Unbend and enjoy it, lad. As long as we can pay for our fare, no one here cares a hoot about us."

"They buried him with his coat, then?" Toby asked for perhaps the fourth time.

"Seems like it," Headley answered patiently. "I'm thinking that we can go to Potter's Field and claim the body, as Price's next of kin."

"The Price brothers? Is that what you're going to do, brother?" Toby's tone was a mite cynical, surprising Headley momentarily, but he put the thought aside. They had work to do.

When Headley paid the bill, he asked the proprietor, Luke Gilbert, about hiring a wagon.

Gilbert was a corpulent man with a nose full of broken veins. "When would you be needing it?"

"Now."

"Why would you be needing a wagon this time of night? Not planning to rob a bank, are you, boys?" His laugh exploded; other customers barely noticed.

Headley leaned toward the fat man. "Our brother lies six feet under in Potter's Field with his throat cut, sir. We've come to take him home."

Gilbert was instantly contrite. "I beg your pardon, sirs, twice over. For my levity and for my fellow citizens of New York. Allow me to be of service. You shall lease our wagon. It's around back and it will cost you one dollar in advance from now till midnight. Coin or greenback; no stamps, please."

"Thank you for your gracious manners." Headley set the silver dollar on the bar; Gilbert snagged the coin and dropped it into the cash box kept on the floor between his feet.

When Gilbert called "Walt," a kitchen boy appeared from a side room. "Take these gents around back and hitch Jenny to the meat wagon." Gilbert's laughter made his large belly bounce. "Oh, that hurts." He clasped his paunch. "And, Walt, better lay some canvas down."

"Yes, sir."

⌒TONNEMAN LET OUT a loud belch.

"You shouldn't have eaten so fast." Jed eyed him with dour humor.

"I was hungry." Tonneman tilted his head, the growler of beer to his lips.

"I never would have known," the Sheriff mumbled.

The two men sat in Jed's hired cart opposite Gilbert's, picking at what was left of the roasted chicken Tonneman had purchased from the tavern.

"I'm gnawing on chicken bones while they're slopping oyster stew and keeping warm by the fire."

"Keep it down, scribbler. You see that?"

"See what?" Tonneman groused. He raised his head. From the back of the tavern, a boy led a tired swayback mare. The dun-colored horse had to work hard to pull the ramshackle wagon. A lit oil lamp swung aft, but there was none up front.

"Thank you, lad," they heard the older of the two men say as he handed the boy a coin. The boy darted into Gilbert's and the two men climbed on the wagon and headed north.

With a twist of his wrist, Jed turned his cart about and followed.

TWENTY-NINE

November 4th, Friday night.

MAYBE A QUARTER MILE above the Central Park," Headley said. "We can go straight up Fifth Avenue. Where did he say we find Fifth?"

"Washington Square. First we have to take Broadway to Canal. Left on Canal and then to Thompson Street, take a right and go through Washington Square Park. Fifth Avenue starts on the other side."

Lower Fifth Avenue was a long elegant street, well illuminated by gaslight and lined with mansions and hotels. At Twenty-second Street, they passed the Fifth Avenue Hotel, lit up like a grand palace.

"Something," Toby said.

"Something, indeed," Headley concurred. "Do you see all the telegraph lines?"

"I see them."

In spite of the dun nag's age and because there were fewer horse-drawn public cars to deal with, they were moving quickly up the avenue.

Cold night had covered the City by the time they got to the massive Croton Reservoir, which extended from Fortieth to Forty-second Street, from Fifth to Sixth Avenue. Here and there street

lamps and house lights relieved the darkness. The reservoir, however, was surrounded by light.

Headley came to a full stop at the side of the road.

"Glory be," Toby exclaimed. The reservoir looked much like the
pyramids he'd seen at a stereopticon show in Lexington.

"This grand edifice holds the City's water supply. If we can't be
effective during the election, perhaps we should destroy this?"

Toby nodded. "Sounds hunky to me."

Headley grinned. "That's the last time you use that word. Do we
have a deal?"

"Deal."

After a moment, Headley said, "Mr. Gilbert left us a jug of lard
oil in the back of the wagon. Would you care to stop and sprinkle
some around the reservoir and light a match?"

Toby squinted at Headley in the darkness. Was he serious?
" 'Twouldn't work, sir. The reservoir's a powder job, and it would
take too much powder and too many men. I wouldn't trust anyone
Longmire sent. Besides, 'twould be a pity to destroy such a wonder."

Headley tilted his head to one side. This boy was a poet. "Perhaps. I'll think on it. We've still got the Greek Fire." Headley didn't
show it, but he was vexed with himself. He'd had the same tender
notion as Toby. The lad was young and sensitive; it was almost all
right for him to think that way. But not Headley. Headley was a
soldier. He snapped the reins. They began moving again.

The farther north they traveled, the fewer the street lamps. While
other carriages and wagons carried two lamps, they had no head-
light to guide them. The November night was bitter. Toby rubbed
his hands together, grumbling, "You'd think for a buck we'd get
two lanterns."

Soon all they had for company was open space, a few farms and
even more open space. But the telegraph wires continued and the
road was paved with macadam. At Fifty-sixth Street, they passed
three farmhouses; then, suddenly, they were in the country. To their
left was the Central Park, gleaming ghostly with gaslight.

Two miles or so more and the Park ended in a kind of wilderness.
Toby turned in his seat as they climbed a hill. The single vehicle
light that had been behind them had disappeared. All around, as far

as the eye could see, nothing but night. Above them, no moon, but the sky was black and full of stars. The road narrowed, as the macadam gave way to dirt.

"Damn," Toby said. "Wouldn't I love to take that tail lamp in my lap to warm my hands. And I could light the way. How about stopping, Headley?"

"Easy, Toby. I've been colder than this and lived through it. So will you." Contradicting his words, Headley pulled the horse to a halt. While Toby moved the tail lamp to the front hook, Headley pointed way off to the faint glimmer of light. "That stingy beacon has to be it." They moved on.

Presently, Toby said, "Here." *Here* was a wooden arrow marked with smudged charcoal: "Potter's Field." Headley turned left onto a rough road.

They followed the road to a slight incline, then into a clearing containing two buildings, a wood cabin and a brick barn. No welcoming smoke poured out of the cabin chimney. The beacon they'd been aiming for was a dim lamp on a peg next to the cabin door. "Whoa," Headley called as they approached.

Both men jumped down. This time Toby had a real opportunity to warm his hands on the lamp. A dog growled, its eyes two bright spots in the lamplight. A long tether tied the animal to the hitching post.

Tugging the whinnying horse, Headley moved them back till they were all out of the dog's reach. The wolf-like creature set to yapping at them.

The faint flicker of a lantern from the road they'd just come off caught Headley's eye. The light wasn't moving. "We've been followed." As Headley spoke, the flicker from the road disappeared.

Toby looked back. "I don't see a thing."

Right then Headley would have been happier with a fighting man like Kennedy at his side, drunken sot or not. "When I lead the dog away," he told Toby, "you take up the slack on that tether and wrap it around the post."

"Yes, sir." Toby went to the post and set down the lamp. The wolf-mongrel went for him, slavering, teeth gnashing.

Headley threw a stick at the dog and the dog changed targets. Headley ran back and forth and around; between them, the two men soon had the dog on a very short leash. When the mongrel realized its situation, it lay down with its head barely resting between its paws and whined softly.

Headley walked straight to the cabin and took the lamp from its peg. He pushed the half-opened door all the way open. "Quickly, Toby."

Toby was right behind him.

The single room reeked with whiskey. Lying on a mat on the floor was a man, drunk asleep, a cold lantern beside him.

"Look, Headley. Those black boots he's wearing. They're Price's."

Headley snatched the broad-brimmed black hat from the hook on the back of the door. "And his hat. See if you can find the coat before that dog sets to barking again and brings those hombres from the road down on us." He tried not to breathe; the dank cabin stank. "I'm going next door."

Headley eased outside; he stood very still. No noise. No light from the direction of the road.

His lamp wasn't much help. Instead of going to the brick building he made his way to where he thought the burial field would be. Suddenly, he was in it. As much as he could see, a barren expanse, its evenness impaired by mound after mound of dirt. The graves were marked by narrow wooden slats. Of the few he saw, most were worn and broken. Some graves had no markers at all.

Headley dredged a deep sigh out of himself. Time to do what he had to do. Still nothing from the road. Perhaps he'd imagined the light. Then again, perhaps they were closing in right now. He shook the thought off and left the burial field. Being a soldier could make a man crazy.

If anything, the brick building stank worse than the cabin. It was a house of coffins. Each box was marked in crayon, with a number cut into the top. In one corner Headley found several coffins that had been pried open. Apparently the gravedigger looted before he buried. In the third opened coffin he found Price, already a feast for maggots, and naked as the day he was born.

THIRTY

⮑November 4th, Friday night.

JESUS," TONNEMAN EXCLAIMED as the Sheriff suddenly appeared out of the darkness.

Instead of answering, Jed spat a slop of tobacco juice and led the gray to the opposite side of the road. "They came to have a look at Price's body. He was naked as a jaybird. They were debating taking the body with them. Going on about a coat, they were. Hush, they'll be here soon."

"When you didn't come back," Pete said, "I thought you were dead."

It was only a low rumble, but Pete thought he heard the Sheriff laugh. "I'm not ready to die just yet, thank you. *Shh.*"

After a while Pete whispered, "I hear them. Can you hear them?"

"Heard them a minute ago. They got smart. No lights front or back."

The dark ride to the City was laborious. Jed and Pete stayed well behind where they thought the Reb cart was, catching a glimpse now and then as the Rebs passed under a street lamp. Otherwise, the road was pitch dark. "What are you still doing in New York?" Pete asked. "I thought you decided Price killed the Government man up in Catskill Station."

"I could be wrong."

"I doubt that."

"Me, too. Let's just say, I like a good hunt. Now shut pan so I can listen."

The street lamps became more than occasional. But now also random sounds of other horses and vehicles, as few as there were, made the cart's task of following the unlighted wagon even more difficult.

"We're going to lose them if we don't get closer," Pete warned. He heard Jed give a mighty spit. The scent of his tobacco was pungent, almost, if not quite, blotting out the familiar stink of horse droppings along the road and the newer intense smells of a rapidly growing city. No manure sweepers out here.

"Have no fear," Jed said softly. "The time I can't pick a swayback's hoof sounds out of the crowd I'll pack it up."

LIEUTENANT THEODORE SMITH stood across the way from the three houses on Gay Street. Waiting. Thinking.

Through Minstrel, they knew that the plot to burn New York was very real and that the plotters would be holed up in Gay Street. But what they knew was precious little.

Smith and Ridley, with the aid of one experienced sergeant—Frank Lonnigan—and nine very green enlisted men, were going to corral the various habitués of Nos. 9, 11, and 13 Gay Street and sort out the lechers from the spies—if any of the latter actually were here.

Ridley, Lonnigan, and the troopers were in position in front and back, waiting for Smith's signal.

THE METROPOLITAN POLICE were represented by Detective Tim O'Connor, who reported to Chief Hays Tonneman. Because he was alone, O'Connor remained on the corner, attempting to cover both the front and the back at the same time, while doing his damndest not to be seen. He knew this was impossible.

Two hours earlier O'Connor had seen a closed wagon pull up in front of No. 9. The wagon was still there, the driver snoozing. Was it waiting for a whorehouse patron, or was it part of an escape plan? O'Connor didn't have any idea. In fact, he had no idea what he was doing here at all. All he could think of were his poor feet. He considered going into the brothel. Not to get a woman, but to take off his shoes and put his feet up.

The brothel had a steady stream of visitors from morning till night. It was unbelievable how many men in this town found the time and energy to have a woman. O'Connor didn't marvel at them having the money. New York was the place with a toll for everything; people expected to pay their way.

When O'Connor heard the screaming, he couldn't tell if it came from the front or the back. Was it a woman? Even that he couldn't tell. He crossed the street and looked up at each building in turn. The screaming stopped as suddenly as it had begun. Seeing nothing, hearing nothing further, he started back for his limited cover at the corner. Whores, he thought. Whores.

꩜THE MAN WITH the bowie knife waited as O'Connor came toward him. Swiftly, the man swatted O'Connor's derby hat aside, grabbed the policeman's thick hair, jerked his head back, and cut with the sharp, single-edged blade. The killer was rewarded with the gurgling sound of blood pumping from the dying cop's throat.

꩜"MOVE IN." SMITH gave the order and raced up the stairs to No. 9, one enlisted man behind him. "Stay in your rooms!" Smith shouted. Doors slammed shut in response to his command. Smith's three troopers, two from the front, one at the rear, would now commence a floor-by-floor search. If all was going according to plan, Ridley and Lonnigan and their teams were doing the same in Nos. 11 and 13.

The flash of light had come from the attic window. At the landing below the attic, he paused and held his breath.

Nothing. He breathed, tasted smoke, but proceeded up the stairs anyway.

His eyes confirmed his fear. An overturned lamp leaked kerosene onto the floor. The burning patch was still contained, close to the body. Cursing, Smith stamped the fire out. Another few minutes and the whole house would have gone up, and Gay Street with it.

Now it was pitch dark. He nudged the body with his shoe. It did not move. He crouched and searched by feel. No weapon. His fingers felt sticky and he lifted them to his nose. The smell of blood was unmistakable.

Smith relit the lantern. A wave of nausea hit him. It was Carl Ridley, his throat cut. Smith's hand trembled as he held the lantern. For God's sake. A match was jammed between Ridley's teeth.

From the street, Smith heard the clatter of a wagon moving away. A horse whinnied. Smith cursed and ran down the stairs and out the front door. "Lonnigan! Lonnigan! Where the hell are you?" The closed wagon that had been in front of the house was gone.

HEADLEY, AFOOT, SLOWED down at the high end of Gay Street, positioning himself next to a large sycamore. He motioned to Toby, expecting the boy to be right behind. Toby had vanished.

At that instant, Headley felt the gun push into the small of his back. "Move and you're dead."

LOW TO THE ground to keep himself a minimal target, Toby saw men coming from all directions. He crept to No. 13. On his knees he pushed at the door under the stairs. It was not locked and he crawled in. Without warning the door slammed shut behind him and a lamp flared. An enormous black man was aiming a shotgun straight at his head.

THIRTY-ONE

⌒November 4th, Friday night.

TOBY TENSED, WAITING. Would he hear the blast that would shatter his skull?

In the darkness voices murmured, a mixture of surprise and fear.

The huge man cradled the shotgun in his arms. A reprieve, for the moment. Behind the man with the gun, someone raised a lamp. As Toby's eyes acclimated, he saw that the man wore white man's clothes, business attire, very much like what Colonel Martin and Captain Kennedy wore, complete to flowered vest and silk cravat.

"What do you want here?" the Negro asked in a low voice. His speech was like a white man's, too.

Toby sat up cautiously. His adversary didn't move. "The war out there on the street. I thought I was going to get killed." Squinting at the shadows around the lamp, Toby began to make out several shapes. Women, hanging back against the wall near the staircase. "I mean you no harm," Toby said, attempting to make his speech sound more like a New Yorker's.

"He's here to take us back, Jeremiah," a woman cried. "Don't let him." The women's voices rose in agreement.

"No, I'm not," Toby said.

"You sound like a Yankee," Jeremiah said. "But underneath I detect the South . . . ."

"No, really. I'd like to stand."

"Easy there, mister." Jeremiah brought his gun back to bear on Toby.

"Let me assure you," Toby said, caught halfway up and halfway down in a crouch. "A friend of mine was killed on the streets of the City and the family sent me to find out the circumstances and to bring him back to his people for a Christian burial."

"Praise Jesus," a woman said.

"Amen" came from all around.

Toby slowly straightened all the way. "With your permission, I'd like to leave."

"No," Jeremiah rumbled, prodding Toby with his shotgun.

"He's performing a Christian duty, Jeremiah," a woman said.

"Do you swear as a Christian not to tell anybody about us?"

"I swear to Almighty God," Toby vowed.

"Amen," the women said.

"Follow me." Jeremiah led Toby through the kitchen. A heavy padlock secured the back door. Jeremiah removed it and he and Toby stepped out into the darkness.

"Go, then," Jeremiah said. "God be with you."

"And with you."

TOBY HADN'T LIED. His intention was to get far from this place as soon as he could. But before he had moved three paces, a rustling noise close by stopped him. He squatted behind the thick slats of a stone bench. If Jeremiah had had a change of heart, he didn't want to give the black man a target.

A silhouette gradually took the form of a cloaked man as it crept from the back of the house where the Lucifer band had been staying. There was no light at all, not even from the clouded sky or the whorehouse. Toby heard only a muffled shout, then running footsteps.

The cloaked figure's steps quickened as he approached Toby's hiding place. Toby stayed very still.

The figure passed so close to Toby he could smell the whiskey on him. The man was carrying a carpetbag.

Bolder now, Toby followed the cloaked figure. He reached the sidewalk just in time to recognize the man in the cloak, who was now leading a horse and sulky away from Gay Street.

Relieved, Toby whispered, "Captain, it's me, Toby Garner."

Startled, Longmire dropped his bag.

Someone shouted. Lights appeared at the corner. More voices. They were coming closer.

After a scramble to retrieve his bag, Longmire tossed it onto the seat of the two-wheeled carriage. He groped for the reins as he scrambled up, then flicked them before he was even seated, urging the already moving horse to git.

Toby ran after him. In a low hoarse voice Longmire called back, "I wouldn't tarry too long if I were you." Then he was gone.

THIRTY-TWO

⌒*November 4th, Friday night.*

AS TOBY PLOTTED a course for the Bowery, he racked his brain. What was the name of the rooming house Colonel Martin and Headley were going to? Well, he would find it. Fortunately, he did remember it was above the Hamburg Drinking Club on the Bowery.

"Are you lost?"

Toby peered up at the stern face of a mounted policeman. Careless of him; he should have been paying more attention. "Just the man I'm looking for," Toby said. "I'm on my way to the celebration at the Hamburg Drinking Club."

"Two more the way you're going will get you to the Bowery and one to the left will put you right there at Stanton Street."

"Thank you, Officer."

"*Gute nacht.* Just be glad my name is Frankenheimer and not Muldoon."

"*Gute nacht,*" Toby responded, hoping he was saying it correctly. He continued on his way.

At Stanton, a street lamp obliged him by casting its light on the drinking club's sign painted on the front of the four-storied orange house.

A more modest wooden sign hanging from a wrought-iron arm

creaked in the sharp breeze that slapped litter and leaves at his legs. This one said, "MRS. McDONALD'S ROOMS. NO VACANCIES." Under that was a smaller sign: "ACTORS WELCOME."

Toby circled the block before approaching the building. Other than two men talking outside the drinking club, the street was empty.

The first of the men was heavyset and ordinary. The second, in the black herringbone mackinaw and spectacles, was more distinctive. He seemed familiar to Toby. His large companion struck Toby as far from harmless, but while it was good to be wary, if Toby played the rabbit he'd never get any food or rest.

On the steps, he took a surreptitious second look at the two men; he could hear piano music and a woman singing inside the house. Laughter, too. Good. Laughter had been in short supply lately. A cord hung to the side of the front door. He pulled it, and was rewarded with the ring of a bell from inside.

When no one answered he tried the door and found it was open. Hanging his hat and coat on the already overburdened rack, he sniffed the air and felt a sense of well-being he hadn't experienced since he'd left Kentucky three months ago.

The odors of corned beef and cabbage, baked apples, and roasted chestnuts filled his nostrils. But the dining room, a big square chamber on his right, was empty. A Negro woman, piling dirty dishes on a huge tray, looked up. "They're in the parlor." Noticing him staring at the two scant slices of beef on the large platter, she said, "Go on, have a nibble. Actors are always hungry and I've got mine in the kitchen."

Toby grinned and shoved the two pieces of corned beef into his mouth. Closing his eyes he chewed, letting the moist salt taste comfort him. When he opened his eyes the black woman was offering him a biscuit. He accepted, saying, "You are the true darling of my life."

The woman laughed. "And you're a sugar-tongued devil. When you're done chewing just go on in."

Opening the double doors, Toby saw a batch of folks, some sitting, others gathered round the piano where a dignified elderly woman was playing "Beautiful Dreamer." That particular Stephen Foster tune was a special favorite of Toby's mother's. Hearing it filled him with a powerful homesickness.

He was struck by the sight of several of the women smoking. He cleared his throat. All eyes turned to him. The music stopped.

"Enter, enter, dear boy." A plump woman waved to him. "I am Mrs. Jane McDonald. You're more than welcome." She had a mellifluous voice, a small trace of the Carolinas still faintly discernible.

"Honored, ma'am. I don't mean to interrupt. I'm looking for a friend. A Mr. Martin?"

"You are Mr. Garner, then." Mrs. McDonald signaled to the woman playing the piano to continue.

The pianist struck a clanging chord and sang, " 'Camptown ladies sing this song . . .' " The others joined in and the room throbbed with their enthusiastic sound.

"Yes, ma'am," Toby said, raising his voice to be heard.

"Well, go on upstairs. Top floor. Last door on the right. Towel and soap are waiting for you. Bath is across the hall."

"Thank you kindly." Toby's stomach emitted a loud growl.

The woman focused on him with a keen eye. "Are you hungry?"

"I'm sorry, ma'am. I am."

"I'll send Susan up with a tray." She gave his arm a squeeze. "We don't want our heroes to starve before they make us proud."

Toby climbed the stairs. He'd seen enough to know that this was an unconventional boardinghouse. First of all, actors were accepted as boarders. The women were all older than he. They wore face paint and smoked cigarettes. He'd love to watch one of them roll one. He found their perfume, their conspicuous hair and clothing . . . exciting.

The men, too, were somewhat larger than reality. They should never try to be conspirators, he thought, they stand out too much.

On the top landing he turned down the hall and proceeded to the door Mrs. McDonald had indicated. When he heard the coughing, he waited a moment before knocking.

"Who is it?" Martin's voice was tense, in a way Toby had never heard before.

"Toby, sir."

The door opened. Martin seemed exhausted. "Where's your gear?"

"Lost, sir. Trouble on Gay Street." Toby stepped into the small room. A double bed and a cot.

"What sort of trouble? What did you learn at the morgue? Where's Headley?"

"I don't know where Headley is. We walked right into it. Police. A fire in the attic of No. 9. We got separated. I ducked into No. 13. Almost got killed for my trouble. Full of darkies scared to death themselves. One with a shotgun."

"Damn. Did you see Price?"

"We got to the morgue too late. They'd moved him to Potter's Field, up above the Central Park. Headley found his coffin. It's for sure. Price is dead meat."

"I thought as much."

"All he was wearing was skin." Toby poured himself a whiskey. "The gravedigger who stole Price's hat and boots was passed out drunk. No sign of the coat, though."

"Then that's that." Martin examined the ash at the end of his cigar, saw it was ready to fall, and poised it over a bowl. "What did you do with Price?"

"Left him. Headley thought we were followed so we got away quick."

Vexed at Toby's information and impatient with the ash, Martin tapped the cigar, knocking the ash off. "Who was following you?"

Toby shrugged. "We weren't showing lights; I reckon we left whoever it was someplace uptown. They never got close enough for us to see them or them us."

Martin frowned. "They might have been part of the police raid on Gay Street. This entire mission has become a fiasco."

"Maybe yes, maybe no, sir. What if it was all because Longmire put us next door to the colored people? What if the raid was meant to flush them out?"

"Comforting thought, Toby. But we're in New York, not Richmond. Still, it is a possibility. If they were after us the best thing we can do is nothing." Martin's dry chuckle was humorless. He poured himself a drink; Toby hadn't touched his. "And it will drive them mad." Snapping his head back he drained the small tumbler. "We'll know more when Headley arrives."

"I hope they didn't get him."

Martin shook his head slowly. "Not John Headley. He's a good man. And he's got nine lives."

There was a soft knock at the door.

"Yes?" Martin called.

"Susan, sir. I've got victuals for the young man."

"Come."

Susan was the Negro woman who'd given Toby the corned beef and biscuit earlier. She set her tray on a corner table and removed the linen cloth. Bread and butter, rice, and black-eyed peas. Bread pudding that smelled richly of bourbon. And a pitcher of milk with two tall glasses.

"Once more," Toby said, "you are the true darling of my life."

Susan grinned at Colonel Martin. "Keep this one locked up, sir. That sweet tongue of his could cause a load of trouble." She shook her head and backed out the door.

Toby set to. When he'd tamed his hunger, he drained his tumbler of whiskey and said, "Longmire is gone."

"He'll turn up soon enough."

"I think not. I expect Captain Longmire is on his way to Canada by now. Last I saw of him he was rattling off in a sulky like the Devil was chasing him."

Martin's lips formed a bitter smile. "I'm not surprised. Longmire never struck me as steadfast."

Toby poured himself another whiskey. What he was about to say might mean the end of their mission.

"Out with it, boy." The faint strains of "My Old Kentucky Home" drifted to them from below.

"Are the greenbacks safe?"

Martin looked at the open wardrobe. Two carpetbags were on the floor of the closet. "Yes."

"I think you'd better have a look, sir. Longmire was toting a bag of his own and it looked awful full."

Martin lifted out one bag and set it on the double bed.

Wiping his mouth with the back of his hand, Toby joined the Colonel as he opened the bag.

Martin lifted away the clothing, then the false bottom. "You were right to be suspicious, Toby. Our comrade Longmire is a thief."

There had been twenty packets of Yankee greenbacks under the false bottom. They were all gone. In their place were copies of the *Evening Post*.

THIRTY-THREE

⌒November 4th, Friday night.

NEITHER MAN SPOKE.

Unaware he was doing so, Toby joined in on the song filtering up from the parlor. " 'Oh, the sun shines bright on my old . . .' "

"He died, January last."

"Who?"

"Stephen Foster. Right here in this City."

"It's a terrible thing, to die away from home."

Martin nodded. "The only thing worse than being destitute away from home."

Unhappy, Toby stated the obvious. "Which we are."

"Which we are not," the Colonel said, lifting out the second false bottom and revealing five packets of greenbacks. "Fifty thousand Yankee dollars. More than enough to do the job."

⌒As HEADLEY AND Kennedy approached the Hamburg Drinking Club, Kennedy was still laughing, slapping his thigh. "You should have seen your face."

"I should have smashed yours," Headley growled, keeping his eye on the hulking man standing outside the club. "Don't ever try a fool trick like that on me again. What are you, ten years old?"

"Come down off your high horse, Headley. Don't take life so seriously."

"I have to when I soldier with a man who thinks nothing of shoving a gun in my back during hostilities and saying, 'Move and you're dead.'"

Kennedy roared. "Oh, my, it was funny, wasn't it?"

THIRTY-FOUR

November 5th, Saturday morning.

DUFF WOKE WITH a throbbing desire for Kathleen Tierney. It was Kathleen who had given him his rosary to take to war. Though she was a whore, she was a sweet girl. But Duff's thoughts weren't of sweetness. He needed a woman. And Kathleen lived a mere ten blocks away on Chrystie Street, this side of the Bowery.

Desiring Kathleen made him think of the Blessed Virgin Mary. Damn Bishop Hughes. Dagger John Hughes had done this to him. The Archbishop, who had sponsored the Irish Brigade of which the 69th was a part, had magnanimously offered to hear confession from the boys going off to war.

Hughes, hearing Duff's confession, which enumerated Duff's carnal doings and thoughts of Kathleen, had not required Duff to say any Hail Marys. Instead he had instructed Duff to picture the Virgin Mother whenever he had his lecherous contemplations for Kathleen or any other woman.

The struggle was constant between the lecherous contemplations and the Virgin Mother, with lechery always a horse cock ahead. Duff dressed, had his tea, and hurried to Chrystie Street.

. . .

⌒" 'I'LL TAKE YOU home again, Kathleen,' " he sang under the girl's window. A workie came out the door, grinning, and walked toward the Bowery.

The sash flew open. "Duff. Is it really you?"

Duff opened his arms wide. "Himself."

"Come up at once, you wicked man."

She was on the third floor, as he well remembered. He'd not seen her since he'd gone off to war.

"Your eye," Kathleen said, her small hand to her lips. She wore nothing but her cotton shift. The sunlight struggling through the narrow window put her breasts in shadow.

Duff wrapped his fingers in her light brown hair, soft against the ruddy blush of her cheeks. He'd forgotten how just the sight of her could make his heart race. "A present from a Johnny Reb, who managed to die in an alley in New York."

She pulled his coat from his shoulders. "You'll have to tell me all about it. After."

⌒LONG AFTER, HOLDING her in his arms, breathing in her musky smell, he said, "Kathleen, love."

"Yes, Patrick."

"Do you know a whore by the name of Claudia Albert?"

THIRTY-FIVE

⌒*November 5th, Saturday, late morning.*

As HE WALKED in the bright sunshine, Duff felt good. His energies were replenished, his step light, his stomach full with his favorite oatmeal and honey. In his pocket was a worn business card: *Claudia, No. 205 Grand.*

Grand Street was but a short walk from Chrystie Street.

Two fat ladies followed him with their hawk eyes as he approached the corner building on Grand and Mott. They spat tobacco juice.

"What the hell do you want, One-Eye?" one of the women demanded, her ear trumpet in her hand like a club.

"Claudia Albert."

The second woman cackled uproariously. "Another one who wants his stick wet! Well, you're too late. Hanna's gone."

"Which is her room?"

"Up there." The deaf woman spat, then nodded at the first-floor window.

"I think I'll take a look."

"Cost you ten cents." Without rising the woman scraped the box she sat on along the sidewalk until she was in front of the door.

"Take a stamp?" Duff asked.

The woman frowned. "Is that all you got?"

"It's all you're going to get."

She flapped her fleshy hand out. "I'll take it."

⌒A DUPLICATE OF Claudia's card nailed to the door marked it as her apartment. Her two small rooms had obviously been better than others in the neighborhood. But they looked as if a plague of locusts had been through. Marks on the floor showed where sofas and chairs had once stood. "Thieves in the night," Duff muttered.

Glass beads glinted on the floor. He picked one up. A broken necklace perhaps.

He opened the window and leaned his head out. "Where did she go?" he asked the fat sentries.

Both cackled. The one who could hear said, "Far, far away, lover."

The deaf one shook her trumpet and put it to her ear. "What he say?"

"He wants to know where Hanna is."

"Hee hee hee. Tell him she got married!"

This set both crones to cackling again.

As Duff closed the window something that had been caught in the sash hit the sill. It was another business card. This one was worn where it had been folded. All he could get from it was ". . . *finest in cigars*," and ". . . *aport*," and ". . . *WERY*."

He shoved the card into his vest pocket and left Claudia Albert's rooms a great deal less happy than when he'd left Kathleen Tierney's.

THIRTY-SIX

November 5th, Saturday,
late morning to noon.

". . . finest in cigars," and ". . . *aport*," and ". . . WERY" was not enough to help Duff search in the City Directory, but it didn't take a professor to calculate that ". . . WERY" was *BOWERY*.

He decided to start at the bottom of the Bowery at Chatham Square, and keep his eyes open for tobacco or cigar shops as he worked his way up. It was only a mile or so to where the Bowery came to an end at Cooper Square.

The wide road called the Bowery was elegant and shoddy at the same time. At any given hour, day or night, a stroller was apt to see jugglers, street singers, and musicians entertaining small groups of people. Beggars proliferated. Cider carts sold applejack for a penny a cup.

To Duff, this was the most exciting thoroughfare in his adopted city. A grand, bright boulevard of theatres and minstrel houses and oyster bars. And, damn it, tobacco shops. Too many tobacco shops.

"Shine your shoes, mister?"

Before he could say yea or nay, the young moke bootblack was on his knees, his box at Duff's feet. "They'll shine like gold."

"Not today, boy," Duff said, passing on.

On the next corner, the *Bouquet Man,* worn beaver hat, hair to his shoulders, a thick mustache under his hooked Hebraic nose, sold chestnuts now, and flowers in season.

One block farther, a boy with his right leg gone to the knee, his crutch by his side, sat on the ground selling ginger nuts, the small brittle cookie flavored with ginger and molasses, from his large basket.

Duff exchanged a penny for two nuts which he immediately popped into his mouth as he continued his search.

A blind beggar, one hand stroking his dog, the other holding out a hat, stood in a doorway only several paces past the boy. Money was low for Duff and he tried to pass the man by, but he couldn't. He dropped a penny in the hat and sped off at the man's blessing.

Broadway swells, in their tall silk toppers, much like the President's, promenaded the Bowery on their way to entertainments, preening and stroking well-barbered beards and mustaches, displaying the latest fashion in men's attire and brandishing walking sticks.

"Letter paper, mister?" A man with a tray hanging from his neck approached.

Duff found himself wanting to write to Kathleen. But that would be a waste; the wretched lass couldn't read. The aroma from a cigar on his left, his blind side, was what made Duff turn. He saw the red wool shirt and the bell-bottomed black broadcloth trousers draped over high-heeled boots and a tail of gray smoke from his butt-ender. A Bowery Boy. The youth turned a corner. Duff went after him but the dandy had been swallowed up in the busy walkway.

Irked at an opportunity missed, Duff resumed his walk. Still, who was to say this was the one he'd seen in Jew's Alley since all the *B'hoys* fancied the same costume and the same gummy hair.

At Houston Street, Duff finally saw the sign. *For the finest in cigars of any sort, talk to Abe Rappaport.*

The shuttered door to the shop was closed. When Duff shook the knob, it did not turn. "Rappaport," he yelled, banging on the door with his fist.

No answer.

Again he called out. "Rappaport."

"Go away." A harsh voice in a thick sheeny accent came from deep inside the shop. "It's *Shabbas*."

Duff knew that meant Sabbath and that Saturday was the Israelites' Sabbath. He sighed, unwilling to profane any man's day with God. He lifted his patch and rubbed the skin around his empty eye socket.

He'd have to come back on Monday. Or, since his Sabbath didn't appear to be as important to Duff as the Hebrew's was to him, he could come back Sunday. Duff gave the knob one final shake simply because he'd been thwarted by God.

"Hanna," he heard the coarse voice say, "tell the *goyisher* idiot it's *Shabbas*."

⯌RAPPAPORT, SITTING WITH his back to the curtain that separated his living quarters from the shop, smiled between slurps of his niece's rich chicken soup. Abe had given up on the rabbis and *shul* when he was still a pup. But that wasn't something he wanted the *goyim* to know.

Besides, he was eating and food *was* sacred to him. He didn't care to have his mealtime interrupted. Thanks to Hanna, he could afford to turn away a paying customer.

"Is the soup good, Uncle?" Hanna wore her red hair hidden under a scarf. Her splendid body was obscured by a brown sack of a dress. At her place leaning over the wood stove, Hanna smiled while she added vegetables to the beef stew she was preparing for their evening meal.

Abe Rappaport smacked his lips. He hadn't seen Ida's daughter for years. Then Thursday she appeared, just like that, and moved in with him. A small burp tickled his throat.

Something had frightened the girl out of her other life, driving her to him. This was good and this was bad. He was, it was true, eating like a king, but the life she lived was what brought him ease in his old age.

No matter, she'd made plenty and he knew she'd put it in a safe place. Hanna was very smart. "I'll have another taste, please, Hanna. With a nice *knaydl*. They're so light, your *knaydlach*, like feathers that would fly right out to the sky if I didn't . . . What's wrong?"

His niece was gaping at him with horror. No, not at him, over his head. Abe turned.

A huge demon was standing in the backyard outside the window, staring at his Hanna from out of his evil eye.

THIRTY-SEVEN

⌒*November 5th, Saturday, midday.*

AWAY, EVIL ONE," Abe shouted, holding his second and middle fingers to his lips and spitting three times.

"I am not Satan." Duff appreciated how similar the old man's actions were to what his own Da's would have been.

"Then who are you?" Abe demanded.

At the telltale *click,* a startled Duff looked at Hanna. Abe did the same.

In her left hand the woman held a wooden spoon. In her right was a derringer. Her eyes were steely calm.

"Niece, put that—"

"I love and respect you, Uncle, but shut up." To Duff she said, "This little toy holds two .22 slugs. I'm not afraid to use it."

"Of that I have no doubt. But there's absolutely no need to. My name is Patrick Duff. I merely want to talk to you."

"Aha." Old Abe pulled the big napkin from his shirt and stood with an awkward shrug. "Business. Why didn't you say so?"

Hanna's face went red, the way she'd turned Meg's face red only four days earlier. Claudia might be a prostitute, but Hanna was a proud Jewish woman. "Uncle Abe!" She whacked her uncle on the arm with her spoon.

"What'd I do?"

"Don't talk what you don't know." Claudia shoved the spoon into her stew pot and gave it a stir. "Sit down, Uncle. I want a clear view of Mr. Duff." As Abe sat she lowered the derringer but kept a firm grip on it. "Why are you here, sir?"

"I'm the one who found Price's body—"

"I can read."

"I don't question that. I need to know about Price and his friend."

"Can *you* read?"

He smiled. She had a sharp tongue. He liked her. "Yes, I can."

"Everything I know about Price and Kennedy was in the papers."

"May I come in?"

Abe dabbed his lips with his linen napkin. Hanna put them out even when they ate alone. "Ask the man to come into our house and sit, Hanna. Give him some soup. Talking like this through the window is not nice. You're not horses."

Hanna wasn't listening to her uncle. She'd made a mistake. What was worse, she could tell by the expression on his face that this Irishman knew it, too.

T H I R T Y - E I G H T

⌒November 5th, Saturday, midday.

HANNA REALIZED SHE'D already let the cat out of the bag when she told Pete Tonneman Kennedy's name. God strike her for a blabber. It was her turn to spit the evil away. "Come in." She laid her derringer close at hand on a worktable.

Duff moved as if to go round to the front of the shop.

"No, you don't," Hanna said. "Through the window. I have to keep my eye on you a while before I can really trust you."

Duff's size made coming through the window a struggle. With one foot in, he had to edge his big shoulders through the narrow opening. Hanna and Uncle Abe watched the effort with amusement.

The room Duff entered had a heat stove and cookstove, a worktable, a dining table, and three chairs. To the right was a curtain that led to the shop, to the left, a door, leading either to another room or out back.

"Sit," Abe commanded, pointing to the place his niece had set for herself. "Hanna's *knaydl* is light as angel breath."

"A fine recommendation," Duff said. "What is *knaydl?*" His tongue stumbled over the exotic word.

"Dumpling." Hanna selected a bowl from the shelf, ladled hot fragrant soup, and set the bowl in front of the Irishman. When her uncle gestured with his empty bowl, she served him as well.

"Thank you." Duff ate voraciously. All he'd had since his morning oatmeal were the two ginger nuts. Famished as a wolf, he was, for sure. He moved his head to get a full look at the woman. She was beautiful even in her plain homespun. Unruly red curls crept from under her head scarf.

Hanna, her arms folded, was doing her own watching. "When you're done, you can leave. And if you're a true gent, you won't say where you saw me."

"That's fair, but only if you tell me about the two men."

Hanna grinned and shook her head. "You're a stubborn one; how'd they ever get that eye away from you?"

"Hanna, shush," Uncle Abe scolded.

"It's all right," said Duff. "With one eye I don't have tears to waste, so I don't. To laugh is better. There's always someone worse off. You like jokes, Hanna? It was Price who took my eye from me. At Antietam."

"*Gottenyu,*" Abe whispered.

"He was a Grayback. I'm trying to find out who killed him."

"Are you a lawman?" Abe asked, doubtful.

Duff shook his head. "I have my reasons."

"It's because he took your eye, isn't it?" Hanna said. "You have to. To banish the Devil."

"Dear Jesus," Duff said.

Abe made a snorting noise but said nothing.

Duff glanced at the old man, then brought his eye back to Hanna. "You understand completely. It's uncanny. I thought we were so different, Israelites and Irish." He thought: *Or is it you who understands so much?*

"My Hanna's a bright girl."

She pulled out a chair and sat at the table. "That night before he died, John Price and his friend Kennedy and I were drinking and having a rip-roaring time in the George Washington Room at the LaFarge House." She paused. "Uncle, I need more potatoes for the stew."

"What are you talking? You have a basketful by the stove."

"Uncle."

"All right, I'll get them from the cellar." Abe shook his head. "Ah, the way she treats me," he said to the air. "I might just as well be married again."

Hanna watched her uncle walk to the back room. Only after waiting several moments did she speak again. She told her story quickly. "I went upstairs with them, did what I'm paid to do, and left with a gold double eagle for my industry. The coin was one of many Price had sewn inside his coat. As I was leaving I met the barmaid, Meg. She was bringing them a bottle of Kentucky bourbon. Their fourth that night."

"Price wasn't wearing any coat when I found him."

"You have it, then," Hanna declared. "Kennedy killed him for the gold."

"That's possible," Duff agreed. "What sort of man was Kennedy?"

Hanna let out a short, mirthless laugh. "A man."

Duff shook his head. "The name says he's an Irishman. What sort? A Paddy right off the boat? A gentleman?"

"He didn't have an accent. Not like yours, at any rate."

Duff squared his wide shoulders. "I don't have an accent."

"And I'm a nun."

The eyebrow over Duff's good eye arched. Hanna had flawless skin and soft full lips. Kathleen Tierney, bless her, slipped out of his mind.

"Kennedy spoke the way Price did. I think they're both from Kentucky."

"The maker's mark in Price's hat agrees with you. Why do you say it?"

"He drank Kentucky sour mash, but to say true, many do these days. And he wanted me to sing 'My Old Kentucky Home' to him. While we were doing it, for God's sake."

"So that's what that journalist Tonneman is sniffing after. These boys could very well be spies, the gold their expense money. And Kennedy killed his partner for the gold, simple as that." Duff laid his spoon down and wiped his lips. "Now all I have to do is find this fellow Kennedy."

"Simple as that," Hanna said, mocking.

"Thank you for the soup," Duff said. "What made you run?"

Hanna mused silently. "I think what you think. Kennedy killed him for the gold. Kennedy knows I can identify him. He might come looking for me."

"Why would he bother? If I killed a man and had his gold, I would be a hundred miles away." As he spoke Duff hoped he was wrong. He had to find Kennedy and . . . What? Kill him? No. He'd done with killing. Take him to the law. That would make him quits with Price.

"It's easier to hide in this City than anywhere else," Hanna said.

"The South is losing. With all that gold Kennedy could be a rich man in Kentucky."

"The South is losing," Hanna repeated.

A door slammed. Hanna looked to her gun, then relaxed. Abe's wheeze could be heard coming toward them.

Hanna leaned across the table at Duff, so close he could see the ripple of her breasts under her dress, smell the sweetness of her breath, her subtle perfume. "What if it's one final terrible Rebel plot to attack New York?"

Reluctantly, Duff stood. He didn't want to leave her. "I doubt that. They're licked; they know it. It's over. Shall I take my leave through the window?"

Duff's fleeting thoughts of the Holy Mother could not erase the picture he had in his mind of Hanna's naked breasts as she smiled and pointed to the back door. What was this fascination he had with whores?

THIRTY-NINE

THE EVENING POST   *New York, Saturday, November 5, 1864*

CITY INTELLIGENCE

Two men died during a fire in Nos. 9, 11 and 13 Gay Street last night. No one else was injured and the three buildings were saved, suffering little damage. The Metropolitan Police are investigating the cause of the fire and as yet have not identified the two dead men. When asked, an aide to General Butler, the new Military Commander of New York, said he knew nothing about the incident.

November 5th, Saturday night.

IT HAD BEEN a long night. And a long day. Pete and Jed had followed the two Southerners in the dark carriage to Gay Street and there walked into chaos. Shots fired, flames, men running around like chickens with their heads cut off. And the end result was no Rebel conspirators and a dead cop and a dead soldier.

Pete's Uncle Hays had arrived. Tim O'Connor and Lieutenant

Ridley had been murdered the same way Price had been. And with a stupid match left between their teeth, too.

Uncle Hays was incensed. Pete understood. One of their own had been killed. O'Connor had been a good man, with four kids and a fifth on the way.

Pete and Jed had stayed with Hays as Hays and Kevin Rourke scoured the City, trying to pick up the scent. But it was cold. Finally Uncle Hays said he was going home for a wash and a nap, but Pete knew Hays wanted to confer with Old Peter.

The night had brought a weather change. Cold winds came in off the East River, rattling shutters, causing gas lamps to flicker and go out.

Jed and Pete were at a work site near the Bowery, where a new building was going up and where an informant had told Rourke that strangers had been seen. The reporter and the Sheriff were standing around the workers' fire, drinking cans of hot tea. Some of the workers had slept at the site on Friday night, but they'd neither seen nor heard anything.

If Price hadn't got himself killed, the Confederate plot as a political ruse would still be gospel. As it was, the only ones who took the damned plot seriously were an old man, a drunken reporter, and a hick cop.

⌒PETE TONNEMAN SAILED a stone across the lot; he was restless and unhappy. Though he'd led a dissolute life, he'd always prided himself on what he considered his one saving grace: He was a good journalist. He'd proved that again and again. But not in last night's *Post.*

The story ran only four lines. And practically every word of it was a lie.

Uncle Hays had said, "It's for the good of the City and for the good of the country." Hays believed if the truth about the deaths got out, there would be rioting in the streets, even worse than the Draft Riots.

If the people learned that there really was a plot to burn New York and that two lawmen had died while investigating, it would impede the election. Maybe even open the way for Southern sympathizers to overthrow the City government. Pete doubted that strongly, but it was his Uncle Hays asking. When Uncle Hays asked, Pete considered it a request direct from Old Peter. For that reason and for that reason only, he'd not told the truth about the circumstances surrounding the death of the two men on Gay Street.

"WE'VE GOT A great deal to mull over," Jed said.

"We?" Pete was surprised. "I surely thought you'd be heading home now to Catskill Station, Sheriff."

"I believe I'll stick around, Mr. Tonneman. I'm a loyal American. I don't want to see New York burn."

Pete scowled and threw another stone. "All right, let's talk about it. Most important—who killed the copper and the soldier in Gay Street?"

"Them, too," Jed said. "I was thinking more about why those two we followed went up to Potter's Field."

"What do you think?"

"To see if he was really dead," Jed said.

"Maybe yes, maybe no. They knew who he was from my description in the *Post*."

"You could have been lying."

"I write the tru—" Pete glared at the Sheriff. The old bastard had a cruel streak in him, but he was right. "When he died, Price had something on his person. They wanted it. Makes more sense."

"Yes, it does. And I'll wager they didn't find it."

"What makes you think that?" Only good manners kept the grin off Pete's face. He'd been holding back on the Sheriff. There was no way now he could get away with not telling him.

"Somehow I get the feeling, City boy, that you know what it was. Or think you do."

"Oh, I know I do. Price was wearing a coat full of gold double eagles sewn into the lining. His killer took it. That may be why he was killed."

"Thank you for sharing that information with me," Jed said dryly.

"You're quite welcome."

"Maybe his killer took it and maybe he didn't. How do you know about the gold?"

"A whore. Claudia Albert. She spent time with Price and a friend of his, named Kennedy, before he died."

Jed shook his head. "People don't use the sense the good Lord gave them. Are you telling me Price went and showed her the gold in the coat?"

"That's one thing he didn't show her."

Sheriff Jed Honeycutt tongued his wad of tobacco to his left cheek and narrowed his eyes at Pete Tonneman. "I suppose you think that's funny, City boy?"

Now Pete couldn't help but smile.

"Damn New Yorkers," the Sheriff mumbled. "You make a joke out of everything."

FORTY

ASHBROOK, JOHN.
SCHOOLTEACHER. LIEUTENANT.
TENTH KENTUCKY CAVALRY.
ARMY OF THE CONFEDERACY.
MARRIED. LUCIFER.

⌒November 5th, Saturday night.

IT WAS A PARTY of three who entertained one another in a private room at the St. Nicholas Hotel. Heavy blood red velvet draperies covered the tall windows. The air was thick with cigar smoke, and Meg was tipsy.

The crystal chandelier dazzled her eyes when she looked about the elegant room. Too much excitement, too much wine. The champagne had gone to her head.

Josie Fallon had shamed Meg into coming with her. "For the fun," she'd said. "I've been an actress for five years now. We work hard and we play hard. You'll never get ahead in this world if you don't know how to have fun. And one thing about Johnny Booth—he's fun."

So she'd gone along with Josie and Johnny. When it got late Meg wondered, in a whisper to Josie, how she would get back to her room at the LaFarge—at this hour, going home was out of the question. Josie said, "You'll come home with me." Josie lived in a boardinghouse off the Bowery. Because Meg so much wanted to be like Josie and to share the life, she accepted.

She'd been troubled about John Wilkes—that he'd take liberties. But he spent the evening drinking and talking politics, worse than her own brothers. Meg hated politics, but she loved the excitement of the City during wartime, with travelers from all over the world and always something happening.

"Mark my words," Booth said. "There'll be rioting in the streets. New York may be 'God's Country,' but it's not Lincoln country."

Josie's constant smile disappeared. "I was on Tenth Street the first day of the Draft Riots. There were fires everywhere. I thought I'd died and gone to Hell. I ran home and drank for three days." Reminded, she drained her glass and refilled it, then flashed Booth a flirtatious smile. Booth took the bottle from her and tipped it to his mouth.

Meg shuddered, closed her eyes. The whole world had gone crazy for three days last year. Dennis had been hurt, not bad, but still, a gash on the arm could be a knife in the heart, excepting for God's grace. It had been a black day for Dennis. Bad enough he was hurt, but he'd been hurt fighting Irishmen. Catholics. Same as Superintendent Kennedy, who'd been horribly beaten himself. The Colored Orphan Asylum on Fifth Avenue had been burned to the ground. By God's grace all the orphans escaped out the back. Meg felt bad for the kids, but she didn't like coloreds; they stole good Irish jobs.

Loud laughter startled her and she opened her eyes. There were two more men in the room. Where had they come from? Her mind whirled. Oh, well, the more the merrier. Josie was refilling her glass.

"In '61," Booth declaimed, "if it were up to New York City, there would have been no War. There would have been compromise. That's why I like this town." He beamed at his companions. "Almost like home, eh, boys?"

Kennedy's smile twisted his face. "If you say so, Mr. Booth." He pulled his chair close to Meg's.

Meg blinked and opened her eyes wide. Kennedy! She was suddenly sober as a stone. She drank deep from her glass to banish the fear. The fiery liquid made her gasp. Josie had given her whiskey. She had to get out of here. But her limbs would not obey her muddled brain.

Kennedy laughed, his breath hot on her cheek. She would ignore him, that's what she'd do. Annie Clancy's daughter was no fool.

"This City is like a voluptuous woman," Booth declared, gesturing elaborately. "When you think she's given you all she has to give, there's always another morsel more."

"I could use a morsel just now." Kennedy clamped his hand on Meg's thigh.

"Sir!" Meg stared at his hand, outraged. "If you please."

"I please. Where'd your friend Claudia ever fly off to? I went by her place on Grand Street but she's not there anymore."

Meg writhed in humiliation and wished for a hero to rid her of this animal.

"The Academy of Music," the third man said. "I saw *Die Zauberflöte*. Charming. I never thought I'd get the—"

"Ashbrook's a professor," Kennedy said, an edge in his voice. His hand was drifting higher.

"Really?" Meg pretended to give Ashbrook her attention. He was an average-sized man with light hair, a thin mustache, and a small beard.

"A professor?" She patted her hair and surreptitiously removed her hatpin.

"Not really," Ashbrook said. "Not so grand. Merely a humble schoolteacher."

Summoning her courage, Meg jabbed.

"Damn bitch!" Kennedy shouted, pulling back his wounded hand, releasing her thigh.

"Schoolteachers, actors." John Wilkes was eloquently drunk. "We're all in the Cause together against that monkey tyrant in Washington City. Darling Josie, 'shall I lie in your lap?' "

"Sir?" Josie exclaimed with mock horror.

" 'Do you think I meant country matters?' " Booth squeaked. " 'That's a fair thought to lie between maids' legs.' "

By sheer determination, Meg tottered to her feet. When she was several paces clear of Kennedy, she asked, "Where is your other friend tonight, Mr. Kennedy?"

"What other friend?" He sucked his hand and glared at her.

"Mr. Price."

"How . . . ?" Ashbrook said loudly.

"I met Mr. Kennedy and Mr. Price a few days ago."

"Oh, Christ," Kennedy said. "You're the barmaid at the LaFarge House. I thought you were one of Claudia's whore friends."

"How long are you going to be with us, gentlemen?" Josie asked, stroking her Johnny's hair. His head was now in her lap.

"None of your affair," Kennedy replied truculently.

"Bob!" Ashbrook warned.

"Forgive me," Josie said. "I was merely hoping that you'd buy tickets for the benefit. The Booths—all three—are performing for one night only. *Julius Caesar.* I recommend it highly. Something to tell your grandchildren about."

John Wilkes spoke without opening his eyes. "Thank you, my dear. November twenty-fifth, it is. To put Willie up in bronze in the Central Park."

Josie arched her neck, her head high. "I'm to play Calpurnia."

Her boast was all but obliterated by Kennedy's words. "We hope to have our business done by then and be gone. Mr. Booth, I wouldn't count on playing that performance."

Ashbrook seized Kennedy's arm.

"What is your business, Mr. Kennedy?" Meg asked boldly, now that she was at a remove from the frightening man.

"Business." Kennedy laughed, his head lolled. He was past drunk.

Ashbrook got to his feet. "We must be on our way."

"But the night's young," Booth proclaimed, not moving from his nest in Josie's lap. "And the women agreeable."

"We have an engagement early tomorrow morning."

"Settle the bill on the way out, if you'd be so kind." Booth let out a deep sigh and burrowed deeper.

Evenly, Meg said, "Would you kindly see me home, Mr. Ashbrook?"

"My pleasure, ma'am. But I do have to deal with Mr. Kennedy."

"I quite understand," Meg answered. "I've had to deal with him myself this evening."

"A hit, a very palpable hit," Booth called out in a sleepy, muffled voice. "Well said."

As big as Kennedy was, Ashbrook put him over his shoulder like a sack of onions, carried him out of the hotel, and deposited him into a waiting cab.

Unfortunately the cab was a brougham, a luxurious box-shaped coach that was made to seat two passengers inside. A quick look about proved that a larger four-passenger double brougham or clarence wasn't available.

With Kennedy sprawled over half the seat, Meg and Ashbrook were practically in a tight embrace in the other corner. "The LaFarge House, if you please, Mr. Ashbrook."

Ashbrook pulled on the driver's leather. "The LaFarge House, and then to—I'll tell you later."

"You have a wife in Kentucky?" Meg whispered into Ashbrook's face as they rolled along. What an adventure she was having.

"How did you know?" the schoolteacher asked, surprised.

"A woman, especially an actress, can sense these things."

At the LaFarge, Ashbrook gallantly descended and offered Meg his hand.

"What is your Christian name, sir?"

"John."

"Good night, John. Get home safely." Meg wondered if he knew she meant to Kentucky.

"With God's will." He knew. "Good night, Miss Clancy." He held her hand for a moment, then climbed back into the cab.

Meg watched the carriage drive off. Her adventure was over. What a nice man. But like Kennedy and the late Mr. Price, he was here in New York City for no good. He'd been in a great hurry to get his drunken friend away before he said too much.

Whom could she tell? Her own brothers were hopeless.

It was obvious. Only one person in New York would believe her. Only one person in New York could possibly do anything about this.

She had to talk to Pete Tonneman.

FORTY-ONE

⌒November 7th, Monday morning.

THREE HUNDRED Mulberry Street," Old Peter's driver called out, as he did whenever he delivered his charge to Police Headquarters.

"Thank you, Steve," Old Peter said to Steve Brent, the man who'd been his sergeant for all these many years, starting when they were both young minions of the law. Steve had come to work for Peter Tonneman after Jacob Hays—the one and only High Constable the City ever had—promoted Peter to Captain.

Three hundred Mulberry was the house that Jacob Hays had built. Not brick by brick, but idea by idea. It was Hays's vision of a modern police force that led to the house on the east side of Mulberry, between Houston and Bleecker. Though only four stories tall, the building was a mighty palace and the heart of New York City's Metropolitan Police Force.

The law and the house it lived in had given Peter Tonneman a life and a calling. And even at his advanced age, whenever he entered or even approached the house, it never ceased to thrill him.

Around the "palace" was an iron fence. Charity had declared it as good as a moat when he and Old Hays were working. Peter Tonneman had loved Jacob Hays, perhaps more than his own father. He'd modeled his life on that of Jacob Hays, married Charity,

Jacob's cousin, and named his son Hays Tonneman. Now Peter found himself referred to as Old Peter.

Old Peter looked over at his son. "You're very quiet this morning, Hays." This was Old Peter's joke. Hays Tonneman was the quietest of all the Tonnemans. He never spoke where a nod or smile or grunt would do the trick.

Hays grunted.

"Good morning, Ned," Old Peter called to Sergeant Corrigan at his high desk. He saluted the desk sergeant with his gold-topped stick.

Hays said his good morning with a nod.

Corrigan licked the powdered sugar from his fat lips and gobbled the last of a sweet cake. "Good day to you, Chief Tonneman. Chief Tonneman."

The two Tonnemans climbed the staircase to the second floor. Hays watched the old man for any signs of age, amazed that Old Peter was not a bit winded. The years had altered his appearance but not his vigor. It was as if Old Hays had been reborn in his father.

Jerry Murphy ushered them right in. "He's waiting for you."

"Good morning, gentlemen." Superintendent Kennedy greeted them briskly, but his eyes were ringed with coal-like smudges and were deeply pouched, as if he hadn't slept in days. "The situation is what you already know. On Friday, Major General Butler arrived from Fortress Monroe to take military command of the City. He and Dix are welcome to the job. Today, as we speak, at least seven thousand soldiers are arriving under the command of a Major Hawley."

"The Army seems well prepared," Old Peter commented.

"As are we. It's not going to be the Draft Riots all over again."

Old Peter nodded. He was not one to take too much pleasure in being correct. When the first draft was due on July 14 of '63, Old Peter had warned Kennedy about the tinderbox he knew the City had become. Kennedy hadn't listened. And had, for his stubbornness, suffered a terrible beating during the four days of rioting. "I'm glad to hear that."

The silence that followed was thick enough to cut with a knife. Finally Old Peter said, "I did what you asked Saturday. Pete wrote the story the way you wanted. Nobody knows what really happened to O'Connor and Ridley on Gay Street."

Kennedy's expression was grim. "I don't like it when a cop is killed. Add him, the soldier, and the similar killing in Jew's Alley on Wednesday night, and we have three more bodies than I want to contend with on the eve of Election Day. All with their throats cut. And all with damned lucifer matches jammed between their teeth."

"Which might mean they were done by the same man."

"Or men," Hays offered. "A conspiracy."

Old Peter and Kennedy nodded.

Kennedy said, "Those troops and all my men have one purpose and one purpose only: To make certain the election comes off without a hitch tomorrow, and to keep this town from blowing up or burning down or whatever our enemies try to do to it. That's my job; I don't have the manpower to do more."

"What do you require of me?" Old Peter asked.

"I'm depending on you and Hays to find this damned killer."

FORTY-TWO

CHENAULT, JAMES. LIEUTENANT.
TENTH KENTUCKY CAVALRY.
ARMY OF THE CONFEDERACY.
LUCIFER.

⌒November 9th, Wednesday morning.

IT WAS CLOSER to dawn than to midnight in Printing House Square, and fog covered the City like a mildewed blanket. Rain had come in spurts; first a drizzle, now a downpour. Still, the crowd milled, waiting resolutely for the election returns. Torchlight held individual groups together.

Returns shouted out through horns from newspaper windows could scarce be heard over the noise. When those closest to the source passed it on, the news rippled to the back, not always as it started out, but close enough. The reaction built as more and more were informed.

Military troops had been placed on steamers stationed at various places opposite the Battery and in the North and East Rivers. They were within call and could be marched to any point in the City within half an hour. General Butler and General Dix were determined that the election wasn't going to be the Draft Riots all over again.

When the vote favored the City's popular choice, General George McClellan and the Democrats, the throng roared its pleasure. On the few occasions when the returns supported Lincoln and the Republicans, the crowd hissed and booed.

Standing at an open window, looking down at the restless horde, *Tribune* publisher Horace Greeley turned to his companions. "What did I tell you? A nest of Copperheads. Have you heard this one? Why are there rattlesnakes in Richmond and Copperheads in New York?"

A smile hinted at Hays Tonneman's lips. "Because God gave Richmond first choice."

Greeley nodded, removed his spectacles, scratched the spare fuzz on the top of his seemingly tonsured head.

Stout and carelessly dressed, Horace Greeley was a tall man, though not as tall as Old Peter. Today he wore black pantaloons to the ankle and a white vest. His unbuttoned black frock coat swung freely as he moved and his black cravat, as usual, had slipped off the collar and worked its way to the side.

Greeley's wavy gray hair nestled against his collar. He wore his beard around his throat and under his chin. Nodding vigorously, he said, "Exactly. Lord save me from a misguided Northern Democrat. What these benighted Copperheads don't understand is that this War is not only about slavery and business." He set his glasses back on his longish nose. His eyes were blue, sunken but intense. "It's about the Union, damn it. It's what Hamilton was talking about. If the Federal Government isn't in charge, the government won't function."

"Changed your tune a bit, haven't you?" Old Peter said.

Greeley didn't answer at first. "What do you mean?"

Old Peter shook his head slowly. "Please. Remember me? I'm one of the people who had to convince you to support Lincoln this time around."

"Bah," Greeley said, vaguely. "Politics."

"And everyone knows you've been pursuing peace on your own." Old Peter enjoyed listening to Greeley spout no matter which side he stood on, but today he and Hays had more important business to tend to. Namely, the two men found dead after the Friday night raid on Gay Street. Although Old Peter had never met Lieutenant Carl Ridley, who worked as a military policeman for General

Butler, he had known Detective Tim O'Connor. Tim had worked for Hays and was an old friend. Old Peter was Tim Junior's godfather.

The publisher turned away and belched. "My apologies. It's true I've been working for a negotiated peace, but Copperheads make me bilious."

Old Peter was amazed at how the publisher could be on both sides at once. "You are one inconsistent cuss."

"Lincoln will lose the City," Hays Tonneman said.

"And win the election," Greeley said as another roar went up. He closed the window.

"You'd think this rain would get them off the streets."

"This mob? Look at that." Greeley pointed to a group of Federal troops standing in front of the *Daily News* building. "The City is overrun with soldiers."

"I don't blame Seward; he doesn't want trouble in New York."

Greeley's expression was bleak. "When Lincoln wins, that's exactly what we'll get."

AT THE *EVENING POST,* the presses were silent now, having rolled out the last edition some hours earlier. Only the clatter of the telegraph could be heard—and barely, for the noise inside and outside.

Pete Tonneman sat with Sheriff Jed Honeycutt while the city room filled with reporters and friends. Pete had been drawing pictures on his pad. He threw the pencil down; it rolled off the desk to the floor. "Give me a few minutes." He was bleary-eyed; his innards gnawed for a drink.

Jed pointed his jaw at the spittoon and let loose. "I'll give you the whole damn day."

Outside, the crowd roared.

Pete went to the window and listened and watched. He walked to the telegraph where a group of reporters hovered over the operator's chair, then came back to Jed, who sat calmly, paring his fingernails with a pocketknife. "Still raining," Pete said.

"Good for the crops."

Amused, Tonneman said, "The news is bad, and the news is good."

"Good and bad for who?" Jed swept his nail bits off the desk and pocketed his knife.

"Take your choice."

⌒THE GEORGE WASHINGTON ROOM in the LaFarge House was closed, as was every legal bar and saloon in the City.

Meg finished her chores in the guest rooms and left the hotel with two of the other chambermaids. When she passed the kitchen, Lotte Schmidt, the cook's helper, sneaked her a loaf of bread and a two-pound crock of butter. With a whispered "thank you," Meg put them in her voluminous canvas bag. She was teaching Lotte how to read English out of the newspapers.

"Ooh, Meg," Maddie called from the street. "You have a hand-some admirer here waiting for you."

Pete Tonneman, Meg thought, her heart pumping, though she couldn't fathom why. She had things to tell him about Kennedy and the others. But how could Pete know that? She hurried down the alley where she saw the other two maids fussing over a great bear of a man with a black patch over his left eye.

How disappointing. Not Pete at all.

"Here's our Meg," Maddie said, which set her and Christine to giggling.

"You're Meg Clancy?" the man asked. His voice was lovely, with the lilt of Ireland to it.

"I am, sir. Go on, girls."

The girls stayed, giggling behind their hands.

Meg stamped her foot. "Will you stop it? Go on home."

"I'm Patrick Duff. A friend told me—"

"Pete Tonneman sent you?"

"No. But I know him. Claudia said I should talk to you. May I walk you home, Miss Clancy?"

Offended, Meg said, "You knowing Claudia does not impress me, Mr. Duff. Before I take a step, what kind of girl do you think I am?"

Duff blushed. "Oh, no, please. Please. In the name of Mary, Mother of God, please forgive me."

She was tickled by his embarrassment.

"I need to talk to you," he said hesitantly. He offered his arm. "Will the omnibus do? I'm just a poor veteran . . . ."

"Could be that you'll be wanting a good Irish meal, Mr. Duff," she said, taking his arm. "Do you like corned beef?"

☞LIEUTENANT JAMES CHENAULT stood smoking amidst the crowd in Printing House Square. The rain had stopped for the while, still his clothing was damp and his boots were sodden. The local results didn't show it, but there was no doubt about it, Lincoln would win.

The Lucifer men had gathered earlier that evening at a lecture presented by the humorist Mr. Artemus Ward at Barnum's Lecture Hall, then separated. Chenault looked around for his companions, but the Square was so jammed with people it was a hopeless cause. Like the one they were fighting for, he mused.

Election Day had passed without disturbance. It was Chenault's conclusion that the mission was a failure. Federal and State buildings were under heavy guard, Price was dead, the gold was gone. Longmire had abandoned them and stolen most of the greenbacks. Why risk capture and hanging to burn a few buildings, when the fight was all but lost? He'd rather die a soldier's death on the battlefield.

So deep in thought was Chenault that at first he didn't comprehend the words being shouted. The reaction from the throng was double—triple what it had been before. People hugged each other. Jammed or not, they were dancing in the street.

"What is it?" he asked the man behind him, who was yelling gleefully. "What's happened?"

"What we've been waiting for." The man hugged him like a long-lost son. "It's burning! It's burning!"

"What?" The mob was so loud and demented Chenault couldn't hear his own shouted words. Had one of his own torched a building already? He broke away from the man holding him. "What's burning?"

The man grinned like a fool. "General William Tecumseh Sherman has set fire to Atlanta!"

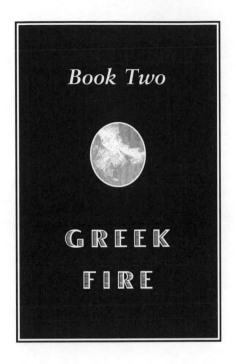

Book Two

GREEK FIRE

FORTY-THREE

⌒November 10th, Thursday evening.

BLACK AND STILL as the grave," Kennedy muttered as he slipped out of McMaster's print shop. He was seething. They'd had words, he and the publisher of the *Freeman's Journal.* "Should have slit his throat." And he would surely have done the man damage had Headley not interfered.

"Damn Headley. All high and mighty because he's second-in-command. I have the rank. I'm a Captain, by God. No justice in this world, precious little in the next. To Hell with you, Headley, to Hell with you, McMaster." Kennedy raised his flask to his lips. Shit, it was empty. He shoved the flask into his coat pocket.

The election had given Lincoln a clear mandate; Sherman had the North's blessing to burn and destroy the South. Not that the bastard needed it.

McMaster no longer spoke of his thousands who would rise up and take the City; the worm was desperate to abandon the mission. "Bastard," Kennedy said. The other cur, Longmire, had run off with most of the greenbacks. "If I ever get my hands on you, Longmire, you're a dead man."

And Price was dead, the gold he carried gone with him. McMaster was a coward. The turd was afraid to die by the hangman's noose. Why the hell had he gotten involved in the first place? Now that the monkey, Lincoln, had won, McMaster was "unwilling to continue."

"Damn all cowards." Through the fog in his brain Kennedy saw himself dangling from a rope. He shook the gruesome vision off. If they got caught and were lucky, he'd be killed by a firing squad. A soldier's death.

But one thing was certain, he wasn't going to die in New York City.

⌁"LOOK AFTER HIM," the Colonel had whispered in Toby's ear. "If there's one thing we don't need right now it's more attention from the police."

As Toby set out after Kennedy, the rest of the Lucifer band waited by the door. It was tacitly understood that the first thing they had to do was get away from McMaster. If he wasn't for them, he was against them.

Sherman's burning of Atlanta had brought them up sharp. It galled them that New York was celebrating.

Martin resolved, and the men agreed, that they had to damage and insult New York the way Sherman had damaged and insulted Georgia. This was their last chance for Lucifer to carry out the contract.

While McMaster was a disaster, Mrs. Jane McDonald was Heaven-sent. The Colonel and Toby would be leaving her boarding-house tonight. Mrs. McDonald had arranged for them to stay in the cottage near the Central Park with her sister-in-law, Mrs. Louisa Van Allen, yet another Southern sympathizer in New York.

"Headley," Martin whispered.

"Yes, Colonel."

They stood in darkness. Charles Street in front of McMaster's shop was quiet. Martin reached into his coat and brought out a packet of Yankee greenbacks, which he passed to Headley. "Tomorrow night I want you to get a wagon and go to Waverly Place, here in Greenwich Village to Henry Stout's Chemist Shop. The day Price was killed, he and Kennedy put in the order." Martin felt Headley stiffen. "Kennedy's a good man. Drunkard or not, if he said they arranged it with Stout, they did."

Headley loosened his belt and slipped the bills under it at the small of his back. "If you say so, Colonel. I'll need a second man."

"How does Toby suit you?"

"Fine."

"I sent him after Kennedy. If he doesn't get back too late, take him. If not him, Chenault. Give the ten thousand to Stout. The password is 'Greek Fire.' He'll give you eighty bottles packed in straw. Be careful with that stuff. If just one bottle breaks you'll go up in flames."

"I'll have him wrap them in wet paper."

"Take them to Mrs. Van Allen's cottage on Fifty-eighth Street and Sixth Avenue."

"What's the plan, Colonel? When do we do this?"

"I'm sharing this with you alone. Kennedy worries me and we can't keep it only from him. I'll tell them all closer to the time. We will burn New York the day after Lincoln's Thanksgiving."

FORTY-FOUR

⌒November 10th, Thursday evening.

THEY WERE BEING FOLLOWED. Or rather he was. Toby didn't relish the idea of lying in wait for whoever was following him and slitting his throat. He also didn't relish the stranger slitting his throat.

Were he on his own it would be simple. He was fast. Escape would be easy. But the Colonel had made him responsible for Kennedy. And though he didn't care much for the man, Toby took the Colonel's order seriously. If they were being followed, he couldn't leave Kennedy in harm's way.

So Toby did what he was good at; he ran. Sure enough, he heard running behind him. Grinning at being right and enjoying the run, Toby circled one block, then looped to another, and finally cut over to a third. Except for a couple of stray cats and the man following, he had the night streets to himself. With each circuit the footfall of his pursuer faltered and grew fainter. When all he could discern behind him was silence, Toby doubled back on his own trail, looking for Kennedy.

He caught sight of his drunken comrade again in the shadows; Kennedy was drifting toward Hudson Street. Good, the fool was safe. Toby was glad not to have to disappoint the Colonel.

That didn't mean he had to hold Kennedy's hand. Or talk to him. Pleased with his logic, Toby slowed his steps and hung back.

On each corner Kennedy would scamper about, dancing to music only he could hear. As long as he didn't start singing, Toby intended to let the man be and continue following him at a distance.

Toby took a quick look back. Turning front again, he saw only an empty street. Where the devil was Kennedy? Tarnation. Toby was running again.

Suddenly his legs went out from under him. He was on his back. Pain. His hair was being pulled back so hard it felt as if his neck would crack.

In the night shades he could see the glint of the blade.

"I'm going to kill you, McMaster," the monster pinning him to the ground shrieked. The blade descended. That damned bowie knife.

"Kennedy! Stop! It's me, Toby."

A club came down before the knife did, whacking Kennedy across the head. Kennedy fell back, the knife still in his hand. Toby rolled away. He saw Kennedy rise, knife poised, on the attack after the man with the club. The man, his spectacles glinting in the street-light, backed off slowly, club ready. "Boys! Help!" He broke, shouting. Then he ran, his herringbone mackinaw flapping.

Kennedy chased after the man, screaming, "Damn you to hell, McMaster, I'll have your guts for breakfast!"

TOBY WALKED IN a daze. Kennedy was insane. First, mistaking him for McMaster and looking to carve him up with that Arkansas Toothpick he carried, and then mistaking the stranger in the her-ringbone mackinaw for McMaster.

Toby reconsidered. The man in the mackinaw was no stranger. He had seen him before. Outside Mrs. McDonald's boardinghouse.

THE STREET LAMP shed only a dim circle of light. Toby heard them first; then he saw the men gathered in an empty lot, voices rumbling.

"Stop!" A woman's voice. They ignored her.

A shot rang out.

Everybody, including Toby, dropped to the ground.

One of the mob yelled out, "Are you mad, woman?"

Then Toby saw her, a tiny figure standing on the stoop of a red-brick building adjacent to the lot, her gun smoking.

"Get out of here," the woman said, sounding as tough as any man.

One of the gang, apparently the leader, started for her. "You can't shoot us all." His companions were right behind him.

She leveled her weapon at the leader. "No. But I can shoot you."

They were boys—young men. After a moment, the leader laughed. "Come on. Let's go. I need a drink." They raced off, hurling insults and stones at the brick building.

Toby and the woman both hurried to the lot.

The woman whirled and shoved the pistol in his face.

"Wait," Toby cried. "I'm not one of them. I think that's my friend."

A silhouette moved. Toby followed the woman. Closer inspection proved his suspicions. It was Kennedy on the ground, stripped down to his underwear, his head bloodied.

"He's alive," the woman said. She turned to Toby. "He's a big one; can you carry him?"

"Yes, ma'am. Lead the way." Draping Kennedy's arm over his shoulder, Toby more dragged than carried Kennedy, but it couldn't be helped.

On the step the woman set down her gun, brought matches out of her pocket, and lit the gas lamps that flanked the door. She then ran her fingers over Kennedy's scalp, and lifted his eyelids. "I don't believe he's suffered a concussion." She felt for the pulse at his throat. "Not too bad. Let's get inside. Phew, he smells like a still."

"Are you all right, Miss Lee?" The question was asked by an angular woman in a white cap who poked her head out the door.

"Yes, Elsie. Help this young man with our patient." Elsie and Toby each took an arm. The building proved to be a small clinic. They placed Kennedy on an examination table in a neat study.

"Is there a doctor here?" Toby asked.

"There is," Miss Lee replied. "And a nurse." As she removed her hat, Toby noted that Miss Lee was wearing a dark green dress and a matching fitted jacket. The dress was elegant, but not like any he had ever seen on a lady. The skirt hung close as if she wasn't wearing any petticoats at all.

Toby shrugged. What did he know about what ladies wore? This woman was obviously a lady. She also proved to be much older than Toby had first thought. Her small face with its sharp dark eyes was surrounded by pure white hair.

Elsie began cleaning away the blood from Kennedy's face and body. The injured man groaned, cursed.

"Excuse him, ma'am."

"I've heard worse. He's your friend?"

"Yes, ma'am. We got separated. His name is Robert Kennedy. I'm Toby Garner. We were visiting friends in the area. He was in a foul temper and he left before me."

"Well, your friend was lucky those toughs set upon him outside the front door of the Northern Dispensary."

"Yes, ma'am. Will the doctor be long?"

"The doctor is here, sir," Miss Lee said. She examined Kennedy's head. "Shave his head, Elsie."

"Excuse me, ma'am. I don't understand."

"I am the doctor, Mr. Garner."

FORTY-FIVE

⌐November 10th, Thursday night.

A WOMAN DOCTOR. TOBY had heard about them but never in his life did he think he'd meet one. He stood back and watched her work on Kennedy, whose head was a mess of bloody gashes.

After shaving around the patient's lacerations, Elsie cleansed the wounds again using a strong-smelling liquid.

Kennedy groaned.

"What's that you're using?" Toby asked.

"Alcohol with sassafras root bark," Elsie replied. "Fenugreek seed and gum myrrh."

Miss Lee laughed. "Would you like the recipe?" She was threading a needle.

Toby put his eyes on the opposite wall and a picture of Mr. Lincoln. He'd never noticed before how much the man resembled Jeff Davis. "No, ma'am. Doctoring is not my choice of vocation."

Suddenly Kennedy roared, "Burn it!" He flailed out, knocking the small doctor against Elsie. He sat up, eyes crazed.

Toby ran to Kennedy. The last thing he wanted was for one of these women to get hurt.

"McMaster!" Kennedy screamed. "You're a dead man."

"Excuse him, ma'am, please," Toby said. "He doesn't know what he's doing." Pinning Kennedy's shoulders to the table, he said softly, "Bob, old fellow, you've been hurt and these nice ladies are fixing you up good as new."

For an instant, Kennedy's eyes cleared. "Burn . . . New York," he whispered, then his eyes rolled up into white and his body relaxed.

"Good," Miss Lee said. "He's passed out." The thread in her needle, she told Toby, "Hold him down, Mr. Garner. Let's get this done."

"Thank you, ma'am." He looked again at Mr. Lincoln when she began sewing.

"You're not from around here, then?"

"No, ma'am, we're from Kentucky. Here on business."

The doctor was intent on Kennedy's head wound. "McMaster . . . Would that be the publisher of the *Freeman's Journal*?"

Toby considered lying but decided it was better to stick with the truth where he could. "It would be, ma'am. Bob's cousin." All at once he felt hot and was aware of the sweat dripping down his face. His arms hurt from holding Kennedy down. "Could you hurry, please, ma'am?"

She straightened and gave the boy a searching look. He was lying. She cut the thread. "I'm finished. Six good ones."

Toby let go of Kennedy and expelled the breath he didn't know he was holding. "Ma'am?"

"Six stitches on his crown. Elsie, plaster." Miss Lee washed her hands over a sink against the wall, dried them, and turned back to Toby. "Shall I have a look at you, Mr. Garner? You've turned quite green."

FORTY-SIX

D

⌒*November 11th, Friday, late afternoon to night.*

D R. LEAH TONNEMAN was bent over the tearful child's leg as Elsie held the limb steady. The physician applied the first coat of plaster over the cloth. The three-year-old girl had been run down by a cart that morning, suffering a fracture of her right fibula. Sad to say, this was not a rare occurrence on the busy City streets.

Fortunately it was a simple fracture; people, especially children, died all too often from compound fractures. Bones piercing skin led to infection as readily as knife wounds.

Dr. Tonneman had read about Dr. Joseph Lister's use of carbolic spray as an antiseptic agent, and used it in her surgery.

Wiping her hands on a clean cloth she said, "I'll hold, you finish the plaster, Elsie." To Mrs. Perkins she said, "With God's will, Sandra's leg will be as good as new."

"Thank you, Miss Lee, thank you. I tell Sandra all the time not to run into the street. I don't know what to do with her, she's such a tomboy, always chasing her ball. Lately there is so much traffic. Will she be a cripple?"

"If you follow my instructions and there's no infection, I don't see why she should." While Dr. Tonneman held the little girl's leg with both hands, Elsie wrapped more strips of linen. "As you say,

Sandra's a little tomboy, very active. We want to give the bone a proper chance to heal. When Elsie is done I want you to wait a good half hour until the plaster has set before you take her home." Dr. Tonneman let go of Sandra's leg with her right hand and fished a chunk of rock candy from her pocket. "Here you are, Sandra, for being such a good girl."

Sandra's grubby hand reached out for the candy. Old tears dried in smears on her round cheeks.

"What do you say?"

The girl popped the sweet into her mouth. "Can I have another?"

"Sandra!"

"Thank you, ma'am."

Dr. Tonneman smiled and gave the child another piece of rock candy.

The next patients were the usual: a man with an abscessed cyst on his ear; a drunk who claimed to have the grippe; and a pregnant woman who had begun to stain.

It was night when at last the surgery emptied. Leah breathed a great sigh. "Go home, Elsie. Tomorrow's another day."

Elsie had been with Lee for the last ten years, assisting and nursing. Her husband had died of yellow fever; there had been no children and she'd never remarried.

"I'll say good night, Miss Lee."

"Good night." Lee's crinoline stood like a statue in a corner of her study. She wouldn't, couldn't work in it. Her mentor, Elizabeth Blackwell, wore Quaker dress but Lee favored current fashion. Besides, the crinoline had its uses; it prevented her skirts from dragging on the muddy streets.

She pulled the crinoline on, fastened it, and straightened her black silk dress over it. She brewed herself a pot of tea and sat at her desk, opening her account books. The years had sped past and here she was with white hair and she didn't know when it had happened.

She had never married. Even so, she was as good as a grandmother to the Tonnemans and related broods through her sister Gretel's two girls, Racqel and Mariana.

The memory of Gretel brought tears to her eyes. The beautiful girl had faded into an old woman after Racqel's birth in 1815. Gretel's heart had failed; she'd become an invalid, dying at fifty-two. Her husband, Isaac De Groat, had been devastated. Unable to deal with his grief, he died a year later.

Lee, still living in the Tonneman family home on Christopher Street in Greenwich Village, had become both mother and father to Gretel's daughters.

In spite of her sudden motherhood Lee had achieved her dream in 1853. At the age of fifty-five, she'd become a doctor, as her father had been. She'd studied medicine at Geneva Medical College in Geneva, New York, from which Dr. Blackwell graduated in 1848. Like Blackwell, Leah graduated with highest honors.

To Leah's great joy, Mariana followed her aunt to medical school and became a physician. Racqel had married Steven Lehman and was now a grandmother herself.

The fire sparked; she let it go out. It was time she went home. Yet she didn't move. The tea had cooled; she pushed it aside.

Her brother's wife Charity lay dying. With all her skills, Lee could not prevent that. The human body wore out. The cancer had spread, eating away at Charity's bones; there was little she could do but give her sister-in-law opium. Medicine was making great advances, finding cures, but few for cancers and fewer still for female cancers. She would stop by and see Charity in the morning.

The sound of a door opening startled her. The door shut. Something dropped with a thump. Footsteps. Her heart beat faster.

The door to her study opened and the shadow of a man filled the doorway.

"Lee." He removed his wide-brimmed hat.

She stood.

The man was of medium height and build; he had a majestic head, thick dark hair to his shoulders—streaked now with white—a square clean-shaven jaw, deep-set hazel eyes. He wore a black coat with a brocade waistcoat and flowing tie. As always, his essence was exotic, of turpentine and oil.

Philip Boenning Tonneman was Charity Tonneman's son by her first husband, Philip Boenning, who'd been an artist of some renown. He'd died before young Philip was born. Thus, Philip was not a Tonneman by blood.

Old Peter was the only father Philip had known. Philip had been ten-year-old Leah's first nephew. They stood now looking at each other, virtually frozen by their history.

"Your mother . . ." Lee said, her heart racing.

"I've been. She didn't know me." His voice cracked. "Lee. I've wanted to come home. I belong with my loved ones while we still have time." He made a beseeching gesture with his hand.

With a soft sigh, Lee moved toward him. "I know." The crinoline swayed under her skirt. "Philip."

"I told Papa I would stay with you." He smiled. "You haven't taken a lover, have you?"

"You know I have only loved one man in all my life." She was standing close to him now, head tilted.

"Do I? Who would that be?" He took her in his arms.

⌒IN FRONT OF Stout's Chemist Shop on Waverly Place, which was an interruption of Sixth Avenue at Third Street, a wagon waited on the quiet street. The only sound came from the restless gelding pawing the cobblestones.

The door to the shop opened; Toby stepped out. He heard the murmur of voices. Turning, he looked at the chemist shop's plate glass window, keeping track of the pedestrians by their reflection.

He had seen plate glass before, but nowhere in his young experience was it used to such extent as in this City. Shops employed it to display everything from pretty frocks to fake legs for the war wounded.

Large, lantern-shaped Venetian bottles were arranged in Stout's window, blues and greens and reds, the colors of Fourth of July sparks, caught in a bottle. Fourth of July made him think of his mother. He was so far from home, on a difficult path.

Had he chosen correctly? The only reflection in the window now was his. He gave himself a wink, opened the shop door, and whispered, "Clear."

Henry Stout, a wispy-haired beanpole, assumed watch while Headley and Toby carried eight wicker baskets out to the cart. Each basket, stuffed thoroughly with excelsior, contained ten damp-paper-wrapped bottles of deadly Greek fire.

The last basket was loaded. Going into the shop, Stout said, "Something else . . ."

"Mr. Garner." A woman stepped into view. Her companion carried a lantern.

"Ma'am?"

"Who the devil is that?" Headley turned his face from the light.

"The lady doctor that stitched Kennedy up last night."

"Get rid of her." Headley climbed to the driver's seat.

Henry Stout appeared, lugging three boxes. "Longmire left these . . . ."

"It is Mr. Garner, isn't it?" The woman turned to her companion. "Philip, these two gentlemen were at the Dispensary last night." She raised her voice slightly. "How are you feeling tonight, Mr. Kennedy?"

"He's not Kennedy, ma'am."

Stout hurriedly placed the boxes in the wagon and ran back into his shop, closing his door and bolting it.

Toby got onto the seat next to Headley. "You'll excuse me, ma'am. Have a nice evening."

Headley flicked the reins; the wagon moved off, its taillight swaying in the darkness.

"Be sure to remind Mr. Kennedy," Lee Tonneman called. "He must come in next week to have his stitches removed."

FORTY-SEVEN

⌒November 11th, Friday night.

THE SIGN IN Walker's window said: "Beer—3¢. No stamps."

Pete and Jed made their way through the usual crowd of workmen gathered at the bar for their constitutional libation after a long day of work. Smith was waiting for them, eating a hard-boiled egg at a table near the bar.

"Go on, then," Tonneman said to Jed. "I'll get the beer."

"Three beers," he said to Benny Walker. Several heads nodded at him; Pete Tonneman was no stranger to Walker's.

"Nine cents," Benny said.

Tonneman dropped a dime on the bar and brought the beers to the table. Smith and Jed nodded their thanks and each had a long pull.

Pete downed his quickly as if he were in a race. "I'll get another round," he said, jumping up.

Jed moved his chaw from one side of his mouth to the other. "The boy likes his drink."

"Just beer."

"It'll be whiskey soon enough," Jed said. "Mark my words."

Jed's words were prophetic sooner than he thought. Only two of the drinks Pete returned with were beer. The third was a healthy ration of Kentucky sour mash.

"Lieutenant Smith, I want to tell you how much I appreciate your talking to me."

"You want me to sit somewhere else?" Jed asked.

"No need," Smith said. "I'm off the case."

Pete stopped the motion of his glass to his mouth. "But this morning when you agreed to this, you—"

"A great deal can happen 'twixt morning and night," Smith said. "Especially in the military. I have to tell you that like everyone else, Butler believes the fire plot is bunkum. Sorry to have wasted your time. Thank you for the beer." He drained his mug and stood.

"Wait a minute," Pete said. "If you can't give me a story on what's going to happen, maybe you can fill me in on the past." Pete was lying through his teeth. He didn't want to lose Smith. He could smell a story in Smith's being taken off the case. "Have a real drink before you go."

Smith grinned and scratched the back of his neck. "After dealing with General Butler all day I could use a tonic." He sat. "Don't mind if I do. But what I just said about the General is not for publication."

"I won't print a word without your say-so." Pete caught Jed's jaundiced expression and looked away.

Five drinks and half a bowl of hard-boiled eggs later, there was nothing Smith wouldn't tell his old pal, Pete Tonneman. "You see, this plot idea is not something that's going to make the General's reputation. Gold, on the other hand, might. He wants me and Sergeant Lonnigan to investigate this Wall Street gold fraud."

"Gold," Jed said, his eyes gleaming.

"Why, you old fake." Pete laughed. "And here I thought you were a simple man of the soil. You are just as greedy as the rest of us down here in Gotham."

"Being country doesn't make you stupid." Jed let loose at a nearby spittoon. "What about the gold?"

"The Beast is on the track of a Confederate scheme to reduce the value of Federal currency." Smith cracked another egg. "He feels that greedy or disloyal factions, or both, might try to force the price of gold up."

"Are you going to buy gold?" Pete asked Jed.

"No. Too risky," Jed replied. "You never know when one of those rascals is going to double-cross you and sell. The smart thing would be to corner produce. Gold going up would influence the price of food and other essentials. When gold goes up, food goes up. Then wouldn't you see some riots."

They went on like this, drinking through the night. Finally Smith lurched to his feet. "Time for me to get to bed. Up with the bugle when you soldier for General Butler."

Pete attempted to focus on Smith; he no longer remembered why he wanted the man to drink with him.

Jed spat tobacco juice but it dribbled on his shirt.

"Filthy habit, chewing. Have a cigar." Pete looked around. Smith was still standing there. "Here, you have one, too." He searched in his pocket for a match. "Do you have a lucifer?"

"What do you know about Lucifer?" Smith looked stunned.

"What?"

"That's top secret," he mumbled.

"What?" The fog began to clear from Pete's mind.

Smith placed both hands on the table, scattering eggshells. He leaned to them. "Lucifer," he whispered, "is staffed by members of the Kentucky Tenth Cavalry, among them previous officers of Morgan's Raiders. Their mission is to burn down New York City."

"Ain't that interesting?" Jed said.

"You know something else?" Smith asked, still whispering. "We have a man inside Lucifer. Minstrel, we call him. But you never heard it from me. Good night." He gaped at them, then staggered out of Walker's Tavern, dreading the morning and General Butler.

FORTY-EIGHT

⌒November 12th, Saturday morning.

A GOODLY NUMBER of the clan Tonneman swelled the house on Grand Street that morning. Leah and Philip had no sooner arrived when Hays appeared. Philip and his half brother greeted each other with gruff emotion that astonished their nephew Pete just making his way downstairs.

On her way with her doctor's bag, Lee, noting how heavily Pete leaned on the banister rail, clicked her tongue against her teeth.

"Don't say it, please, Auntie Lee. Last night was different, believe me." A hammer beat behind his temples.

"How so?"

His smile was sheepish. "Whiskey greases reluctant tongues."

"I'm sure," she replied tartly, continuing toward Charity's sickroom.

"You're a hard woman, Auntie Lee." Pete went down the stairs. What he needed was strong black coffee. He peeked into the dining room. His uncles sat at the dining room table, filling the room with their presence. Nellie had put out coffee and cakes.

Philip looked up. "Don't tell me—Pete, you're the image of your Papa." Turning to Hays, "Looks just like Johnny."

"Can't stay away from the booze, either," Hays said.

"Family curse, uncles."

They were interrupted by Old Peter's heavy footsteps on the stairs. He entered the room, Lee behind him.

Both Philip and Hays stood. Old Peter appeared drained, exhausted. "Papa," Philip said.

Lee placed her hand on Philip's arm. "Go up. She drifts in and out."

"Is she . . . ?" Philip did not finish the thought.

"She was lucid just now and may know you."

Philip headed for the stairs.

Lee poured coffee for herself and Old Peter.

"Sit, Papa," Hays said, helping the old man to an armchair.

"Lee's had an odd experience, Hays." Old Peter calmed his mind in order to concentrate on Lee's story. "Lee."

She sat at the table. Pete, curious, poured himself coffee and leaned against the doorjamb.

"Thursday evening I treated a man who was set upon by a gang in the lot next to the Dispensary. I stitched up a bad gash in his head. His young friend, Toby Garner, called him Kennedy."

"Aha!" Pete wanted to dance a jig but he controlled himself.

They all turned to him.

"No. Go on. Sorry to butt in." The coffee had sloshed over his cup into the saucer; he set it on the table.

"The two had Southern accents. Kennedy was half conscious, ranting about McMaster and cowards. When I asked, Garner confirmed that he was talking about James McMaster of the *Freeman's Journal,* claiming McMaster was Kennedy's cousin."

"Hays," Old Peter said sharply.

"McMaster is on our list of avowed Southern sympathizers."

Lee went on. "Last night, as Philip and I were on our way to Christopher Street, Mr. Garner and another man—not Kennedy—were loading a wagon with what appeared to be wicker baskets, from Stout's Chemist Shop on Waverly Place."

This time it was Old Peter who said, "Aha!"

FORTY-NINE

⌐November 12th, Saturday, late morning.

PETE TRAILED ALONG after the two detectives, his uncle and his grandfather. He would have a story out of this. But on second thought, perhaps his Auntie Lee should be the reporter. She'd stumbled upon the plotters. And she hadn't even been trying.

"Burn it," Lee had heard Kennedy say. "Burn New York." The story was unfolding before him like a Walter Scott novel.

Their first stop was McMaster's print shop on Charles Street. The smell of the nearby Hudson was strong here. Pete felt the tug, as he always did near the water. That was the life, sailing the seas. Pieter Tonneman, the first Sheriff of New York and the first of that name, had been a sailor.

"Trouble," Hays said, a protective arm in front of his father.

The door to the shop was standing open. A bad sign. No smoke came out of the chimney.

In his mind Pete already could see James McMaster. On the floor, his throat cut, a lucifer sticking out from between his teeth.

But that didn't prove to be the case this time. The shop, smelling of sweat, cigars, and ink, was empty. And the disarray indicated it had been left in great haste.

"Time to talk with the neighbors," Old Peter said.

McMaster's print shop was bounded on one side by Banghart's

Emblematic Signs and Banners and on the other by Whitney's Painter Supply Store.

A. E. Banghart proved to be a garrulous little man. "Of course, my neighbor's business is of no consequence to me, but McMaster was anti-Union with his journal. Our brave lads are off fighting to uphold the Union—"

"Mr. Banghart," Old Peter said. "Have you seen anything of an unusual nature going on at McMaster's shop?"

"Unusual nature? Let me think." He looked over at the row of seamstresses working on a red-and-blue banner.

"Groups of people coming and going," Hays said.

"Maybe last night?" Pete interjected.

"Unusual?" Banghart pressed his fingers to his forehead, wrinkled his brow, pondering mightily. He shook his head. "No. Can't say that I have."

"Get word to me if you do," Hays said. "At Police Headquarters."

They were already on the street when the little man chased after them. "Chief, wait. McMaster loaded up his carriage at five this morning and drove off. Is that unusual?"

"MR. WHITNEY IS pricing a paint job uptown," Mrs. Whitney said. "He took Caleb with him."

"Caleb?"

"Our Negro hired man. He's very reliable. Sleeps in the back. Mr. Whitney gave him a room to fix up for himself."

"Thank you, ma'am," Hays said politely. This was the plodding way of detective work; he was used to it.

"We'll be back later," Old Peter said.

"Caleb said he heard shouting last night from the print shop, if that's any help to you."

STOUT BELIED HIS name. He was thin as a rail. And he kept his squirming hands under his apron and his eyes fixed on his counter.

"Are you here about the break-in?"

"What break-in?" Hays said with agonizing patience. The air in the shop was scented with sweet herbs and chemicals.

"Closed up at six last night. When I came in this morning, I saw that the glass in my new door was broken. Someone went off with eight of my baskets."

"What was in them?"

"Nothing. But they were nice baskets. I sell them. Good for arranging flowers, drying herbs. I had the big window and the door put in because I saw that Stewart's had glass like that and thought it would help business. If people could see in. Thank the Lord they left the big window alone. I'm trying to sell more varied items."

"Like baskets," Hays said.

"Like baskets."

Old Peter glanced at the door. "Do you notice anything odd about the broken glass, Chief Tonneman?"

"Nothing much. Unless you mean that it's obvious by the broken glass outside that it was broken from the inside."

"That's what I mean."

"How do you suppose that happened, Mr. Stout?"

Pete loved watching Old Peter and Hays when they were working like this. It was like going to the theatre.

Without even bothering to let Stout come up with a lie about the glass in the door, Hays pressed on. "Let me get this clear, Mr. Stout. A thief broke the glass in your door. From the inside. He then opened the door, stepped inside. And all he stole was some baskets."

"That's the size of it," Stout replied, setting his pointy jaw.

"Do you consider yourself a stupid man, Mr. Stout?"

"No need to be insulting."

"My son means if you were smart you might have told us something more valuable was stolen."

"For instance," Hays said, "morphine. You do stock morphine, don't you, Mr. Stout?"

"Yes."

"Had you told us someone stole morphine, that would be more believable."

Stout knocked his scales and a stone mortar to the floor in his rush to a drawer behind the counter. The mortar cracked in two but he paid it no mind. "You're absolutely right. They did steal the morphine."

"Before I only thought you were stupid, Mr. Stout," Old Peter said. "Now I'm positive."

"Why don't you tell us what you know," Hays said, "before we bring the Army in and they hang you for treason by your scrawny neck."

"I don't know what you're talking about. You are both of you lunatics," Stout sputtered, shifting his eyes to Pete, seeking an ally.

"Don't look at me," Pete said, "I'm kin to these lunatics."

FIFTY

November 12th, Saturday, midday.

WAVERLY PLACE was warm with autumn sunshine. A last spell of mild dry weather before winter. Children played with hoops and balls in the street and an old woman sat in the sun shelling peas.

Pete Tonneman was warm with Kentucky mash. From his vantage point on the east side of Sixth Avenue, and through an Indian summer bourbon haze, fuzzy around the edges, he tried to keep his eye on Officer Frank Dorsey across the street. Dorsey, in his shiny black coat, looked like and was dumb as a rock.

Still, Uncle Hays had too few men for this assignment, so he had to use what was available. Since Pete knew what Stout looked like, he'd been drafted to work with Dorsey.

Dorsey trotted across the road. "Mr. Tonneman, I need to piss real bad."

"Go ahead, Frank. I'll keep my eyes peeled. There's an empty lot on Third Street."

"I know it well. Many's the weed I've watered there."

"Go. I'll watch Stout's shop."

While Dorsey ran to do his business, Pete looked about. Nothing unusual. Across the street a wagon with two racks of glass sitting high in its bed stopped in front of the chemist shop. Two men came down from the wagon and immediately set to work replacing the broken glass in the door. On Pete's side of the street a scowling woman in gray passed him carrying a market basket.

He watched her on her way uptown, then took the pint bottle from his coat. He uncorked the bottle, leaned his head back, closed his eyes, and took a long swallow. He felt that wonderful sense of well-being as the drink made its way down his gullet.

Dorsey returned. He could smell the whiskey on Tonneman and thought to ask for a taste; another copper would have shared without being asked. "Anything?"

"Just those two fixing the door."

Dorsey squinted at the two men, crossed the street, and talked to them as they worked. Then he came back to Tonneman.

"What did they say?" Tonneman asked. The sun was too hot; he was in serious need of a lie-down.

"They haven't seen him. He sent word and money to fix the door and that's what they're doing."

"Good," Pete said. "Stands to reason if he's spending money on repairs he means to stay for a while."

Soon enough, the glaziers collected their tools and left.

Tonneman shifted his position. Dorsey said, "Maybe I'll take a stroll past and see what's doing." The policeman's face had turned pink from the sun. He wiped the sweat from his brow with his sleeve.

Just then a boy carrying an envelope stopped in front of the chemist shop. He looked at the address, then marched up to the door and rang the bell. Impatient, he immediately pounded on the door.

Dorsey laughed. "Stout don't watch it he's going to need those glaziers again."

The boy left his envelope leaning on the chemist's door.

Finally Pete pulled himself out of his haze. "Come on, let's see what that kid has to say."

They caught up with the boy, who couldn't have been more than ten years old. He opened his eyes wide at Dorsey's approach.

"I didn't do nothing," he whined.

"Take it easy, lad," Pete said. "We only want to know about Mr. Stout."

"What?"

"You left an envelope for him."

"That's what I was told to do. The fellow gave me two bits."

"What fellow?"

"Skinny. Hair like spider web."

"Where was this?" Murphy asked.

"Around the corner. He was in a hack."

"Shit." Tonneman was already running back to the chemist shop. He picked up the envelope which was addressed simply: "Cops." He tore it open. "I'm innocent of all wrongdoing," it said. "But I do not relish being beaten by the New York coppers. Respectfully, Henry Stout."

PETE TONNEMAN ROAMED along the City's edge at South Street, stopping at the docks to watch bales being loaded onto an English ship. Probably illegal cotton, smuggled in from Dixie.

Time was when he had a thought like that, he would have torn open a bale, uncovered the truth, and written the story. But that was then. Now it had come to this: Pete Tonneman was dumber than a dumb cop.

The whiskey was still in his blood, almost but not quite deadening his sense of failure. So why did he want to cry like a baby?

Pete pulled the half-empty bottle from his coat. It was warm from the heat of his body. He uncorked the bottle; his nose trembled. He breathed in the whiskey fragrance as if he were sniffing a desirable woman.

Now he brushed his lips against the glass for one last kiss and sent the bottle, drizzling bourbon, sailing over the water.

FIFTY-ONE

⁀November 12th, Saturday afternoon.

CHARMING AND VINE-COVERED, the cottage was filled with richly ornamented furniture. It was set in a rural part of the City near the Central Park. Mrs. Van Allen, Mrs. McDonald's sister-in-law, a dressmaker, had access to the finest homes in the City.

Mrs. Van Allen employed two Irish girls, Bridget and Nora. They had replaced Dolly, the Negress, who had been set upon and beaten to death during the Draft Riots the previous year. Mrs. Van Allen missed Dolly, but things always seemed to happen for the best. The two Irish girls were clever with their needles, though they each did cost more than Dolly had, more was the pity.

The Irish girls worked separate from the cottage in a small one-room cabin, with a cookstove and a fireplace. The work cabin was behind the herb garden and a grove of chestnut trees; thus her guests in the cottage need never be seen by someone who could tell about them.

Her hired girl, Eva, who lived in a small attic room, was both deaf and dumb. She had come with the cottage and was a fair cook and housekeeper. Mrs. Van Allen had never felt the need to replace her. Best of all, she didn't chatter.

These fine boys with their lovely manners were no hardship.

Opening her home to them for a short duration was certainly not
too much to give to the War for the Southern Confederacy.

With Election Day come and gone and that awful man President
again, there was no more in the newspapers about a plot to burn
the City. Of course that story had been a Republican lie. Her guests
were just not that sort. They were Southern gentlemen, here to ar-
range for food for the starving South. The mothers and their little
babies.

They had arrived last evening, five of them. Then another two.
One had been set upon by thieves. He'd had his head sewn up, but
he seemed ill and his eyes burned feverish bright. She'd heard move-
ment and had peered out her second-floor window when two had
gone out again, much later. She'd not noted their return.

But she'd fed seven young men bacon, grits, and biscuits that
morning, so they were all here now.

⌒MARTIN'S FACE WAS gray with fatigue. He looked ill, worse than
Kennedy, and Kennedy's head was broken. Martin's cough had returned and he was spitting blood. "How is Kennedy?"

"Toby's seeing to him." Headley was troubled. He sensed that
Martin had lost his stomach for the mission. Even for the War. They
had to work quickly or everything would fall apart.

The City of New York had wrapped her arms about them and
was holding on for dear life, draining them of their will. He would
be happy to be long gone.

"I should never have brought him into Lucifer," Martin said.

"How could you have known?"

"Some men can change; I should have known Kennedy wouldn't.
Not after he and Price went out on those renegade raids, robbing
banks and farms, against Morgan's orders." Deep lines etched Martin's face.

"That's in the past. In the present it's the lady doctor I'm worried
about. She saw Toby and me at the chemist shop."

"I don't think that need worry us," Martin said. "Toby told me
you'd finished loading the baskets into the wagon by the time she
came along. An innocent activity. I wouldn't waste any more
thought on it."

"Yes, sir. I believe we've overstayed our welcome in New York. We should do what we came to do and get the hell out of here."

"What targets?"

"Well, with all the Blue-bellies around in the City, and the way they're guarding the Government buildings, we wouldn't get close enough to light a cigar. But if we can't strike at the Government directly, we can strike at the City. Each of us armed with ten bottles can register at various hotels, using aliases. If we do our jobs right and time it properly, we can burn much of this City to the ground."

The Colonel coughed into his handkerchief. Although Martin tried to hide it, Headley saw the pink-stained linen.

"Call a meeting, Headley."

"Yes, sir."

Ten minutes later they were assembled in Martin's room: Headley, Ashbrook, Chenault, Harrington, Toby, and a subdued Kennedy, his head wound covered with a fresh bandage.

Before they could begin there was a light tap at the door. Martin opened it. Mrs. Van Allen stood before them. "Mr. Martin. My sister-in-law has just sent an urgent message." She handed the Colonel an envelope and left.

Martin opened the envelope. After scanning the first few sentences he read aloud. " 'Sir, Mr. Stout was visited by the police this morning. He closed his shop and came to me. He has not given your presence away, but he feels he might succumb to brutal treatment, so by the time you read this he will have left the City.' "

"The fool," Kennedy said. "The coward."

"More the fool," Headley said, "if he was followed to Mrs. Mc-Donald's boardinghouse."

Martin paused. The moment had come to tell them the plan. It was simple. Headley would assign the hotels. Each man would go to his designated target and familiarize himself with it. When the time was right, they would strike.

"When do you think?" Ashbrook asked.

"I'm not certain. What with Stout's defection, I believe we must be more circumspect. No member of Lucifer shall go out of this house alone. Two or more together at all times."

"That's insulting, sir," Chenault said. His cheeks then went red at his lapse of military courtesy.

"Chenault."

"It's all right, Headley," Martin said. "Boys, what if one of you were captured?"

"We'd never talk," Harrington said.

"I am sure you believe that. But I can't risk this mission on how even I would behave if a Yankee soldier put a red-hot blade to my eyes."

"They wouldn't." Toby was shocked.

"Yes, they would," Kennedy said. "And laugh while they did it."

FIFTY-TWO

November 13th, Sunday afternoon.

A BLACK DRIVER in fancy livery was handing Abe Rappaport a greenback in exchange for a box of Daniel Webster cigars, when the bell above the old man's door rang, signaling a new customer.

The elderly man's visitor waited until the coachman left. Even then he didn't speak. In the doorway he watched the driver tap on the door of the waiting brougham and hand the box to his passenger, then climb up to his seat and drive off. Only then did the new customer close the door.

Abe spoke first. "Again? You want this time a fine cigar?"

"No, Mr. Rappaport. I—" Duff stopped when he saw the set of Rappaport's jaw. "Well, a good cigar might be just the thing." He fished into his pocket, extracted a nickel, and laid it on the smooth wood counter. Duff had spent the previous day finishing the carving of a gravestone for his pal Aemon Kelly's granddad. And miracle to behold, Kelly had paid him.

Smiling, Rappaport handed Duff a cigar. On the counter was a dish holding wooden tokens. He handed one to Duff.

"Good for two cents' trade at Uncle Abe's," was crudely marked on the wood. Duff nodded and dropped the token into his coat pocket.

"Hanna, visitor." Abe Rappaport pointed to the back of the shop with his impressive nose just as the bell rang and a new customer entered.

Since there was just the curtain that divided the shop from the home, Duff tapped on the jamb. No answer. He glanced back at Hanna's uncle, but Abe Rappaport was fawning over a fat gentleman in a tight-fitting coat.

Duff drew back the curtain.

Dressed only in a shift, she was drying her hair with a towel in front of the stove.

Taken by surprise, Duff was speechless, awestruck. It had been eight days since he'd seen her last, and he hadn't remembered her being so beautiful. Her hair, thick and curly, red as blood, hung down almost to her knees, which he could make out through her thin shift.

Not at all concerned, Hanna kept smoothing her hair with the towel, fingering for snags. "You know what I am?"

"What do you mean?"

"Don't play the fool. Meg told you. I'm a whore."

"You're one of God's creatures."

"Jesus. You sound like a priest."

"Don't I, though?" He thought of the Blessed Mother. "Please don't take the Lord's name in vain; He loves us all." Duff was unable to keep his eye off her.

"Your Lord, not mine. My Lord is God up above."

"Really, I thought it would be money."

"You're mean enough to be a priest." She shook her head vigorously and the towel fell away; her hair draped about her. It was magnificent. She knew it; she knew the effect it was having on Duff. "Did you know that Chinese men wash their lovers' hair?"

He could see the outline of her heavy breasts under her shift. "Have you had Chinese men?"

"Does that thought revolt you or intrigue you?"

"Don't talk like that."

"Like what? A whore? That's what I am." She picked up the amber brush and comb from the worktable near the stove. "Would you like to brush my hair?"

Silently he crossed to her, set his cigar on the table, and took the brush from her. Their hands touched. It was as if he had placed his hand into the fire. He put the brush to her hair, inhaling her scent. Leaning forward he lightly kissed the nape of her neck.

She turned and pulled him close to her, kissing him fiercely. When they stopped she didn't pull away. "You're not a priest, that's for certain."

His hand played along her throat and down to the swell of her breasts.

"Not here," Hanna said—and it was Hanna speaking, not Claudia. "Not in my Uncle's house."

Duff stepped back as if the fire had increased a thousandfold. Hail Marys chanted by a legion of archangels thundered in his head. "I didn't mean it that way. I don't want to buy you. I respect you."

"Oh, good," she said, taking Duff's cigar from the table. She bit the end and lit it from the stove. "I thought you were going to say you loved me."

FIFTY-THREE

⁓*November 14th, Monday morning.*

MEG, A GREEN BANDANNA covering her hair, twisted the mop until it stopped dripping, then ran it over the floor of the George Washington Room, all the while repeating her speech to Edwin as Caesar:

> " 'They would not have you to stir forth today.
> Plucking the entrails of an offering forth,
> They could not find a heart within the beast.' "

She was down on her knees scrubbing a tight corner when she felt a hand touch her shoulder. "Jesus, Mary, and Joseph," Meg cried, jumping to her feet.

"Shh." Pete Tonneman put a finger to his lips. About five paces behind him stood an old fellow with wild hair.

"Who's that with you?" she whispered. "He looks mad as a loon." She dried her hands on her apron.

Pete laughed. "He's a Sheriff from a burg up north, Catskill Station." Pete raised his voice. "Meg Clancy, may I present Sheriff Jed Honeycutt. Meg's the girl that first spotted the Rebs and told me about them." To Meg he said, "Jed thinks one of these fellows might have killed someone in his town."

"Oh, my," Meg said. "How terrible." Her mood changed as she realized she was being paid attention to at long last. She drew her five feet up as tall as she could. "Where have you been? Didn't you get my message?"

"I'm sorry to be so late. I've been working with the Sheriff here and haven't been by the *Post* the last few days."

"What you got, girl?" Jed asked. These two dancing around each other like courting birds were making him itch. At the rate they were going, he wouldn't hear what she had to say until next Easter.

Meg was suddenly aware of the bandanna over her hair. She removed it and tucked it into her apron pocket. Pete Tonneman was real nice-appearing when he wasn't drunk, when he was smiling at her like that, his hat tilted back on his head. "I saw him."

"Saw who?" Jed demanded.

"Not the one that was killed, but the other. Kennedy. Bob Kennedy. He was with another man. John Ashbrook. A very nice polite man, a schoolteacher. I met him through an actress, Josie Fallon. She's playing Calpurnia. I could do it better."

"They were here?" Jed asked. "You talked to them?"

"No. It was at a . . . party after I did my first part. At the St. Nicholas Hotel. A week ago Saturday last." She hesitated. "Mr. John Wilkes Booth gave the party." Meg was embarrassed to admit to Pete that she had been in Wilkes Booth's company. Everyone knew of his reputation with women. "That Mr. Kennedy is a wicked man. He wanted to know where Claudia is, but I wouldn't tell him even if I knew."

"Do you know?"

Meg knew enough, a name, but she'd promised. She couldn't tell, not even Pete. "Patrick Duff. He says he knows you. He's talked with her."

"Duff." Pete and Jed exchanged nods.

"Have you any idea where Kennedy or Ashbrook is?" Jed asked.

"None at all," Meg said. "Mr. Tonneman . . ."

"Pete."

Jed persevered. "What do they look like?"

Meg frowned at Jed. "Kennedy is a very big, frightening man. Black hair and thick mustache. His eyebrows are thick, too, and grow straight across. Mr. Ashbrook is not as tall. He's got light hair and a thin mustache with a small, pointy beard." She gestured with her fingers at her chin. "He's strong, though; he hauled Kennedy down to a carriage by himself. He wore a brown sack suit and a green-and-red flowered brocade waistcoat."

"Thank you," Jed said.

"You're quite welcome. Mr. Tonneman. Pete. Perhaps you would enjoy seeing me in the benefit of *Julius Caesar* on the twenty-fifth. All the Booths are in it and I have a small part." She added modestly, "It's the first time I say words."

Pete stared at her, charmed.

"It's for a good cause. The statue of Shakespeare in the Central Park."

"I know. I already have tickets. They're my grandfather's. My grandmother is too ill to attend."

Tears came to Meg's eyes. "Oh, I'm so sorry. I'll light a candle for her recovery."

Touched by her concern, Pete saw Meg Clancy as if for the first time. The damp golden curls around her sweet face. How beautiful she was.

FIFTY-FOUR

⤚November 14th, Monday afternoon.

IMMEDIATELY ON LEAVING the LaFarge House and Meg Clancy, Pete and Jed by mutual agreement went to Mulberry Street. There they found Chief Hays and Old Peter on their way out of a crowded and noisy Police Headquarters.

"I think we have something," Pete said.

"What?" Old Peter asked. "Let's get away from the commotion." They went out to the steps of 300 Mulberry Street.

"Meg Clancy, the barmaid, just informed us that a week ago Saturday, at a party at the St. Nicholas Hotel, given by John Wilkes Booth—"

"A son of the South if there ever was one," Hays said.

Pete repeated Meg's description of Bob Kennedy and John Ashbrook. He ended with, "Josie Fallon, a member of Edwin Booth's company, was also there. Meg has no idea where Kennedy or Ashbrook is."

"Good report, Pete," Uncle Hays said, winking.

"After we see this Claudia woman," Old Peter said to Hays, "I'll go to the St. Nicholas Hotel and you call on Miss Fallon."

"You've located Claudia!" Pete exclaimed. "May we go with you?"

"Yes," said Old Peter. "Get a carriage and follow us. My brougham won't hold us all."

⌐HAYS HELD THE door to the little shop open. Old Peter stepped in followed by Pete, Jed, and Hays.

"This shop doesn't seem to be able to hold us, either."

Abe Rappaport greeted them effusively. "Gentlemen, gentlemen. Good day to you. How may I help you?"

Jed said, "We're looking for a woman . . . ."

Abe kept the smile on his lips, but his guard went up.

Old Peter stepped in front of the Sheriff. "Some Garcia cigars would be nice."

"Garcia cigars," Abe said loudly. "Let me see, Garcia cigars." He was practically shouting. "Garcia. Garcia."

Hays moved to the curtain to the back rooms and pulled it aside.

"That's all right, Uncle," Claudia said. "I heard you. Step in, gentlemen. I believe you know Mr. Duff." She turned to the one-eyed man seated at the table. "You told them, didn't you?"

"No, on my sainted mother's grave," Duff was swearing as the four men filed into the tiny living quarters.

"Grandfather, Uncle Hays, this is Patrick Duff, the man who found the body in Jew's Alley."

Nods were exchanged all around. "How do you come to know Miss Rappaport, Duff?"

"I found her with good police work."

Hays smiled. He liked this fellow. "He didn't tell us, Miss Albert."

"Rappaport."

"Rappaport. Your description was known and the patrol officer in this precinct recognized you."

Claudia nodded. "If you found me, they can find me. Your police will sell their mothers away for a nickel."

"Sad to admit," Old Peter said, "there's some truth to what you say."

"An honest copper," Hanna replied. "I've seen the Promised Land. What can I do for you, honest old cop?"

"Please describe Mr. Bob Kennedy."

"A nasty piece of ice," Claudia said. "Big man. Black hair and mustache. Mustache and eyebrows are thick. No break in the eyebrows."

"Thank you. Do you know a man named John Ashbrook?"

"No."

"If you see Mr. Kennedy again will you let us know?"

"If I see Mr. Kennedy again, I'll run for my life. If ever a man had murder in his eye, it's Bob Kennedy."

FIFTY-FIVE

⌒November 15th, Tuesday night.

ASHBROOK PAID the coachman. With a restraining hand on Harrington's arm, they waited until the coach was out of sight. Their whispers formed frost puffs in the cold air. Above them the sky was overcast. Dark-edged clouds hid the stars from view. Satisfied that they had not been followed, they entered the cottage.

The two men had been to the Academy of Music at Fourteenth Street and Irving Place to see and hear *Il Trovatore*. They had sat in awe among perhaps four thousand people, many in evening clothes. The theatre itself was a thing of intense beauty with its tiers and boxes, its immense stage, carved figures, and plasterwork.

Harrington, who had dreams of being an architect after the War, was overwhelmed. And then there was the opera itself; the splendid voices and orchestra.

The two were still drunk with the experience and at first were unable to shake the magical event, but when they found Chenault waiting for them his mood banished all magic. He led them upstairs.

"At last," Martin said, haggard.

"What is it?" Ashbrook searched the faces of the others.

"Sherman is leaving nothing of Georgia but fire and brimstone," Martin said, his voice rasping.

"And we'll do the same here," Kennedy said loudly, picking like a demented rooster at the dark stitches on the shaved patch of his head. "Now. And get the hell away."

"No," Martin said. "We'll keep to the plan." He nodded to Headley.

His second-in-command said, "Tomorrow, Toby, Ashbrook, go together. Harrington and Chenault, you go to another part of town. We need twenty-eight black canvas bags, for the bottles of Greek fire. Do this in separate trips; I don't care how many times you have to come back here. No more than four bags per two men each time. What I don't want is one merchant recalling the sale of ten bags to two men. Questions?"

Toby was the only one who spoke. "No, sir."

"Headley and I will reconnoiter the targets," Martin said. The Colonel stifled a cough. "Any business?" No one spoke. "Good. Let's all get some sleep. Headley, Kennedy. Stay." Martin didn't intend for Kennedy to learn anything he shouldn't, but he didn't want to alienate the man. It was bad enough he had to treat the other four so shabbily.

"Stout," Headley said. "He's gone, but we've not been discovered."

"Our best hope," Martin said, "is that he didn't talk and that he got away clean. Our worst fear is that he led them to Mrs. McDonald and she led them here and we're being watched."

"Then again," Kennedy barked, "they could be complete fools and have botched their watch over us. Fools."

"Yet, they're winning the War," Headley said. It was the first time Headley had voiced the dismay Martin was feeling.

Hearing a noise outside their room, Headley opened the door.

Toby stood there, holding two wooden boxes.

"Oh, good, Toby," Headley said. "Colonel, I wanted you to see this." He brought one of the boxes to Martin and opened it for him to inspect. "Stout told me Longmire had them made to hold the Greek Fire bottles, but never gave Stout more than the first two."

Martin sneered at the box as if it were Longmire. "Here Kennedy and I agree. Longmire is a coward and a traitor. What he did no longer makes any difference."

Headley shook his head. "Some carpenter still has a half dozen or so more of these lying around."

"Loose ends," Martin said. "They'll burn with the rest by the time this is over." Now he shook his head. "What madness could have inspired Longmire to have them made? These boxes are too odd-looking; if we carried them we would be noticed immediately."

"Maybe . . ." Toby paused. He was still at the door, his hands running over the dovetailed corners of the box he held. "Maybe that's exactly what Captain Longmire had in mind."

FIFTY-SIX

⌒November 16th, Wednesday night.

HARRINGTON ROLLED the cigar in his hand. A good smoke and some air would help him sleep better.

"Where are you going?" Headley's voice called to him as he reached for the front doorknob.

"Just out," Harrington said.

"Not alone."

"We thought we'd go out for a quick drink," Kennedy called, coming down the stairs.

Headley narrowed his eyes at Kennedy, and worked hard at not revealing how much he disliked him. "One drink, then, and back," Headley said. "And don't you think it's time for you to have your stitches pulled?"

"Tomorrow," Kennedy said. "Tomorrow." Outside, Kennedy laughed. "Come on, Harrington, my lad. I've discovered a blind tiger, Crazy Bill's at Fifty-ninth Street, below the Central Park. Let's have a few and put our cares behind us."

•   •   •

November 18th, Friday night,
to November 19th, Saturday morning.

Lying three in a bed didn't help him sleep. At least he wasn't in the middle. Kennedy felt as if his dome was about to split wide open. He fingered the top of his head. Hot. Those stitches had to come out; it had been eight days. But he wasn't going back to the lady sawbones. Who ever heard of lady doctors?

She'd seen Headley and Toby in front of the chemist's. And she asked too many questions to begin with. It was too chancy to go back to her. He had a job to do.

Pushing aside Chenault's foot, Kennedy got out of bed. He found purchase in the first stitch with a fingernail, and pulled. Shit, that hurt. He caught his bottle from under the bed and drank, emptying it with one swallow. Damn, that was the end of the bourbon; another dead soldier.

He sat on the edge of the bed, pulled his bowie from his sheath, and ran it across his palm, smiling when the tooth drew a drop of blood. He rubbed the blood away on his trouser leg and got to his feet.

Turning up the gaslight and putting his face close to the glass over the bureau, he poised his knife over the top of his head. He knew he should put the tip into gaslight flame, but he cherished his beautiful blade too much to do that to her.

There it was, dip and hook, then just like for a snakebite, he cut. A larger trickle of blood ran down his face, but he felt much better. The pressure, though not gone completely, had been relieved somewhat. The rest of the stitches could wait.

Pleased with himself, he placed a handkerchief on his head to stanch the blood, covered it with his hat, and slipped down the stairs. He needed another bottle. He crept from the house by the back way, past a dozing Harrington who sat in an easy chair in the front hall.

He'd spent well two nights before at Crazy Bill's, so they took his twenty-dollar gold piece and gave him two bottles without comment, and didn't say a word when after his first drink he poured some whiskey on the top of his head, shouting, "Fuck, that hurts."

Kennedy finished half of one bottle, then started back to Mrs. Van Allen's house.

As he approached the cottage, he saw someone coming from around back, covered up tight in a coat and a hat. Who the hell was it? Was it one of them sneaking out? "Mighty suspicious," Kennedy mumbled, giving no thought to the fact that he himself had sneaked out. Or was it a spy? McMaster? Longmire? Maybe the chemist?

"Halt! Who goes there?" Kennedy shouted, drunk as a skunk.

The fellow hesitated, rocking between dashing back in and running. He chose to run. Kennedy gave chase, staggering along the empty street.

Just as Kennedy reached out to seize a handful of flying coattails, he heard a crash and smelled the whiskey. One of his bottles had fallen. He hoped it was the half-full one. Distracted by his misfortune, he lost a step, and his prey slipped out of his grasp. Kennedy picked up the pursuit.

Now he had him with both hands. Kennedy sensed rather than saw the ripple of the man's knife. He threw up his arm, blocking his opponent's arm, and drew his own blade.

Again, his adversary attacked, this time with a meant-to-be-gut-stabber from the ground. Kennedy parried. Clumsily. From the impact and the clanging sound of the blades, he suspected that his opponent also was armed with a bowie knife. And had the skill and strength to use it.

Then, by the light of the half moon, he saw he was right. A bowie. His eyes shifted to the man's face, but it was too dark. All Kennedy knew was that his opponent was smaller. Kennedy also knew few could match his strength. His toothpick darted out, twisting, intending to eviscerate.

The other man fooled him. He didn't parry; instead, he side-stepped and kicked Kennedy between the legs.

Kennedy screamed, nearly fell. This gave his adversary room to slash out. Both grunted and went on guard again.

Blood oozed from Kennedy's right wrist; he switched his bowie to his left hand and feinted with the blade. When his opponent moved to counter, Kennedy hammered the man's ribs with his bloody but not disabled right hand, stopping him.

"Uh," the fellow grunted, staggering back, dropping his knife with a clank.

"Yes," Kennedy shouted, scooping up the second bowie. Now he had two.

"What's going on here?" A lantern glowed in the darkness. "This is the law talking. What's going on?"

The combatants each took this as a signal. They turned and ran, in different directions. "Good." Officer Horace Mulroony yawned loudly. "That's what I hoped you'd do. Now, I can get back to my nap."

⌒MINSTREL WAS BOUND for a saloon at Forty-second Street and Sixth Avenue. When he finally arrived, the place, Harry's Dog, was closed and all his rappings and calling brought only a streetwalker.

"Can't I help what ails you, sweetheart? I'm Judy." She wore a man's cap over her dull blond hair, a soldier's blue coat covered her limp skirts.

He was tired and he had to get back before he was missed. For all he knew Kennedy had roused the house and now they all knew he was gone.

"Do you know Harry?" he asked the prostitute.

"Everybody knows Harry."

"If I give you a letter for him will you pass it on?"

"Of course I will, if you make it worth my while."

"How much?"

"A dollar would be fine." When Minstrel didn't react, the prostitute said, "Two would be better."

"How would five be?"

"For five, I'll deliver your letter, and . . ." Her hands touched his face, stroked down his chest.

"Ow." He felt his ribs.

"I'm sorry, sweetie. Am I too rough?"

"It's all right."

"You're hurt."

"I'll live." Kennedy had whacked him good; he could feel it now. But he hadn't cut him, that's what counted.

"I have a room on Forty-first. I'll take you there and fix you up. You can spend the night. In the morning when you feel better, I'll make you real happy. And all you have to give me is . . ." She hesitated and said, tentatively, "Ten dollars?"

Minstrel wasn't listening. He was using a pencil stub to write along the border of his map of New York City. "Give this to Harry.

That's all I ask. It's important. Tell him Minstrel gave it to you. It's going to happen soon." He shoved the map and a coin at her. "Do you promise? It's very important."

"You're in trouble." Tears glinted in her eyes.

Real or fake, the tears touched Minstrel. "Promise, Judy."

Her hands closed over the coin. "I promise."

Minstrel nodded, kissed her on the brow, and hurried back to Mrs. Van Allen's house.

Judy sighed and held the map to her spindly chest. This was so romantic. A good night. She looked at the coin he'd given her. Good, hell! It was the best night of her life. The coin he'd given her was a twenty-dollar gold double eagle.

BACK IN THE cottage, Kennedy's first concern was his whiskey. Closing himself into the bathroom, he brought the bottle out gently. When he saw it was the full one, he examined his wrist. Only a slice; the tendon was fine. He wrapped it with his handkerchief and reminded himself to keep the new wound covered with his shirt or coat sleeve.

Now he looked at his newly acquired Arkansas Toothpick. The sturdy, long, single-edged blade was hand-inscribed with the battle flag of the Confederacy, encircled by the words "Our flag and our RIGHTS." John Price's bowie knife.

ASHBROOK WAS DOWN in the kitchen. Chenault was out, a snoring babe. As Kennedy fell into troubled sleep, he wondered which other Lucifer he had surprised.

A LITTLE LATER, Minstrel crawled past the dozing Ashbrook in the kitchen, cautiously inched upstairs, and locked himself in the bathroom.

A spot of blood on the rim of the tin bathtub indicated the possibility that Kennedy had returned and that Minstrel had cut him. Minstrel washed away the spot and touched his ribs, cautiously. They didn't feel cracked, that was a blessing.

His roommates were snoring away. The whore seemed square, he thought, as he wrapped himself in his blanket. Maybe the message would get through.

⟐THE QUESTION BUZZED around Kennedy's sleeping brain, forcing him awake. He slipped out of his room again, crossed the hall to the other bedroom, and opened the door a crack. Two asleep in the bed, Martin seated at the desk, head down, Toby on the floor. Kennedy returned to his room.

Only when he finished the bottle could he get back to sleep. In the morning he woke with a terrible headache.

FIFTY-SEVEN

⌒November 20th—23rd, Sunday morning to Wednesday afternoon.

FOR LIEUTENANT JAMES HARRINGTON, the service at St. Thomas's Episcopal Parish Church on Fifth Avenue and Fifty-third Street was a chilling reminder of how far he was from home.

The minister's sermon was rich with Bible imagery and parables of thanksgiving and forgiveness. The church was magnificent, a cathedral really, and the parishioners were obviously well-to-do.

Harrington had meant to block out the minister's exhortation to "pray for our brave boys in Blue," but after he'd prayed for his parents, and his wife Louisa, and the child—his son—he'd not yet seen, and for all the men of Lucifer to get home safely, he couldn't help but say God bless to every soldier—Gray or Blue—in this terrible War.

⌒NEXT TO HARRINGTON, Lieutenant Tobias Garner closed his eyes and bowed his head. This church and preacher were too fancy for him. Methodists kept their sermons and their prayers like their churches, plain and simple.

Toby prayed for the successful completion of his mission, for his safe homecoming, and for his mother's good health.

John Ashbrook looked sideways. He was sitting shoulder to shoulder with James Chenault. They'd known each other since childhood. When the War came, they'd made their choice. States' rights. What did they care for slavery?

Ashbrook's father had a small horse farm, and Chenault's was a harness maker. Though Ashbrook was married, when Chenault joined up, he was, too. They'd been sworn in as lieutenants on the same day. Now neither had worn a uniform for months. Soon it would be over and, God willing, they would get on with their lives.

Chenault kept back a yawn. He never held much with religion. He cared more for sleep than hymns and homily. And why did they have to come to the eight o'clock service? There was one at nine and another at eleven. Still, when his friend John Ashbrook closed his eyes to pray, so did he.

Robert Martin, Lieutenant Colonel in the Army of the Southern Confederacy, looked over his men. Except for Kennedy, they were a group to be proud of.

His gut told him that somehow Kennedy was responsible for Price's death. No two ways about it, Captain Kennedy was a drunk and not to be trusted. But here he was trusting him. There had been no time to pick and choose. The damn War, forcing him to trust a man like Bob Kennedy.

Head bowed in prayer, Kennedy looked like everyone else, but at any moment he could explode. The man was less predictable than Greek Fire.

Kennedy wasn't praying. He was thinking about his comrades. Which one had he fought with? Could it have been Headley?

Martin's gaze moved to Lieutenant John Headley. Headley was a rock, and Martin thanked God for him. Martin had doubts about himself and his damn weak lungs; he kept going by pure will. But with Headley watching his back he felt confident that they would succeed.

Headley felt Martin's eyes on him. He turned his head. They exchanged nods and went back to their own thoughts and prayers.

Outside, after complimenting their minister on his sermon and wishing him good day, many parishioners stopped to gossip with one another. Mrs. Van Allen lingered, passing the time of day for a moment with her fellow parishioners, then joined Colonel Martin, who had waited for her. The Lucifer men started their stroll up Fifth Avenue, singly and in pairs.

"You'll be happy to hear we'll be leaving you soon," Martin said to Mrs. Van Allen.

"Relieved, of course, but not happy, Mr. Martin. This has actually been a pleasant experience. Too much time has passed without men in my home."

"We thank you for your gracious hospitality, ma'am."

AFTER A MIDDAY meal of honey-baked ham, white potatoes, cornbread, and a rich bread pudding soaked in brandy, the men sensed without being told that this might be their last Sunday in the comfort of Mrs. Van Allen's home. All but one wrote letters to their loved ones and handed them to the Colonel to give to Mrs. Van Allen, who would mail them when they were gone. Kennedy sat and smoked and watched everyone carefully.

They went to bed early.

IN THE MIDDLE of the night Kennedy startled the household by waking from his sleep, screaming. Harrington, with Toby's help, calmed Kennedy down.

Minstrel slept fitfully till dawn.

FIRST THING MONDAY morning, Harrington and Ashbrook had a bitter argument over an apple. Colonel Martin realized he had to ease the tension. He sent Headley and Toby into the City to buy equipment, and told them to meet the rest of Lucifer at the Green, a clearing he knew of in the Central Park at Sixty-sixth Street.

When Headley and Toby arrived with the balls, bats, and gloves, they were surprised and amused to see that the grassland the Colonel had chosen for their baseball game was being used by the New York National Guard as a drill field.

Lucifer passed part of the day heckling the New York soldiers. Martin realized he was tempting fate, but it felt good and right. In fact, it was necessary. His men had gotten soft. This propitious little incident would give them some of their edge back. He and Headley stayed alert so it would not get out of hand.

When the Guard left, with blood boiling over, the much-heartened Lucifer men relaxed further by tossing and hitting the ball around.

TUESDAY WAS TENSE, a day spent putting clothes and equipment in order and bantering how they'd showed the Yankees what-for yesterday in the Central Park.

ON WEDNESDAY AFTERNOON, the waiting was over. More than a week had passed since Stout's defection, and it appeared that the authorities knew nothing about Mrs. McDonald and that Lucifer had not been exposed.

Headley brought out an empty Greek Fire bottle. "It's time to review the use of the incendiary bomb. Item one. Make certain the window is closed tight. We don't want telltale smoke to give us away before each man escapes. Item two. We are dealing with Greek Fire, a self-igniting firebomb. You will gather blankets and sheets and hang them on the headboard. After that you will pile anything of wood in the room on the bed. Next you will stuff the newspapers you will bring in your black bag among the wood. Finally, only at the last minute, before leaving the room, uncork the bottle and spill the contents over the bed. When the liquid is exposed to air, it erupts into flame. Then get the hell out of there."

"We go on Thanksgiving, don't we?" Ashbrook asked.

All Headley would say was, "Patience."

MINSTREL PLANNED TO sneak out that night, but, following Colonel Martin's orders, Headley and Ashbrook were at the door, barring the way.

FIFTY-EIGHT

⁀November 24th, Thursday,
Thanksgiving day and night.

MY HORSE IS MEAN, he's bound for jail. Buy my 'taters so I can make his bail. Sweet potatoes, sweet, at your beck. A thin tiny dime for a peck."

Robert Martin awoke tight as a spring. Outside the window, the potato man kept chanting as he moved farther and farther away.

The first business of the day, at the Colonel's insistence, was Kennedy's stitches. Obliging his request, Mrs. Van Allen drew them out with her tweezers. She then went to the kitchen to see to Thanksgiving dinner, which Eva was preparing.

The women served a succulent turkey with sweet potatoes and pumpkin and apple pies. Afterward, they all sang hymns around the piano, gathering together to ask the Lord's blessing and acknowledging that He hastened and chastened, His will to make known.

When the hired girl and Mrs. Van Allen were snug in their beds, Martin and Headley called the men together.

"It's tomorrow, isn't it?" Chenault asked.

"Steady," Headley cautioned.

"Chenault's correct," the Colonel said. "Tomorrow."

"Finally, the fun begins." Kennedy grinned.

Martin looked at Kennedy but did not comment. "Headley has

already registered in his hotels. Tomorrow all of you will go to your hotels and register, using assumed names and toting one of your black canvas bags, which will contain the bottle and some newspaper. You'll have to keep coming back here for replacements. That can't be helped. Carry several spares on your person, just in case. We thought about having one man with a wagon to carry the bags, but such a display would draw too much attention. Headley."

Headley nodded. "The Greek Fire bottles are simple enough to use, you've all seen that. Don't forget to close the windows tight so as not to let the smoke give you away. We want you clear before the blaze begins. You'll each plant bombs in four hotels. Every man has a subsequent target after the prime targets. After that, if you have any bottles left, seek out targets of opportunity." He handed each a piece of paper. "Don't lose these; read them now, memorize them, and destroy them. The plan is to start myriad fires, thus spreading the volunteer firemen's ranks thin and allowing most fires to cause a great deal of damage."

"Precisely," said Martin. "We'll all meet back here, at which time I'll distribute what's left of the money, and we'll make our separate ways out of the City during the confusion. We will meet once again in Saint Catharines."

"I'd prefer to meet you all in Richmond," Kennedy said.

Headley said, "This is it, then."

They shook hands all around.

"Hallelujah," Harrington shouted. "I am reborn."

SOME TIME BEFORE midnight, Kennedy started awake. He was parched; dry as a bone. It was their last night. What did it matter if he went out to Crazy Bill's one final time? A thirst was like an itch, he thought, scratching his head. It had to be soothed.

Slipping into his boots in the dim hallway, he made his way down the stairs. The creak of a chair sliding along the floor below alerted him. Damn it all. Someone was awake.

He moved forward, the carpet softening his footsteps. Toby and Harrington were on guard at the front door. Both heads were nodding.

Harrington came awake, rubbed his eyes, and looked about the room.

Kennedy watched as Harrington's head slid to his chest. Still, the back door was more inviting.

Kennedy waited five minutes in the dark, then followed his nose to the kitchen where leftover food sat overnight covered with linen cloths.

Thoughts of whiskey made him salivate. He opened the back door. Cold air rushed in.

"Going somewhere?" Headley rose from the rocker in the corner.

"Needed a breath of fresh air, is all."

"Take your breath and say good night. We have a full day tomorrow and it's nearly here."

Kennedy gave it up and clumped back through the house. Toby had turned his chair around and was staring at Kennedy. Kennedy stared back.

MINSTREL DID NOT sleep well that night.

FIFTY-NINE

⌒*November 25th, Friday, late morning.*

You AGAIN?" Hanna's smile as she looked up from her ironing belied her words.

"Get your cloak," the big Irishman said.

"Why? I'm not going anywhere." She rested her hot iron on the stove, placed a hand on her hip.

"Yes, you are. I've come to take you to a picnic."

"Too cold."

"Well, then, a ride. We can have our picnic in the spring."

She resumed her ironing. "Who knows if we'll be alive in the spring."

"Not only will we be alive," Duff said, "but we'll be together."

"You are crazy."

"No, I'm not. We'll be together, have many children, and grow old together. Come, get your cloak."

"Patrick, you are absolutely mad."

"I admit to that. For the love of you, Hanna. Come out with me."

"It's Friday." She put the iron down and folded the sheet she'd been pressing.

"The day is young. Oh, are you telling me you observe the Jewish Sabbath, shameless hussy? I'll have you home before sundown, if you insist, but your friend Meg gave me two tickets to *Julius Caesar* at the Winter Garden."

"It is the Sabbath."

"Did Claudia keep the Sabbath?"

"Claudia is no more. But she did keep God's day when she could."

"I have hired a hackney for our ride in the Central Park. You can't say no to me."

"Oh, very well. You are as stubborn as an old Jew."

Duff laughed, took her blue cloak from its hook on the wall, and wrapped it about her shoulders, nuzzling her as he did.

She tied a scarf around her hair and pinned a red hat over all.

"I suppose we can't be rid of you," Abe Rappaport said as they passed through the shop.

"You suppose right, Uncle Abe. I plan to marry your niece and I am not known for my patience."

"Marry? Hanna, what have you done?"

"Don't listen to him, Uncle. He just talks, like all the Irish."

"Are you a drinker, boy?"

"I like my whiskey, Uncle."

"Do you have a trade?"

"I'm a master stonecutter."

"My niece likes to live good."

"We will continue to care for you, Uncle, after we're married. I have no family. You will be my family, too."

Abe Rappaport stared at Patrick Duff.

"So what do you say?" Duff asked.

Abe's answer was a shrug and, *"Abi gesund."*

"What does that mean?" Duff asked a laughing Hanna as he led her out.

"It means being healthy is a good thing."

SIXTY

⁀*November 25th, Friday, midday to night.*

WHEN THEY SET OUT, Martin told Kennedy, "I want you and Toby to work together. Look out for the boy."

Kennedy glowered. "When did I become a nursemaid? It won't work. We have different targets."

"Nonsense," Martin said, clapping Kennedy on the back. "You know you can do it."

Outraged, Kennedy stalked off.

In the meantime, Headley took Toby aside. "The Colonel is worried about Kennedy. The man is a firebomb all by himself. Colonel Martin wants the two of you to work together today."

"But—"

"No buts. It's an order. He's dangerous. Keep an eye on him."

⁀THE BRIGHT SUN notwithstanding, a winter chill was undeniably in the air. After they went once around the Central Park, Duff was flummoxed. He had many plans and no money. "Will you marry me?" he asked abruptly.

"You are serious." He was a handsome devil. And the patch over his eye made him seem so dashing. Could she marry him? She had already begun to turn her back on Claudia and the old life. It would be wonderful just to be Hanna again.

"Of course, I'm serious." He put his arm about her shoulder. "Will you have me?"

"You know what I am, Patrick."

"Was, Hanna. Don't fight me on this. I've made up my mind."

"We are Christian and Jew. I will not take your religion."

"We'll remain what we are under God's eyes. Can you be a stonecutter's wife, my love?"

"A master stonecutter's wife." She touched his cheek under his wounded eye. "Will you come home drunk and beat me?"

"Not very often. Will you have me?"

At her slight nod he turned her in his arms and kissed her. The carriage came to a halt.

"Where to now?"

Claudia nibbled at Duff's right ear. "Tell him the St. Nicholas Hotel."

⌒THAT EVENING, ANYONE could see that the man with the eye patch was definitely more intent on his companion than on the exhibits at Barnum's Museum.

The woman in the green velvet dress accompanying him, a girl really, was distinctly beautiful, with the face of a Renaissance Madonna, her red hair, emerging in tendrils from under a modest green bonnet.

They wandered past the jugglers, the living statuary, and the rope-dancers, hardly noticing, lost in their own world. From time to time she would take a brief look at her escort as if attempting to see through to his soul.

When they came to the Lecture Hall, they jointly decided, without discussing it, to take seats in the last row. An organ played. People were coming in to hear a piano concert; a piano stood in the center of the stage. The concert mattered to most of the crowd. It mattered not at all to these two.

Duff hadn't let go of her hand since they'd walked into the Museum. "You haven't given me your answer."

"True."

"Is it the children? Is that it?" When she didn't respond, he said,

"It doesn't matter to me. You do. The children can be Hebrews. What do you say?"

Hanna was awestruck. "You're Catholic," she said. "You would do that for me?" She had never thought to meet anyone like Patrick Duff. Never in this life. How could she let him go? "I will."

"What?" He was shouting. "You will?"

"Shh, Patrick." Every gaze turned to them.

"I will shout it to the rooftops." And he did. "This beautiful girl has agreed to be my wife."

Applause and laughter came from all around; it spread through the entire hall.

In the midst of it the pianist came out on stage and believing the applause was for him, smiled broadly, bowed deeply, and sat down to play.

Hanna giggled. "I think you should take me home, Patrick."

Standing, he lifted her up and kissed her sweet lips. To more applause. Then they slipped out of the hall. "Let us marry right away." Duff was joyous. "So we can be together till the end of our lives."

They came down the stairs and stepped out onto the street through a side door. Hanna, her hand in the crook of Duff's arm, felt secure. "Together."

The noise and commotion on the street startled them. Fire bells rang and people scurried. Shouts of fire swirled about them. Flames showed in a window of the building across the street. "Fire," Hanna whispered.

"What's happened?" Duff asked a man.

"Confederate spies. Burning down the City. The Astor's on fire. And the St. Nicholas."

"Oh, my God," Hanna said. "We were there." For no reason she could understand, she looked away from the fire across the street to the nearby curb. A man was looking at her. His glare was pure hate. He walked into the Museum.

"Hanna?"

But Hanna did not hear Duff. She was staring after the man.

"Patrick. It was him. Kennedy. He went into Barnum's." She walked rapidly toward the entrance, her hoopskirt swaying madly.

"Wait, Hanna. What's going on? Where are you going?" He ran after her.

She wasted precious moments looking about the ground level. "Hanna!" Duff yelled. "Tell me."

"Kennedy," she screamed. Unsure, she started up the stairs. Duff seized her arm.

"For God's sake, let me go," she screamed, nearly hysterical.

"Here you, let her go," a man called, grabbing Duff's coat.

Duff punched him in the stomach; the man half collapsed, released him and backed away.

On the first level Hanna saw the flames.

Kennedy came at her, a savage bull. She was slammed against the wall. Something flashed in his hand.

"Got you now, you bitch of a whore."

It was as if the fire had swept down and burnt her throat. Her bonnet slipped. She had to fix her bonnet.

"Hanna," Duff cried. He was thrown back by Kennedy's might. The bowie knife slashed at him, slicing through his coat.

The crowd was surging up the stairs.

"Fire," someone called. Kennedy pushed through them. His force and the people's fear of fire caused them to fall among themselves in their effort to retreat.

The flames ahead of him, the chaos behind him had no reality for Duff. He lifted Hanna from where she lay at the foot of the stairs and was immediately soaked with her blood.

Alarm bells sounded.

Hanna looked up at him and mouthed his name; she made no sound before she died.

SIXTY-ONE

⌒November 25th, Friday night.

STANDING IN CITY HALL PARK, Headley looked south on the broad, tree-lined avenue of Broadway. On his left was Barnum's Museum, garishly decorated. On his right next to the Astor House was St. Paul's Chapel. The gaslight made it almost bright as day.

And from where he stood, he could see the spire of Trinity Church on the west side of Broadway, at the head of Wall Street. All would be destroyed. Lucifer would see to that.

Though it was quarter past seven, the thoroughfare was crowded with omnibuses and hackney cabs, people on horseback. Headley crossed the street carefully. It wouldn't do to be run down carrying his bag of Greek Fire bottles. He'd go up in a pretty blaze if one broke, wouldn't he? Headley felt a tremor of excitement. At last, the mission. And its success.

The Astor House stood between Vesey and Barclay Streets in the heart of the City. Its destruction was crucial. The area was clustered with buildings and commercial houses four or five stories high, fine shops selling haberdashery, clothing, gloves. Bookstores, too, tailors, jewelers, daguerreotype salons. All wore signs on their storefronts, heralding their specialty.

At seven-twenty, Headley passed through the four-columned

marble portico and entered the Astor lobby. He already knew that the hotel contained a garden with a fountain and a renowned dining room serving continental cuisine.

The entire ground floor of the elegant Greek Revival Astor House was given over to shops. The shops had chosen the Astor House because of its location and its clientele.

Headley had no interest in the shops and their luxurious wares. His mind was on the mission.

From here he would go to the City Hotel, then the Everett House at the northeast corner of Union Square, and finally to the United States Hotel. The plan was for them to set as many fires as possible within the same period of time: between seven-thirty and eight-thirty. As the fires spread, the City would give way to inferno and havoc.

⌒ THE ASTOR'S LOBBY was fitted with plush furniture and broadleaf plants in large pots. Beautifully dressed people were on their way to dine or to their rooms, or out for an evening's entertainment.

Headley had registered the day before as W. L. Haines from Ohio. The desk clerk acknowledged him and gave him the key to room 204.

He did not rush. He did not want to be remembered. Ambling, he climbed the carpeted staircase. His heart was pounding; it would start here.

The lock to 204 turned easily, like a well-oiled machine. A good omen. In the room Headley leaned against the door for a moment and took a deep breath.

The room was dark. He set down the black canvas bag and turned on the gaslight. A bed with a carved headboard, a bureau, two chairs, a wooden washstand.

He made certain both windows were shut tight before he stripped the bed, lest the first whiff of smoke lead to early detection. He covered the headboard with the bedclothes and heaped the bureau drawers, the chairs, and the washstand on the bed, stuffing newspaper from the canvas bag into the collection as he went along.

Hearing voices in the hall outside his room, he paused. The

voices faded. It came to him that he wasn't sure the Greek Fire bomb would function as expected. Or how. Would it explode? How much time would he have to escape?

He opened the door and placed the key in the outside keyhole, then closed the door again. Now he drew one bottle from the bag.

Removing the cork, Headley dribbled the flammable mixture on the heap on the bed.

With a small, swift sound, not unlike a gasp, the Greek Fire trembled to life. The bed roared into flame. The heat from the shimmering flames was blistering. First dizzy, then mesmerized, he had the peculiar sensation of wanting to leap into the fire.

By force of will he jolted himself back to his senses. He ran from the room, locking the door behind him.

Headley walked slowly down the stairs. At the front desk he left the key with the clerk and took a stroll along Broadway.

S I X T Y - T W O

⟲November 25th, Friday night.

A̲T THE CITY HOTEL, Headley bought a copy of the *Evening Post*. He didn't read it. He needed it to bolster his diminishing supply of newspaper for the fire. Using half of the *Post* he followed the Astor procedure.

When he left the City Hotel on his way to the Everett House, he looked back toward the Astor. He could easily discern a glowing blaze from where he thought 204 would be. But apparently no one else had noticed.

The Everett House on the northeast corner of Union Square was a bit of a walk. He stretched his legs and made it in good time. After setting fire to his room there, the Lucifer conspirator moved on to his last target, the United States Hotel. Headley smiled at the irony: He was burning down the United States.

To his delight, bells began screaming from every corner of the City. Church bells pealed with deafening regularity. Immediately, the streets streamed with people.

Unruffled, Headley kept up his pace. He set the United States Hotel fire with more speed than he had the others. Practice was making perfect.

This final time when he left his key, the clerk looked at him strangely. And here Headley thought he'd been doing so well. On the street he scrutinized his reflection in the glass of a shop window. His nose told him what his eyes did not. The smell of smoke was palpable. He sniffed his coat. Sure enough, there it was; the cuffs of his coat were singed.

He should have been more careful. Thinking back on his progress, he realized he'd made one other glaring mistake. In order to avoid suspicion and seem the proper traveler, he'd toted a black canvas bag to each hotel. But the only thing in each bag had been bottles of Greek Fire nestled on crumpled newspaper. Had the United States Hotel desk clerk somehow discovered this?

It made no difference. Lucifer was doing what it was supposed to do, and succeeding. It was too late to worry about minor details.

ASHBROOK'S LAST HOTEL target was the LaFarge House. As he came down the street, he saw a woman rushing toward him. To his horror, he recognized her. She was the girl, the actress, what was her name? Margaret? She was the one he'd seen to this very hotel.

In that instant, she recognized him as well. Smiling, she said, "Good evening, I'm in the play tonight," and rushed past him into the Winter Garden Theatre.

He tipped his hat to her fleeing figure and sauntered up to the desk. Shifting his black bag to his left hand, he signed the guest register with his father-in-law's name, Edwin P. Margate. The crumpled newspapers in the bag sounded like the crackle of fire.

Apparently he was the only one who thought so.

It took him longer than he'd planned to set the LaFarge fire. The girl's recognition had shaken him. She could identify him and Kennedy, and now she could place him at the LaFarge on this night and this time.

Even before the bedding fire flowered into full flame Ashbrook was out of the room, door closed firmly behind him. It took all he had not to bolt from the hotel.

She'd gone into the Winter Garden Theatre. Ashbrook patted his coat pocket. He had one extra bottle of Greek Fire left. There was no doubt in his mind how he would use it.

.   .   .

SHOULDERS BRACED, DEMEANOR certain, Headley, the good soldier, walked back to Broadway. The sound of all the alarms and church bells was music to his ears.

Throngs of people clustered around Lucifer targets, now all aflame. The mission appeared to be a success.

COLONEL ROBERT MARTIN, standing in front of the blazing St. Nicholas Hotel, viewed the ravenous flames with sad satisfaction.

Judging from the surging crowds and the screeching bells, New York was burning. He was glad of a job well done, but didn't like the idea of innocent civilians being trapped in the flames. That monster Sherman had changed the rules with his vile rampage through Georgia.

A cough caught him sharply; the smoke seared his lungs. Someone grabbed his elbow. He closed his eyes and waited for the policeman's words.

"It's them Rebs, ain't it?" The hand on Martin's elbow was gnarled. The rest of the man was equally distorted, hunched back, twisted leg, toothless. "Tie them to the stake and burn them alive, is what I say." Martin tore his arm free, his lungs burned in his chest. The man's howl followed him as he pushed through the throng and got as far away as he could.

AS CHENAULT DRIFTED over to the Hudson River waterfront, he could still feel the glow of the fire on his skin and the glow of triumph in his heart. His first fire, his room at French's Hotel, had been a pretty sight. A pity that lack of time had not allowed him to stay and see the entire building go.

Looking out across the river, he saw that the ships moored there were sitting low in the water, fat with cargo bound for Europe. More riches for the Union, while the Confederacy starved.

The ships were all in a line. The nearest was less than twenty feet away. A fire on one would surely spread to the others. He reached into his coat and pulled out a bottle of Greek Fire and sent it sailing toward the near ship.

It hit the deck with a crash, shattering, and caught at once. He watched the flame creep until it reached the foremast. Fire danced up the sail, consuming it, then another and another. Someone shouted. The entire ship was ablaze.

More shouting. "Fire! Fire!" Horns sounded, bells went off. Shapes ran helter-skelter. Chenault, smiling, backed away into the darkness.

He walked along the docks again, saw something.

A distance away, someone staggering, falling, rising to his feet. A drunkard, no doubt. Chenault drew closer. Damned if it wasn't Toby Garner.

"Garner." He ran to him. What were the odds of their crossing paths this day? He supposed Toby had thought of the ships, too. "Are you all right?"

"I believe so." Toby patted his coat pocket. "Kennedy's insane. Colonel Martin and Lieutenant Headley wanted me to work with Kennedy today, but after we did my last primary target, he went crazy on me and punched me in the head. I thought he'd killed me." The young man, still dazed, pulled a bottle out of his coat pocket. "I fell on this."

Chenault whistled softly. "You must be in a state of grace. Only with a guardian angel watching over you could that not break. It's amazing that you didn't go up in a ball of flame."

Toby nodded, then winced at the pain.

After a moment, Chenault waved a dramatic hand at the burning ship, whose fire, unfortunately, was still contained to itself and seemed to be under the control of its crew. "See that? That's mine." Chenault knew he sounded like the boy who'd burnt the parson's gate, but he couldn't help it. "My handiwork. Proud to say."

Toby's head had begun to clear. "I have this one bottle left."

"As do I."

"I was trying to decide what to do with it."

"Let's do one together," Chenault said, eyeing the crews of several ships with resentment. They had put out the fire on his ship and were climbing the riggings of others to see where the enemy was. "That warehouse at the end of the pier. Quick, before we're spotted."

Toby squinted. "Why not?"

"On three." Chenault pulled his last bottle from his coat. "One, two, three."

Two bottles flew, were lost against the night sky. One hit the target. The other dropped into the water. The warehouse burst into flames.

"Well," Chenault said with a boyish grin, draping his arm about Toby's shoulder. "One of us has a better arm than the other." His grin grew even wider. "We're done. It's back to the cottage. And then home."

"No. Not me. I think I should try to find Colonel Martin or Headley and tell them about Kennedy."

"Those are not our orders, old chum. We finish the Greek Fire, we go back to the cottage. The Colonel and Headley and the rest will be waiting for us. Whatever Kennedy's done, he's done. Lucifer has struck, come Hell or high water."

SIXTY-THREE

⌐November 25th, Friday night.

MINSTREL WAS CAUGHT between Scylla and Charybdis. Every time he thought he had a chance to report what was going on, he was hemmed in. He'd failed.

It didn't matter now.

⌐THE CLAMOR OF the bells was music to Headley's ears. All along Broadway as he walked south, great confused throngs of people milled in the streets. Panic was on their faces, but not yet evident in their behavior.

From lower Broadway he turned west for the Hudson River, where all along the waterfront ships and barges were tied. He had six bottles of Greek Fire left.

Furtively, employing his bombs as grenades, he threw them at the harbored craft. One by one his bombs found their mark. He waited only long enough to see the first fire catch hold; a hay barge made a spectacular blaze.

Well done, Headley, he told himself as he traveled a circuitous route on the narrow lanes back to Broadway, his eyes watching everywhere, everyone. From there he went to City Hall on Chambers Street. What a pity they couldn't burn that marble palace. It was a lovely thought but he would pass; too many guards. The City Hall clock let him know it was nine-fifteen.

Unable to resist the impulse, he retraced his steps to the Astor to assess his handiwork. He was disappointed. Although the Astor was burning, the volunteers were keeping the fire in check. No hysteria in the streets yet.

He was suddenly aware of shrieking. Amazingly, Barnum's Museum across the way was emptying; crowds of terrified people were spilling out onto the street, screaming. Alarms were deafening. Headley was puzzled; no one had been assigned Barnum's.

People began gathering outside of Barnum's and pointing at nearby scorched hotels. Not as bad as Atlanta, Headley thought, but it would have to do.

Still wary, he made his way through the mob and boarded a northbound horsecar. Many excited conversations about Reb spies burning the City raced through the car. When the car reached Bowery and Prince, Headley saw flames coming from the Metropolitan Hotel. He jumped off to get a better look. The hotel was burning like a great bonfire. It was beautiful. They wouldn't get this one under control.

Casually, he walked past the firemen. One was talking to a large man, who wore a beard but no mustache.

"You!" a strange voice behind him said.

Headley turned slowly. "Yes?"

"Do you know who that is?" The stranger nodded toward the large man. "That's Mayor Gunther. He loves fires."

"Maybe he loves them so much he set them," Headley said, unable to control his tongue.

The stranger stared. "That's not funny."

Headley shrugged and continued on his way, his heart pounding. Only a short distance ahead, even in the garish light from the fire, he recognized a familiar form.

Before he joined his fellow conspirator, Headley looked behind for the stranger. The man was gone. Now, remembering Kennedy's little trick on him on Gay Street, Headley sneaked up behind his cohort and whacked him on the shoulder.

Captain Kennedy went to a crouch and spun around, his hand to his weapon.

Headley laughed.

Kennedy righted himself. "You son of a bitch." He raised his hands. They were shaking. His chuckle was hollow. "I ought to shoot you for that."

"We're even." Headley peered back down the Bowery. "Barnum's is burning."

"I did it," Kennedy whispered. "I had an extra bottle. Cracked it open on the steps like an egg and watched the liquid flame and flow down the stairs like a burning river of Hell. It shot up along the walls, made a wonderful fire. You should have seen their faces."

"I saw," Headley said, keeping his voice low, too. "Everyone's talking about it as if they know who we are."

"It was in all the papers, man. We should have struck then."

Headley suddenly realized something was wrong. "Where's Toby?"

"How the hell should I know?" Kennedy said, no longer whispering.

"Jesus, Kennedy. You were supposed to look after the kid."

"We got separated. He probably went scared and ran off. Like Longmire. We'll never see him again."

Headley looked hard at Kennedy. "No, not like Longmire. Maybe like Price."

SIXTY-FOUR

F
OLLOW ME, THEN."

Junius Booth, as Brutus, led other players offstage, ending Act Two, Scene One.

Immediately they were into Scene Two. Thunder and lightning. Enter Caesar, in his nightgown.

Meg stood in the wings. Her moment was near; she gave thanks to Jesus she hadn't eaten, for surely by now she would have disgraced herself and vomited. The Winter Garden was sold out, even though five dollars per ticket was double the usual price.

Edwin spoke. She couldn't hear him. Take a deep breath, my girl.

"Who's within?"

Edwin's line was her cue. She entered. *"My lord!"* The words thundered in her ears.

"Go bid the priests do present sacrifice,
And bring me their opinions of success."

"I will, my lord." Meg rushed off, nearly knocking the entering Calpurnia—Josie—down. She had done it. She had stood on the stage of the Winter Garden Theatre and spoken lines to Edwin Booth in *Julius Caesar*. She was an actress. But they were easy, she

thought smugly. In a little while she would go back on and prove how good an actress she was.

"They would not have you to stir forth today," she mumbled. Oh, she was going to be grand. And next time *she* would play Calpurnia.

Edwin began his speech that would end with her cue to enter.

> *"Cowards die many times before their deaths;*
> *The valiant never taste of death but once.*
> *Of all the wonders that I yet have heard,*
> *It seems to me most strange that men should fear;*
> *Seeing that death, a necessary end,*
> *Will come when it will come."*

Meg flowed onto the stage, settled herself, and listened to the great Edwin Booth say to her: *"What say the augurers?"*

She breathed deeply as Miss Florette had taught her. But before she could begin, a shout rang out. "Fire!"

Smoke was pouring as if from the walls of the theatre. Almost as one, the finely dressed audience rose.

Edwin Booth stepped offstage and quickly returned, holding a pair of brass cymbals. He crashed them together and intoned, *"We have heard the chimes at midnight."*

The frightened audience stopped in its tracks. Nervous laughter bubbled from the crowd.

"Thank you. One doesn't expect to get laughs doing *Julius Caesar*. Yes, thank you very much. Now, dear friends. I implore you to stay calm." The great Booth sniffed the air as only he, or perhaps his father, the first Junius, could. "I wouldn't worry; it doesn't smell like much of a fire."

The laughter this time was more subdued and several people were shifting their feet, preparing to run.

Meg, who'd been frightened, now was relieved. She wondered at the brilliance and bravery of her Edwin.

"I have a good nose. My father gave it me. *'When the wind is southerly I know a hawk from a handsaw.'* Not much of a fire at all. Mostly smoke."

"He's quite right," a voice called from the back of the house. It was Pete Tonneman, followed closely by Jed Honeycutt. "We've just come through the front," Pete said. "It's all smoke. Some brave men stamped the flames out and opened the doors to let in some air. If it's all right with everyone here, we're going to take our seats. And maybe after a while Mr. Booth will honor us with the rest of *Julius Caesar*. I mean, at five bucks a head I would think we'd get more than a little smoke of an evening."

Now it was Pete who got the laugh. And at that instant he also captured Meg's heart.

Julius Caesar continued to thunderous applause. After which, Jed Honeycutt, who'd had his fill of the City of New York for all time, fairly flew to catch his train back to Catskill Station.

⌒SINCE THE FIRE had done little damage to the LaFarge House, the party was held, as planned, in a private room there.

Meg was now a guest in her place of employment. Tomorrow she'd have to return to being a chambermaid. But not for long. *Hamlet* would open the following night, and she wouldn't be in it. But perhaps the play after that. For now, there was the thrill of tonight . . . .

She left the celebration and the admiring gentlemen and stood at the far end of the room looking out an open window. She loved her new theatre friends and the gaiety and the compliments. But all evenings ended, even enchanted ones. If it was so wonderful why was she so sad? Perhaps because it had only existed for a brief time and was gone, like a fragile flower.

The crowds drawn to the fires had dispersed; the night was cold and crisp, the sky full of stars. An omen.

"Well, my dear, you handled yourself like a professional." The words were whispered, hot breath in her ear, on her neck, their essence lascivious.

"Thank you." She was trapped at the window.

"I see you as my Juliet," he breathed again, his hands at her waist.

Meg knew he meant offstage as well as on. She pulled away from Booth, wondering how to prevent him from following her.

John Wilkes raised a sardonic eyebrow. "I would coach you. Day and night. What is your answer, fair maiden?"

"Her answer is that she is otherwise engaged," a voice said.

Meg didn't even have to turn around. Pete Tonneman.

"Go away, Tonneman," Wilkes Booth said. "She's not interested in what you have to offer."

"Au contraire," Meg heard herself saying. She turned and looked at Pete. She knew it wasn't possible, but was that a nimbus round his head? She offered him her hand.

OUTSIDE THE DOOR to her room, Pete looked at Meg's animated face, her lips parted with excitement. "I'm going to kiss you."

She felt the blood race through her. She knew her cheeks were two patches of crimson. No need for Miss Florette's makeup now. "Who said I was going to let you?"

Arms at his sides, Pete stepped forward. Meg didn't move. Their bodies were almost touching.

Meg swallowed. Her mouth was dry. She stood on tiptoes and brought his face to hers.

He thought, *Her lips are soft as warm milk.*

She thought, *This is better than going on the stage.*

SIXTY-FIVE

⌐November 26th, Saturday, early morning.

KENNEDY LOST TOBY," Headley told Martin when they arrived at the cottage. Martin was alone; none of the others had returned.

"Don't know how." Kennedy's tone was contemptuous. "He was right behind me. When we did the hotels, I told him if we were separated, to meet me on the waterfront, South Street. . . ."

"That wasn't in the plan," Martin said. They sat in the parlor.

The wood in the fireplace crackled, then all at once blazed brilliantly. Headley felt there was a flame inside him, as if he'd ingested Greek Fire. "What's wrong with your wrist?" he asked Kennedy.

"Cut on a piece of glass when I was burning Barnum's."

"That was you?" Martin relented. "Good thinking."

They could hear the front door open cautiously. Headley was at the ready. He relaxed. "Ashbrook."

Lieutenant Ashbrook was soot-covered, more than the rest, a glow of triumph in his eyes.

"Report," Martin said.

Headley handed whiskeys all around, giving one to Ashbrook first, then the Colonel. Martin nodded his approval.

Ashbrook took a long swallow. "Kentucky mash. Oh, how I long for home. Finished up at the LaFarge House, then tossed a bottle into the Winter Garden Theatre right next door. Both fires took right away. I didn't stay around because they were all yelling about Confederate spies."

At that point Harrington arrived, red-eyed and weary. He looked about the room. "Where are Chenault and Garner?"

"No one has seen them since early on." Headley glared at Kennedy while he gave Harrington a glass of whiskey. "We can only hope they're on their way."

"I'll wait up," Martin said. "You'd all best get some sleep. After I divide what's left of the money, we'll leave tomorrow morning, separately, and meet in Saint Catharines on Monday."

⌒MARTIN SNAPPED AWAKE. Someone had just entered the house. He stood, ready to give the alarm.

Smoldering embers were all that was left in the grate. Two familiar figures were silhouetted in the doorway. "Toby," Martin said, rushing forward, shaking his hand. "Chenault. Good lads." He pumped Chenault's hand. Except for Price, Martin had brought them all through.

Now he embraced the two of them together. "Thank the Lord you both made it back safe." To Toby he said, "When Kennedy came back and said you'd been separated, I was worried."

"Separated, ha! Kennedy—" Toby caught himself. What good would it be to say that Kennedy was a madman? Best to let sleeping dogs lie. Lucifer was over. "Kennedy gave me the slip, but I met up with Chenault."

Chenault nodded. "Did the rest get back?"

Martin poured them each a drink and one for himself. "They did."

⌒EXCEPT FOR MARTIN, they slept until ten, resting in their beds, confident that they had done their duty and advanced the War for the Southern Confederacy. When they were dressed and ready, Martin doled out what remained of the money.

Hands were clasped, but not by Kennedy and Toby and Headley, who only looked at each other. Then, one by one, Kennedy, Harrington, Ashbrook, and Chenault slipped out of the cottage, eager to see the damage they'd done before leaving. Martin had cautioned them not to let Mrs. Van Allen know their plans.

"Don't trouble yourself about the soot you brought home," Mrs. Van Allen told Martin. "I'm very proud to know that you helped the firemen."

"We did our best," Martin replied. An elegant coach pulling up in front of her cottage was in plain view through Mrs. Van Allen's front window. She set her bonnet on her head and gathered up a covered bundle. "I have a fitting to do in Gramercy Park and will be out most of the morning."

⌒JUST BEFORE NOON, the last three of the conspirators, Martin, Headley, and Toby, stopped for breakfast at a restaurant on Broadway and Twelfth Street.

As they gave the order for their food, they couldn't help noticing how the crowded restaurant hummed and trembled with excitement. Impassioned people were reading several newspapers at once, excitedly brandishing them, pointing to articles, exchanging ideas about the conflagration of the previous night. Headley worried that at any moment they'd be singled out as spies.

The phrases, "Nineteen hotels," "two theatres," and "Barnum's Museum," circled round their heads like flies.

Toby bought several different papers and brought them to the table.

"A most wonderful escape," one said.

Another told of the "discovery of a vast Rebel conspiracy. One of Morgan's Guerrillas implicated."

"Good God," Headley murmured, showing Martin a story. "They found the black bags."

"It says here," Toby said, "that 'the Army and the Police had complete intelligence about the conspiracy. Suspects had been apprehended.' Do you hear that?" He stopped reading and looked at his friends' faces before reading again. " 'All escape ways are blocked. It is expected that the criminals will all be captured.' "

"I wouldn't believe everything I read in the papers, boys," Martin said. Now he whispered, "Especially Yankee papers."

"I'd like to agree, sir," Headley said. "Especially after reading this: 'The desk clerk at the United States Hotel has given a description of the arsonist to the police, his appearance, conduct, and habits. The clerk further testified that the suspicious-looking man had left an empty black canvas bag.' That's me he's talking about."

"I won't tell if you won't tell," Martin quipped.

"It's good to hear you've regained your sense of humor, sir," Toby said.

"And, have you noticed," Headley added, "you haven't coughed since we all got back."

Martin smiled and resumed reading his newspaper; the other two followed suit. It was only as they read the newspaper reports that the Colonel and Headley finally understood that they'd been observed from the first day.

"They're either crazy or stupid," Headley said. "If they had us, why the hell didn't they arrest us?"

"Maybe," Toby said, "they had us and then they lost us."

"We're not out of the woods yet, my lad," Colonel Martin said. But his lips hadn't lost their smile. "Did you read this? 'Mrs. McDonald, who operated the boardinghouse the arsonists stayed at, has been arrested.' "

"She won't give us away," Toby said, remembering the woman fondly.

The Colonel drummed the table with his fingertips. "She doesn't know where we are now anyway."

The shout of "Twenty-thousand-dollar reward!" preceded a boy who burst into the restaurant, waving the latest edition of the *Herald*. "Read all about it," he shouted. "A twenty-thousand-dollar reward is being offered by the New York hotelkeepers."

Most everyone bought the new report, including Martin. After several moments he put the *Herald* down. "Except for the St. Nicholas Hotel, the destruction from the fires is negligible. And New York has rallied behind Lincoln."

Headley barely heard. He was reading about Haines—the name he'd used at the Astor. "Here are all the names used to register at the hotels. They have our descriptions, and they're watching the depots and ferries."

"This is—" Toby broke off when the waiter brought their food.

The waiter was a taciturn man with bleak eyes, who didn't speak. He served the food and left.

"We'll never get away," Toby said. "Maybe we shouldn't try. Maybe we should hole up somewhere and wait them out?"

Martin shook his head slowly. "We're soldiers, son. It's our duty to report back."

They ate their meal in silence, like efficient machines stoking up for the long haul.

The Colonel finished his coffee. "Let's go, then."

Headley paid the bill. They walked to the Hudson River Line depot, newspapers under their arms. Only Martin carried a bag, not black, not canvas.

⌒As THEY APPROACHED the depot, horsecars abounded; travelers seemed to be moving about with more energy than when the Lucifer team had first arrived twenty-six days earlier.

Two types of policemen were immediately evident, those in uniforms and those who wore suits and black derby hats. And then there were soldiers.

"I'll take my leave here," Headley said. Without warning, he moved away from them and entered the depot.

When Martin and Toby got on the ticket line for the Albany train, Headley was already walking away from the window, a ticket in his hand. Toby looked around. He was doing his best to act casual.

The train was boarding when they reached the platform. Porters were transporting luggage. A conductor called, "Albany train. Albany."

Martin swung aboard the second car. A mother with a little girl came between Toby and Martin. Toby handed the girl up to her mother. He did not see the man in the herringbone mackinaw appear on the platform.

Martin, hidden from view, looked back for Toby. His eye caught the urgency in the mackinawed man's pace.

Martin tapped on the glass. "Toby. Hurry."

The train began to move.

From their different vantage points, Colonel Robert Martin and

Lieutenant John Headley saw the man in herringbone reach out and clamp his hand on Lieutenant Tobias Garner's arm, pulling him from the moving train.

Toby felt the wrench, the rush of air from the departing train. Heard the whistle, the beginning roar. He crashed to his knees. It was over.

People swarmed about, whispering.

"Stand back." The man in the herringbone mackinaw stood over Toby, menacing, as if daring him to rise.

People gave him room.

"Who are you?" Toby gasped.

"Captain Matthew Wayne. I work for General Dix." The man in herringbone gathered Toby's fallen newspapers, glanced at one, shook his head, and said, "Quite a mess, isn't it, Minstrel?"

SIXTY-SIX

THE EVENING POST *New York, Saturday, November 26, 1864*

CITY INTELLIGENCE

MORE OF THE HOTEL BURNING PLOT

The Astor House on Fire This Morning

The proprietor and guests of the Astor House were congratulating themselves on their escape this morning from misfortune that occurred last evening when an alarm of fire was given about eight o'clock by Detective Devon. Room 204, on the top floor on the Vesey Street front, near Broadway, was all in a blaze, the bed having been ripped and its contents scattered over the floor, saturated with turpentine, and then set on fire.

The flames were soon extinguished by the persons employed in the house, but not before the floor had been burnt through and damage done to the amount of about $1,000.

THE EVENING POST   *New York, Saturday, November 26, 1864*

CITY INTELLIGENCE

THE INCENDIARY PLOT

A Reward of $20,000 by the Hotel Proprietors

A meeting of the Hotel Proprietors' Association of this city was held last evening at the St. Nicholas Hotel, at which it was resolved to offer a reward of $20,000 for the detection of the incendiaries who fired the hotels on Friday night and Saturday. The following resolution was unanimously adopted:

"Whereas many hotels were fired on the 25th and 26th instant: Therefore,

"Resolved that a reward of $20,000 be offered by the New York Hotel Keepers Society, as follows:

"Five thousand dollars for the first arrest and conviction.

"Three thousand dollars for the second arrest and conviction.

"Two thousand dollars for the third arrest and conviction.

"One thousand dollars for an additional number of ten, or for either of said number, to be paid upon the conviction of each or either of them; provided that the above rewards be paid only upon the condition that the reward offered by members of this society and published in the New York Herald of the 27th instant, be hereby revoked.

"Richard French, of French's Hotel, President.

"Samuel Hawk, of St. Nicholas Hotel, Vice President.

"H. L. Powers, of Powers's Hotel, Secretary."

SIXTY-SEVEN

⁀December 23rd, Friday, late afternoon.

DESCRIPTIONS OF THE Lucifer conspirators had been telegraphed to all points from New York State.

When Robert Kennedy was reported in Detroit and believed on his way south, Captain Matthew Wayne went after him.

In Detroit he found the Confederate captain just as he was boarding a train for Kentucky and arrested him. Wayne dragged his prisoner across the tracks and got them on the next train for New York City.

Four days later, Wayne stood before General Dix's desk at Department of the Army of the East Headquarters at 37 Bleecker Street in New York.

"Be at ease, Captain." Dix didn't require the sort of accommodations General Butler always demanded. His headquarters and his office were spartan affairs meant only to inspire work, not adulation. "Get your prisoner off all right?"

"Yes, sir. He's on his way by ferry to Fort Lafayette at the Narrows. The military commission convenes tomorrow morning."

"And will condemn him by tomorrow afternoon, I would hope. They wouldn't want to miss Christmas Eve. He will hang. The official charge may be espionage, but you and I know that we'll be executing a murderer."

"Yes, sir."

"It must be gratifying; you've avenged your partner."

"Yes, sir. Dave Corwin was a good man. We'd been in tandem since '62."

The General nodded. "You both came to work for me in '63."

"I'll miss him sorely."

"As will I," the General said, leaning back in his chair.

"Sir, I know it's not my place to ask, but will you be informing General Butler of these final events and results?"

Dix's laugh was the sound of a contented hog. "That Yahoo, I wouldn't tell him what time it was on the last day of Judgment. Let's hear your report."

"Yes, sir. Price, as assassin for Lucifer, killed Dave Corwin. Kennedy killed Price, motive being greed for the Lucifer gold. On the train ride from Detroit, Kennedy didn't admit killing anyone, but I assume he murdered Ridley and O'Connor to protect Lucifer."

"And the girl killed during the Barnum fire?" Dix glanced down at a sheet of paper on his desk. "Hanna Rappaport, also known as Claudia Albert."

"When I asked about that he only smiled. I'm a fairly hard man, sir, but that smile made me sick."

Dix nodded. "Did you recover any of the money?"

"Only greenbacks, no gold."

"Spent it all?"

"Hidden, I would think."

"What about the nonsense with the lucifer matchsticks?"

Wayne shrugged. "Who knows? Something Price started. I reckon Kennedy imitated the lucifer matchstick touch for the fun of it."

General Dix rubbed his ample stomach. "Lucifer did a piss job on New York. And by and large, Butler—and the Metropolitan police—and we—did a piss job on Lucifer. But kudos to you for looking out for Minstrel and for bringing Kennedy back. You have my word he'll hang. They may say it's for arson and espionage, but you and I know it will be for all those cut throats. Well done."

"Thank you, sir."

"Happy Christmas."

"Yes, sir. A Happy Christmas to you, too."

. . .

⌒WHEN MATTHEW WAYNE left Department of the East Headquarters, he was pleased. Not because Dix had praised him for apprehending Kennedy but because the young Lieutenant's secret was safe.

Captain Matthew Wayne, who understood about vengeance, was the only one who knew that Toby Garner had killed John Price.

SIXTY-EIGHT

On April 9th, 1865, General Robert E. Lee surrendered to General Ulysses S. Grant at Appomattox Courthouse in Virginia, and on April 26, General William Tecumseh Sherman accepted General Joseph Johnston's surrender in North Carolina. The terrible War was over.

 *September 1st, Friday, early afternoon.*

"All aboard."

Philip Tonneman kissed the lips of the woman, his lover, his aunt. They were not related by blood, but she had accepted what society might say about a marriage between them.

He was home for good now, and he would never leave her again. But he was leaving her now. He climbed aboard and leaned from the moving train until he could no longer see her.

Leah Tonneman sighed. Philip had a commission near New Haven, ironically, to paint a bridal portrait.

She never had done what was expected of her. If she had, she would have married, had children, and never achieved her life's dream to be a physician.

According to the clock in the stationmaster's office, it was two o'clock. She still could do all her errands and be home before six, in plenty of time to light candles for the Sabbath.

Leah walked through the crowded depot, distracted, thinking about Philip, her errands, her family, and the death of Philip's mother, Leah's own sister-in-law, Charity. "Oh, my goodness!" She'd walked right into a solid young man carrying a suitcase. "I beg your pardon." She peered up at the young man. "Why, it's Mr. Garner, isn't it?"

Toby Garner couldn't have been more surprised. He tipped his hat, smiled, and set his valise down. "Dr. Tonneman, a genuine pleasure, ma'am."

"Is it now? And how is your friend, Mr. Kennedy?"

"I believe you know he was hanged, ma'am."

"I do know, Mr. Garner. It was in all the newspapers. I shouldn't be tweaking you. I noted that your name was not among those wanted. Is Garner your real name?"

"Tobias Garner, at your service."

"Are you taking a train?"

"I'm on my way to Boston, to Harvard College. My train doesn't leave for an hour."

"Do we have time for tea?"

Toby looked down at the little lady. She had only kindness and humor in her eyes. "We do."

On the street she opened her parasol against the sun and held onto his arm.

Madison's Tea Room was close by, frequented, Toby saw, by well-dressed ladies.

They were seated almost immediately.

After tea and cakes arrived, she said, "Please tell me your story. I feel you owe me some explanation for the events I witnessed." She spoke sternly, but the kind look remained.

"My Pa managed the Maysville Branch of the Northern Bank of Kentucky. In June of '64, he was killed when some outlaw Morgan Raiders attempted to rob the bank. Trouble was, there was no money. One of the Raiders got angry and blew my Pa's head off. My mother almost died from grief."

Leah listened intently. "The poor woman."

"Do you have any idea what it feels like to see someone you love shot down like a dog?"

"None."

"I saw the man who did it. He had a white streak in his hair."

"How terrible for you and your mother."

Toby nodded. "A fellow came to see us one day. He said he was a drummer, selling musical instruments. That night he told me he really worked for the Federal Department of State and asked if I wanted to be a spy. In one week I was a Union Lieutenant working directly for State; in the next I was a Confederate Lieutenant in the Kentucky Tenth Cavalry with a letter of recommendation from Robert E. Lee in my hand, and being introduced to Lieutenant Colonel Robert Martin." The young man sipped his tea. "The group Colonel Martin enlisted me into was called Lucifer."

"A letter from Robert E. Lee?"

"A forgery, ma'am."

"Did you find life as a spy interesting, Mr. Garner?"

"Interesting and terrible."

"Ah, yes, the danger."

"No, ma'am, the deceit. Except for two, those men were my friends. I betrayed them."

Leah Tonneman nodded. "How is your mother, Mr. Garner?"

"She is well, ma'am, thank you."

A FOOTNOTE

WHAT? A CIVIL WAR THRILLER set in the City of New York? Can that be? New York was not a battlefield. Or was it?

The mission we describe actually took place. New York newspapers of the day labeled it The Incendiary Plot. The original target date was Election Day, November 8, 1864, but the conspirators lost the moment.

Truth to say, the conspirators got swept up in the magic of the City. Only the news of Sherman's burning of Atlanta brought them up short, and according to Lieutenant John Headley's diary, they did set the fires as we have described.

Historically, Judah Benjamin, the Secretary of State for the Confederacy, supplied Senator Jacob Thompson, former U.S. Senator from Mississippi, with $300,000. Thompson allocated some of the money to the Sons of Liberty, as Southern sympathizers in New York City were calling themselves; the rest went to Colonel Martin and his men.

There was even a Yankee double agent. In real life he was one of the couriers who took messages between Richmond, Virginia, and Saint Catharines, in Canada, just northwest of Niagara Falls, where the Confederacy maintained an outpost. So, ludicrously, the U.S. Government and the Army and the New York Police all knew about the plot on November 2, 1864, having been informed by telegraph by Secretary of State William Seward.

Mayor C. Godfrey Gunther passed the word to Police Superintendent John A. Kennedy and to General John A. Dix, who commanded the Department of the East, with headquarters at 37 Bleecker Street in New York City. The Police Superintendent and the General had trouble believing the information, but they notified their subordinates.

Why didn't the authorities act on this information? We have no idea. We do know that the suspected plot was even known to the newspapers, but the *Daily News,* as well as other newspapers, regarded Seward's warning as an electioneering trick in order to get Lincoln reelected.

We have used the conspirators' real names. Only one man was unknown. We chose to call him Tobias Garner.

Also, apparently, in 1864, John was the name of choice for men.

Mayor Gunther, like his successor in the twentieth century, Fiorello La Guardia, loved the excitement of fires. He was often seen at them, cheering the firemen on.

After the fires, General Dix issued General Order 92, proclaiming that the raiders would be tried by a military court or commission and if found guilty, executed within twenty-four hours. Arrests were made of local collaborators, but all were released. The conspirators, seemingly content with their slipshod results, boarded a train and went back to Canada.

Captain Robert Kennedy was the only conspirator captured. He tried to make his way south, was captured in Detroit, returned to New York, tried, and hanged. To our knowledge, he didn't cut throats and he was no more "villain" than the others.

As for Captain Longmire, he really did vanish. We do not know if he took the money.

General Dix reinforced the order requiring persons coming from "insurgent states" to register. Anyone who failed to do so would be judged a spy. In addition, keepers of hotels and boardinghouses were to submit the names of those guests arriving from Rebel states to the Department of the East.

Our conspirators were from Kentucky, a Union state, but they supported the Confederacy, as did many in Kentucky. This support led to the formation of groups like Morgan's Raiders, a guerrilla organization.

Kennedy, Martin, and Headley did in fact ride with Morgan's Raiders in and around Kentucky. There is no record that Price did. We don't know that any of the three were among Morgan's officers who were imprisoned in the Ohio Penitentiary.

On June 8, 1864, a renegade group of Morgan's Raiders did attempt to rob the Maysville Branch of the Northern Bank of Kentucky, to no effect. No money was stolen and no one was killed.

It came as a surprise to us that initially many New Yorkers were against the War, and for the South, for slavery. The City was violently anti-Republican, anti-Lincoln, pro the Democrat George McClellan. The War was bad for business. The draft was anathema, and only a year earlier, the Draft Riots had torn the City apart.

All three Booths, Junius, Edwin, and John Wilkes, performed in a benefit of *Julius Caesar* the evening of November 25, 1864, at the Winter Garden Theatre in order to raise money for a statue of Shakespeare in Central Park in honor of the bard's three-hundredth birthday. The fire interrupted the performance, was put out, and the performance went on.

The next night, Edwin Booth opened in *Hamlet,* which he would perform for a record-breaking one hundred performances.

In general, the volunteer firemen performed admirably. Hotel managers conducted inspections of every room. During one of these inspections, the last fire was discovered at nine A.M. on Saturday at the Astor. And it soon became clear that the fires were not coincidental.

The major mistake the conspirators made was battening down the hatches. By closing doors and windows tight, the Rebs suffocated their fires, which needed air to expand. It was a case of more smoke than fire. Slight damage, no lives lost. New Yorkers were fortunate that the Rebel infiltrators were not better arsonists.

In 1864, there was a shortage of coins in circulation. Stewart's and Lord and Taylor (department stores) began giving their customers postage stamps as change. Some stores had their own hard times tokens made. The postage stamps were annoying. People, concerned at being stuck by and with gummy messes that fell apart with too much handling, or with counterfeits, passed them on as fast as possible. The Federal Government wasn't issuing enough change. A nickel or a dime was hard to come by. Consequently, the Government issued more paper currency. In addition, *shinplasters,* paper money of amounts less than one dollar, therefore money of little value, were being put out by private companies and small towns in the New York area.

Antietam (where Duff lost his eye) was a creek near Sharpsburg, Maryland. On September 17, 1862, it was the site of perhaps the bloodiest battle of the Civil War. The battle was a draw. The Union declared victory because General Lee pulled his troops back to Virginia. Union commander General George B. McClellan, later presidential candidate McClellan, was harshly criticized for not pursuing Lee. He was soon replaced.

By state law, the Green the high-strung Lucifer men played baseball on was no longer in use as a military drill field at the end of 1864, but it pleased us to give Lucifer this little confrontation with Yankee soldiers. Once the drills were banned, one hundred and fifty sheep were brought to the Green and the name, appropriately, was changed to Sheep Meadow.

Several months before his death on September 4, 1995, William Kunstler told a group at the National Arts Club that his house on Gay Street was a stop on the Underground Railroad.

The first draft in New York City was met with four days of violent rioting. It began on July 14, 1863 (eleven days after Gettysburg). Mobs of men who didn't want to fight wrecked conscription offices, beat and robbed people, looted and burned homes. The mobs put the torch to the Mayor's home, a Negro orphanage, and more than a hundred other buildings. It was estimated that between two thousand and eight thousand people were killed. Business was crippled. Property damage exceeded $1,500,000.

Order was reestablished only when soldiers brought cannon and howitzers to bear on the streets.

In 1857, the New York Municipal Police Department was abolished and replaced by the Metropolitan Police Department.

The Federal Government paid high prices for many wool uniforms and overcoats that turned out to be made of old rags, cut into pulp and compressed into a type of cloth known as shoddy. Many shoddy clothes and shoes were sold to the Government. "Shoddy" became a common term for deception and corruption. Profiteers were called the "shoddy aristocracy."

Because of the potato famine (1845–49), one million Irish escaped hunger and death by coming to America or Canada. They packed vessels that were not much better than the slavers used to transport Africans. They arrived here sick with hunger and fever. By 1850, one out of four New Yorkers (133,000 of 513,000) was Irishborn. A similar situation existed in Boston, Philadelphia, and Baltimore. Irish sweat and brawn dug the tunnels and mines and laid the railroad tracks of America.

In the Civil War, two thirds of the troops on both sides were under twenty-two years old.

The Jew's Alley at the bottom of Chatham Square in 1864 is a different Jew's Alley from the one we refer to in *The Dutchman*. That Jews (no apostrophe) Alley existed in 1664, and eventually became South William Street.

As the election approached, fear of a repeat of the Draft Riots was in the air.

General Benjamin Butler, known as the "Beast of New Orleans," was sent to New York by Secretary of War Edwin Stanton. Butler's jurisdiction and that of his superior, General Dix, was vague. Much of the press considered Butler, whose infamous occupation of New Orleans had added to his family's wealth, a tyrant; others thought he'd make a good president.

On November 4th, 1864, Butler set up his headquarters at the Fifth Avenue Hotel. Later he moved to the larger Hoffman House.

General Dix was not certain who was in command of New York, he or Butler. Still, Dix prohibited Butler from sending out provocative proclamations.

Butler communicated with Washington to get carte blanche. He intended to take over the State Militia in New York, commanded by Major General Charles Sandford. The Militia was antiadministration. Sandford would not report to Butler. Stanton, at Lincoln's behest, warned Butler against any collision between U.S. troops and New York Militia.

Rankled by not having a battle command, being sniped at by Secretary Stanton and told not to cause trouble with the New York Militia, and being questioned at every turn by General Dix, Butler turned a suspicious eye toward Wall Street.

The Beast was on the track of a Confederate scheme to reduce the value of Federal currency. He felt that greedy or disloyal factions, or both, might try to force up the price of gold. Gold going up would influence the price of food and other essentials. The working class would be disgruntled and prone to unruly behavior.

The often repeated date for Sherman's burning of Atlanta is November 15, 1864, but newspaper accounts of the day report the first fires starting as early as November 9th.

In 1791, a Southern Dispensary was established near Town Hall to offer medical help to the poor. The people who lived at the northern edge of the City (Greenwich Village) felt they, too, needed a poor people's clinic. After several transient homes, a Northern Dispensary was set up in 1827, on a small triangle bordered by Christopher Street and Waverly Place. The Northern Dispensary ministered to the working and nonworking poor, including dockworkers, stewards, and hacking valets. And drunks such as Edgar Allan Poe who, in 1837, arrived at the Dispensary claiming to have a cold. The building still exists. It was serving as a dental clinic that supposedly refused to care for AIDS sufferers when it closed in 1989.

By 1827, John Walker, an apothecary of Stockton-on-Tees, England, had invented and was selling Sulphurata Hyperoxygeneta Friction matches. These three-inch matches were tipped with antimony sulphide, potassium chlorate, gum, and starch. To ignite them one pulled them through a pleat of "glass paper."

In 1829, Walker exhibited his matches in London. Canny Samuel Jones realized there was no protecting patent and went into the match business. He dubbed his matches lucifers.

Striking a match brought about a profusion of sparks and obnoxious smells. A warning was placed on the boxes that held them: "If possible, avoid inhaling gas that escapes from the combustion of the black composition. Persons whose lungs are delicate should by no means use lucifers."

In 1830, a Frenchman, Dr. Charles Sauria, substituted phosphorous for the antimony sulphide that Walker used, making the matches more efficient.

One of the challenges we had was trying to write a news story as it would appear in newspapers of 1864, when the inverted pyramid used in later stories had not yet been invented. There were no by-lines. The two City Intelligence articles we used at the end of the book were verbatim from the *New York Evening Post,* except for the date of the second one.

We put Duff in the 69th Regiment. The 69th, the 63rd, and the 88th were all members of the *Irish Brigade,* whose patron was Archbishop John Hughes.

Archbishop Hughes, a forceful man, not nicknamed Dagger John for nothing, was concerned about the hundreds of thousands of Irish famine victims pouring into New York's slums. Concerned they might be victimized and abused by employers looking for cheap labor, he urged bankers to establish the Emigrant Savings Bank in lower Manhattan. The bank offered a safe haven for Irish money, where it could mount up or be sent back to Ireland for impoverished relatives.

Hughes was responsible for transforming the poor and despised Roman Catholic Church into an honored and awesome entity, and for the beginning of construction on St. Patrick's Cathedral.

The Bowery was a theatre in and of itself, and was the "Broadway" of its day. There was street theatre as well, and actual houses showing minstrels—or Ethiopian Delineators—which became Variety after the War. In 1859, Bryant's Minstrels introduced *Dixie's Land* by Dan Emmett. Minstrel shows contained an Interlocutor and Endmen. The instruments were banjo, tambourine, and bones.

The typical Bowery Boy (*B'hoy*) was in his late teens or early twenties and older. He liked to fight. He was a volunteer fireman. He was most likely a thief. He smoked and drank and was a bit of a rough dandy in his costume of red woolen shirt with buttons on the side and a bright-colored or black silk cravat. The flaring bell-bottoms of his black broadcloth trousers were either draped over his high-heeled boots or tucked in. A clump of whiskers adorned his chin. His hair was combed to the front, locks pasted to his brow with soap. A butt-ender (cigar) was usually clenched between his teeth. Once seen, he couldn't be forgotten.

Around his neck the *B'hoy* proudly flaunted the large brass or gold medallion which showed the number of his fire company.

Our conspirators would have boarded the Great Western Railroad at Suspension Bridge, a town named for a bridge designed by John Roebling a long time before he did the Brooklyn Bridge, on the border between Canada and New York. The next stop would have been Niagara, where they picked up the N.Y. Central, which they took as far as Albany. The fare was six dollars from Niagara to Albany. They would have left Niagara at four-thirty A.M., gotten to Buffalo at five o'clock and to Albany at three-fifty P.M. There was no bridge across the Hudson yet—it was in the process of being built; they would have seen the construction from the ferry—so downtown Albany was the end of the line. They would then have taken the ferry across the Hudson to Rensselaer, where they picked up the Hudson River Line to Manhattan. Today AMTRAK still calls that stop Albany-Rensselaer.

In 1863, Commodore Vanderbilt, who owned the N.Y. Central, was already buying up the stock of the Hudson River Line. The merger came in 1869.

At the time of our story and before, every town, city, and hamlet had its own official time, so it was possible to arrive in a city before one left the other. The railroads pressed Congress for standard time, and this finally became law in 1884.

On October 3, 1863, three months after Gettysburg, Lincoln bade Americans to thank God for their blessings on the last Thursday in November. He proclaimed it a national day of thanks.

The Thanksgiving (on November 24, 1864) that takes place during our book is the second of Lincoln's Thanksgivings.

We're not surprised that our conspirators were dazzled by the amazing City of New York in 1864. We were born here, and the City still has this effect on us.

A.M., M.M., *New York*

ABOUT THE AUTHOR

MAAN MEYERS is the pseudonym of husband-and-wife writing team Martin and Annette Meyers. Annette Meyers is the author of six Smith and Wetzon mysteries. Martin Meyers is the author of five books in the Patrick Hardy series. Together they have written six historical mysteries featuring the Tonneman family.